THE FLIGHTLINE

For everyone that has thought about working on the Flightline—or for any poor soul that has endured the insanity and lived to tell the tale.

Written by T.M. Lander

Printed in the United States of America
Hardcover ISBN: 978-1-961624-05-4
Paperback ISBN: 978-1-961624-06-1
Ebook ISBN: 978-1-961624-07-8

Canoe Tree
Press

4697 Main Street
Manchester Center, VT 05255
Canoe Tree Press is a division of DartFrog Books

Acknowledgments

To my amazing wife Erica and children: Hannah "Will," Lucy, Michael, and Luke. Thank you for humoring my insane idea to put my thoughts into words creating this new universe of characters and stories. Your support and unconditional love have made it all possible.

This book is dedicated to all branches of the U.S. Military. Especially those that served on the Flightline and all for that are still out there persevering through the never-ending cycle of hard work and dedication. To the pains, struggles, shenanigans, laughs and memories...cheers! Thank you all for what you sacrificed and continue to endure. Keep moving forward. Good luck and God bless.

Prologue

The Flightline looks different to different people. The point of view of someone that doesn't work here is limited. They see endless rows of parked spaceships, maintainers walking with toolboxes, and bread trucks driving around in circles. Every now and then a spaceship drives off its spot, taxis to the runway and takes off.

When the Flightline engulfs you, like it does every maintainer over time, you see every fine detail. I don't just see a row of ships. I see our unique spaceships. These are our lives and maintaining them is our sole purpose. When we deploy, every aspect of that place is foreign; nothing looks the same, nothing feels the same. The one constant, the one familiar thing we have, is our ships. It doesn't matter where you are, stepping onto these ships feels like coming home.

The spaceships are our children that we raise and protect. I know every ship's name and all the struggles they have been through. Tail number 3034 has always had hydraulic problems. Ship 2046 has had landing gear issues ever since that cocky pilot had a hard landing on Viridis. We won't send 222, a.k.a. Triple Twos, to Nix due to its chronic air conditioning problems. There is nothing worse than being on Nix when the heater isn't kicking in. Then there's tail number 0060, a.k.a. Balls Sixty. This has always been my favorite ship; it flies like a beast with very little maintenance issues.

The Flightline is dark, but in the far distance I can just make out the silhouette of a maintainer walking to one of the ships carrying his toolbox. That's Specialist Fisher an Electro-Environmental troop. He must be going to 3086 to look at the intermittent air conditioning system. Just by seeing Fisher's silhouette and the way he walks, I know exactly who it was. I can name every maintainer we have, I know their ranks, their career field, their skill level, and most important, their attitudes. I know who I have on shift and everyone's current location at any given time. I know what's wrong with every ship and when they're scheduled to fly. This is my job. I am an expeditor.

Work on the Flightline is 24/7. We have different shifts that tag-team each other on their way in or out, giving each other turnover as to what work needs to be done. The shifts are long, twelve hours each. As an expeditor, I'm part of the Production team. We start our shifts about an hour before the rest of the maintainers. I check the status of every ship. I know what's being worked on, what still needs to be fixed, and what inspections are due. I have the flying schedule, a list of when each ship is scheduled to take off and land.

With limited people, I need to prioritize where to put everyone, constantly changing the plans as ships come back with unexpected breaks. Every maintainer is from one of several career fields that have a range of skill sets. I need to know which Hydro troop knows how to run the landing gear through, which Engine troop can power through an engine run, and which Avionics troop can change out a radar antenna. Not only that, but I also need to know who doesn't know how to do these things, in order to get them trained on it. They need to assist in the work to become proficient enough to do it on their own. In the long run this opens up my options. The more people are trained, the stronger we are. Once the next shift of maintainers come on shift, it's time to assign who goes where and control the chaos.

The sounds of the Flightline still resonate in my head today, or maybe that's the tinnitus. On a still night, all is quiet. You'll hear a power cart revving up in the distance; just hearing that in my head takes me back. Power carts are used to power up all the ship's systems, without powering up the engines. These generators can be heard from halfway across the span of the Flightline. It feels like yesterday—walking out in the cold, looking across the rows of spaceships, thinking to myself, *What will tonight bring?* Hearing multiple power carts humming, a reminder that work is going on somewhere, work is constantly needed somewhere.

The systems on these ships fail at times, but it's not just the unexpected problems, it's all the preventive maintenance as well.

There are endless routine inspections done by all career fields to ensure these systems continue to work properly. Inspections and operational checks before and after every flight. There are inspections at time intervals as well. Just like your car, you get certain things checked and serviced after so many miles.

The amount of work we have is never-ending. Our maintainers are constantly chained to the Flightline like a prison work crew. Even if you think you're caught up, there's always more. You aren't caught up unless every ship is fixed and even the newest troop is proficient in every task. This includes every part change and every type of inspection. This will never happen. Eventually the older maintainers will move up and out and it'll be up to the younger crew to lead the charge and train even more newcomers. It's a never-ending cycle.

As a maintainer, there are typically two paths you can take once you reach senior sergeant. You can go the path of the Maintenance, staying on the Flightline in a manager type position as an expeditor or Production Superintendent, or take the path of the Resource Office and deal with all the personnel problems, making sure people make their appointments, deal with any issues outside of work, and endure the ever-dreaded writing of APRs. The Annual Progress Report is a detailed report highlighting the accomplishments of every single maintainer, every single year.

I sit in the driver's seat of the launch truck, taking it all in. These vehicles are also called bread trucks due to their boxy style. The driver and right-hand passenger seats are up front with a large area behind them to transport maintainers. The back area normally has a couple benches on each side and is almost tall enough to stand up in. The front and back are not separated, so one can easily talk between them. I look behind me to see my launch crew. I have a bunch of maintainers behind me. On the floor of the truck, there are a few toolboxes and a couple of spaceship parts. Earlier, our troops replaced these bad parts with good ones. We'll have to return these to Parts Supply before the shift ends.

Spaceship 0060's engines are running as it's about to taxi out of its spot to the runway. A Crew Chief walks from the nose of the ship forward. He stands poised with his marshaling wands ready. A few minutes pass as the pilots finish their preflight checks. I'm waiting. Crossing my fingers that we won't have a redball. A redball is an unexpected maintenance issue. If this is the case, we'll be called over the radio and will have to climb aboard the ship fast to diagnose the problem. This is the whole point of riding the launch truck. Having a group of various maintainers with toolboxes ready, just in case there's a redball.

The ship flashes its forward light as a sign that all the checks were good and it's ready to taxi out. The Crew Chief waves his wands in a forward motion, and the giant ship creeps forward. His hand motion changes to indicate *right*, as the ship goes into a turn. Once it's turned, the marshaller gives a brisk salute and Ship 0060 is on its way. It's time to check on the rest of my maintainers. Work never stops on the Flightline.

CHAPTER 1

Flying

Max: How do we start this?

Roger: May I ask what your name is?

Max: Max Morgan, but just call me Max. What should I call you?

Roger: Roger is fine. I understand you used to be in the military.

Max: Yep, the good old US Space Military.

Roger: What was it like in space?

Max: I hate flying.

Roger: You hate flying? Weren't you in the Space Military for your whole career?

Max: What does that matter? It's like asking someone if they're Irish if their birthday happens to land on Saint Patrick's Day.

Roger: Okay, you got me there.

Max: It's the whole process of flying. Get there early, stand in lines, wait around, then wait some more. The flight always seems to be delayed. I think it's the whole relying on others part I hate. I always prefer to just get in my truck and go, on my own terms, when I'm in control.

Roger: Getting in a truck isn't so easy in space.

Max: Very true. Have you been to space?

Roger: Oh no, I prefer to be planted here on Earth.

Max: I understand that.

Roger: Is *waiting* the only reason you don't like to fly?

Max: Well, there's that whole death thing.

Roger: That bad? Tell me about it.

Max: Like I said, I hate flying. The first time I flew was one of the scariest days of my life. That was when I left Earth, headed to Space Station Prime.

Roger: That's the one in the Stella system, over eight light-years away, through that Space Bridge?

Max: Yeah, Space Bridge. They always come up with nice simple names to prevent fear. I'm surprised they didn't call it the Rainbow Bridge. It's basically a giant unstudied, unstable, and unreliable wormhole. I doubt anyone really understands it. Do you ever think to yourself, "What have I gotten myself into?"

Roger: Take me back to that day.

I'm locked in now. There's no turning back. I'm about to go into space. Am I insane? If I'm insane, that means everyone else on this spaceship is insane. That can't be the case, right? We're still on the ground. We just boarded the ship. The pilots and ground crews are still going through their checklists. There's time—I can turn back, right? I can refuse my orders and go back to my old life.

Did I mention I was locked in? I was literally locked into place. This ship has hundreds of us on it. We were bused in, wearing nothing but our underwear. Guys and girls, no shame here. Led up the rear cargo hold ramp like cattle onto this enormous transport ship. There were no seats. Just rows of vertical gurneys against the side walls. We were then placed standing side by side with each other. Across from us on the other wall were more passengers put in the same configuration. When I say side by side, I mean side by side. The guys to my right and left are pushing up against my arms. We have no choice but to touch this entire trip. My ankles were belted in. There was a strap just above my knees, another across my stomach that my arms were secured to. Over my head and pushing against my chest was a huge harness locked in place, like the ones you encounter on roller coasters.

Roller coasters start off by climbing higher and higher, very slowly creeping—click, click, click, up, up, up. For a new rider, this is a terrifying experience. Their heart is beating like crazy with each click as this death machine gains altitude. Then at the top, the coaster sits there for a few seconds, letting the passengers view the ground so far below as they hover up top. At this point, some riders would do anything to escape, to run away. You've seen it, people screaming with all their might to stop the situation. It's human nature to flee from danger, but they don't give them that option. Roller coaster engineers know they can't trust passengers that want to escape. They can't give them a way out—it's just not possible. They need to lock them in.

I was trying to rationalize these restraints. I was trying to find any reason. I know they don't want us to move about. It's for safety, right? I've seen one of these transport ships take off. They roar down the runway and lift off like an airliner, climbing higher and higher. Then the rocket boosters ignite sending this transport through the stratosphere into space.

Standing shoulder to shoulder, strapped in, harness over the head across my chest. Not knowing when this thing would take off. I could only see straight ahead since I was against a wall. Luckily, peering to my right, I could see one of the side entry doors to this ship. It was still open. At least I knew that as long as that door was open, we wouldn't be taking off yet. Then I saw a group of people come in wearing all white, carrying all sorts of equipment. They had to be a medical team, I thought. From the looks of it they were putting oxygen masks on each passenger and hooking up IVs to their arms. I hate needles. Actually, I don't hate needles. I hate thinking about blood and veins. Needles going into the vein. It just creeps me out. My biggest fear is that of my blood cord being snagged on something, ripping out my veins and bleeding everywhere. That's all I was thinking about. I knew our arms were strapped in, but standing shoulder to shoulder with others and being launched into space with an IV? None of this passed the logic test.

I think the guy to my right was thinking the same thing. He started getting agitated as I felt him moving around.

Then he started screaming, "Get me out!"

Great, I get situated next to *this guy*.

He continued, "Get this off! I gotta get off! I can't...like...this!"

I heard another voice down the line. "I can't like this? Who talks like that? Maybe they should let him off. More space for the rest of us!"

Another chimed in, "Too late now, dumbass!"

Two medics in white garb came over. They held his head back and strapped on an oxygen mask. I still heard his screams, however muffled. The medic took out a needle and poked him. Good thing too, his screams ceased immediately, I think they knocked him out. Looked like I was next—an oxygen mask was placed on me. I could still see through the clear plastic, but it was limited. They also stuck a couple of things on my chest with wires coming out. I could only assume they were to monitor my heart rate. Then I could feel my wrist as they wiped it clean, then stuck me with my IV. I couldn't see it, probably for the better, but I knew it was there.

Now my biggest fear was that the one next to me would wake up, fidget around, and rip this thing out of my vein.

The ship was a lot quieter now with the passengers stuck with masks on. They closed the entry door. It appeared it was time to go. All I could hear and feel was the rumble of the engines, but we hadn't started moving yet. It looked like most were trying to sleep. My mind started wandering. All I could think of was that old footage of the space shuttle *Challenger* breaking apart as it tried to go into space. It was an O-ring. That whole catastrophic event was due to one enormous O-ring exposed to the cold for too long. An O-ring, one small piece of the puzzle, creating such a destructive chain reaction. One part that failed. *How many parts are on this spaceship? Have they all been checked?* I was imagining us being torn apart during launch. Then I saw the entry door open.

What now? Just then two technicians came in holding a toolbox and a computerized tablet. These maintainers looked no older than eighteen. They both went towards the flight deck, to talk to the pilots, I assumed. Then I saw one leave through the entry door. It seemed like forever. I never saw the other one leave. The door remained open. Eventually the one came back holding a black rectangular part the size of a large shoebox. It looked like an avionics box similar to the ones I'd learned about during my technical training.

Roger: How long was your technical training?

Max: After boot camp, technical training was about six months. My job would be a spacecraft avionics technician. Everyone in my class was to become Avionics troops, yet we didn't know where we would be stationed. Most would be working on ships on the ground, while others might spend time on one of the space stations orbiting Earth. Very few of us were dumb enough to volunteer to be transported far from Earth to the distant galaxy.

At school we learned all about radios, radar, defensive countermeasures, infrared sensors and navigation systems. This was part classroom, part hands-on. Class lectures consisted of how the systems worked from a general perspective. Hands-on consisted of learning hand tools and how to remove and install parts. There was enough knowledge to have a basic overview, but not nearly the wisdom to understand how it all works on a real spaceship. The real training would be to experience it hands-on once I got to the Flightline.

Roger: I suppose you will tell me about this Flightline?

Max: Yes, of course. In detail, I may add. Let's get back to these so-called maintainers that have my life in their hands...

Sometime later I see them both leave with their tools and an old part. The entry door closes. Here we go..., I think. The rumble of the engines continues. I may have drifted to sleep. Then the entry door opens again. This huge spaceship still hasn't started moving. I see the same two maintainer kids climb aboard, both looking pissed and agitated as they head back to the flight deck. The one leaves again only to return with what looks like the same part as before. What the heck is going on? Did they just change out the same part? If the first part didn't fix it, why are trying a second one? I wish someone would tell me what's going on. These guys don't look old enough to make a decision that could cost the lives of me and everyone on this ship. After another half hour or so, they depart.

I was sweating, breathing hard. My heart was racing. The enormous spaceship then shifts its weight as it lurches forward and starts taxiing towards what I can imagine as the runway. Staring across the ship, all I see are the others shifting forward and back as we all embark on an unknown future. The ship stops temporarily. I feel like a drag racer waiting for the green light, only I can't see the light nor hear the countdown. It's the waiting that's killing me.

Suddenly I feel the abrupt movement and I feel like my insides are being thrusted to the side. The craft roars down the runway and then I hear a brief change in noise as we've lifted off. I still feel my body leaning as we continue to climb. Now my second and most prominent fear kicks in. At any time now, they will ignite the main boosters to escape Earth's atmosphere.

The acceleration was intense and would not stop. I felt myself being shaken and pushed from all sides. I honestly didn't know if we were still going up or we had been thrown off course like a ship that had just been separated and exploded from its fuel boosters. At some point I blacked out.

If all went to plan, once we reached space, we would be transferred to an even larger transport ship, then prepped for cryo-sleep, putting us into a sort of coma where we wouldn't wake nor age. Then we would be boosted through the Space Bridge light-years away. This large transport, which departs every four months, would also carry a city's worth of supplies that Earth sends to the Stella system. They say the trip through the Space Bridge takes eight weeks.

I found myself waking up in a hospital room. I wasn't sure if I was at Space Station Prime, back on Earth, or dead. I felt like I should be dead. My head was pounding, I was nauseous, my whole body ached. When I tried to get out of the bed, my legs instantly collapsed. A medic came over quickly and helped me off the floor and back to bed. I was told this was all part of the process.

They said all was good, we had made it safely through the Space Bridge and onto Space Station Prime orbiting the Stella Star. I hate the name Stella Star. That's what people call it, the *Stella Star*. The redundancy seems similar to D.C. Comics I suppose. Anyways, we were told by the medical staff we'd have to be in the Medical Bay for at least four weeks to regain our strength from the cryo-sleep.

Four weeks I'm stuck in this Medical Bay with everyone else that was on this transport from Earth. Four weeks and I can finally get to see my barracks, meet my team, and start work. Four weeks is a long time with nothing to do but work on my exercises.

It took me a while to be able to move my legs again, and this was with the aid of a walker. We all had to take exercise classes, take special medication, and try to get back to eating solid foods again. The worst part of these four weeks was sitting through countless briefings. We had lectures from every agency on station: Personnel, Food Services, even the chaplain's group. They taught us things like how to conduct yourself on the space station, how to cope with your emotions on leaving Earth, and what to do in the unlikely event that the gravity simulators stop working. I was so sick of briefings.

My time was almost up. All I had to do was pass a physical and I'd finally be able to leave the Medical Bay to see the rest of the space station and get to work. I'd heard horror stories about people not passing it and having to wait longer or being sent back home through that wormhole. On the day of the physical, I had to fill out a bunch of forms about my health history, then the medic walked in. I don't know if she was a doctor, or a nurse, or an assistant, heck she could have been part of the janitorial staff. All I knew was I needed her to sign me in good health so I could get to my job. I will say she was pretty good looking. Let me take that back. She was okay. Well, she was deployment hot.

Roger: Deployment hot?

Max: I'll save that for another story. Where were we?

Roger: The physical.

The medic started asking me a string of questions. "Did you do your exercises? Did you take your medication? How many sexual partners do you have? Have you been sexually harassed? Did you sexually harass anyone? Do you plan on sexually harassing anyone?"

It's not like she was asking me these questions personally. She was reading them from a form. She said it was standard. She then asked if I could touch my toes without bending my knees. I haven't been able to touch my toes since I was a toddler.

She then asked, "When was the last time you had a bowel movement?" I didn't even understand the question.

"A what?" I asked.

"Bowel movement," she responded, "you know, gone poop?"

I was so embarrassed, I just wanted to get out of there. I told her it was earlier that morning. In all truth it had probably been about a week. I hadn't been eating much since the cryo-sleep. I felt nauseous at the sight of food and could only get a few bites down. I wasn't going to let this issue keep me in here any longer, though.

Roger: So, did you pass the physical?

Max: I did. The medic told me to be ready tomorrow morning. She said I need to be in my military dress uniform to meet my commander and squadron members. Someone from my unit would come and get me in the morning.

Roger: What's the dress uniform?

The US Space Military dress uniform consists of black shoes, dress slacks, button shirt, tie, and suit coat. The shirt and coat each have a name tag, ribbons, devices, and rank insignia. I stayed up late preparing my uniform, knowing someone from my unit would be coming to escort me out of there. I ironed my pants sharp to ensure the hem line was centered and showing one straight line down each leg. The button shirt was ironed without wrinkles. Each sleeve was pressed to a crisp, revealing a sharp edge along my rank insignia. I shined my shoes using warm water and cotton balls.

Small circles around and around for nearly two hours getting it to a pristine mirror finish. I made sure my name tag and devices were aligned perfectly without any imperfections. I even shined up my belt buckle and adjusted my belt so, when worn, the remainder belt piece would align perfectly with the edge of the buckle. It was then I realized how much weight I had lost from this whole ordeal. I was already fairly skinny. Now I looked like a wet starved dog.

I hate flying.

CHAPTER 2

Getting Hammered

The next morning, I awoke early, showered, shaved, and donned my near-perfect uniform. I couldn't even eat breakfast. I was nervous and nauseous about meeting my crew and even more scared of dropping food on my pristine clothes. The door opened and in came a senior sergeant.

Senior Sergeant Tillhammer from my maintenance unit was a large man, well over six foot. Looked like he never skipped gym day. Short flat-top hair. The expression on his big face always looked like he had better things to do.

He looked at me standing in my dress uniform, then at his computerized tablet, then back at me. "Specialist Max Morgan?"

"Yes, sir."

He nodded in disappointment and said, "Get out of that dress uniform. You look like a fucking Nonner! Go put on your maintenance coveralls."

"Yes, sir. The medical person said I was to see my commander."

"Hell no! Colonel Fredrick doesn't have time to meet with every Frank that comes here. You'll see him during the monthly commander's call, and don't wear that uniform for that either. Except for a few rare special occasions, the only time you'll ever see a maintainer wearing the dress uniform is when they're in serious trouble, having to stand in front of the *man* for screwing up something. Promise me you won't do that."

"No, sir."

"You won't promise me that?"

"No—I mean, yes...I, I won't get in trouble."

This sergeant had me all sorts of nervous. I quickly changed into my coveralls and boots. These were a hundred times more comfortable. It consisted of a simple zipper suit with my last name, rank insignia, and Velcro areas to put different patches on.

I grabbed all my clothing bags and followed the senior sergeant.

"Where you from, Morgan?" asked Tillhammer.

"California."

He only responded with a quick nod of disappointment, then said, "Well, you look like an Avionics troop, that's for sure."

Roger: There's a look to an Avionics troop?

Max: There are too many systems and areas of expertise for just one person. Every single aspect of these ships is broken done by several unique groups of maintainers: Crew Chiefs, Engine troops, Hydraulics, Electrical-Environmental and a few more career fields. Some people may include the Weapons troops in the list of maintainers, but I wouldn't.

Roger: So, the Weapons troops work on the Flightline, but you won't call them maintainers?

Max: Nope.

Roger: So, who does call them maintainers?

Max: Only other Weapons troops.

Roger: What do they do?

Max: Load the munitions onto the ships—you know, the bombs.

Roger: That's all they do.

Max: Yep.

Roger: Okay, then.

Max: We all start as the rank specialist. All maintenance specialists start at technical school, yet we went to different classes. Like I mentioned before, most have a certain look to them. Avionics guys are typically your computer techs. You know, nerds and geeks. You won't normally see them out playing football.

Roger: Do you consider yourself a nerd?

Max: Nerd...no, maybe a bit of a geek, but then again this was early in my career. Lots has changed since then. Crew Chiefs are your jocks, often called knuckle draggers due to their caveman instincts. If it can't be fixed with a hammer, they may have to call on someone more familiar in that area. Crew Chiefs do all the basic maintenance, such as configuring the spaceship, servicing, pre- and postflight inspections, and so forth. They lead towing teams and marshall the ships.

Roger: Marshall the ships?

Max: Directing the ships as they taxi in out of their parking spots. The pilots can travel hundreds of thousands of miles without direction, but they need help with the last few feet. They need a marshaller to direct them the last bit so they're exactly on the spot so we can chain down the spaceship.

Roger: Chain it down? Where's it going?

Max: Working on a space station has all sorts of problems. I'll get to that.

Roger: Sounds like Crew Chiefs do a lot.

Max: They do. They're constantly on the Flightline—they live with those ships. I don't envy them. They do the same thing almost every day. Inspection after inspection, washing windows, towing space crafts, servicing the ships. These tasks don't change, just repeat. I love these guys. Whereas the Avionics team never know when something will break. We're constantly troubleshooting trying to find the answer.

Roger: The other groups?

Max: Engines—these guys specialize in the spaceship's ion engine system.

Roger: Sounds easy, only one system.

Max: I wouldn't call it easy at all. They need to know every single aspect of these enormous ion engine beasts. How to differentiate between the air and space modes. How to troubleshoot, which parts to change. This may include replacing the entire engine assembly. Not to mention the engine runs. They sit in the pilot seats and bring the spaceship's engines to power, ensuring everything is running right.

Roger: Hope they don't try to take off.

Max: Yeah, we all hope that.

Roger: So, what's their look?

Max: I would go with grease monkeys, car guys, a little rough around the edges. They can be your best friend or worst enemy; it all comes down to respect. On the Flightline, no one cares what you look like or what you do on your off time. The only thing that's valued is how hard you work. That's what gets you respect.

Roger: Got it.

Max: Hydraulics are your glorified plumbers except when there's a leak, they don't get sprayed with water. You can always tell if there is a Hydro guy behind you due to the smell of hydraulic fluid. We call them bubble chasers. If there's a bubble in the line, it pinpoints where the leak is.

Roger: Makes sense.

Max: Next is the Electrical-Environment team, E&E for short. They deal with the ship's electrical power, air conditioning, gravity systems, and pressurization systems. They don't have much of a look, but there's a certain know-it-all attitude to them.

Roger: Is that good or bad?

Max: It can be great or bad. It's the best thing in the world when they can walk the walk—I'll take that any day. It's bad if the overconfidence doesn't support their work.

Roger: What about the Weapons troops?

Max: I don't know their look. The only time we see them is the rare time when munitions need to be loaded. Other than that, they're never on the Flightline. So, where were we in the story? You got me way off track.

Roger: Your sergeant was leading you somewhere.

Max: Right...

Senior Sergeant Tillhammer led me through the maze of corridors on Space Station Prime. This place was basically a small city. I wasn't sure if I would ever remember where anything was. Multiple hallways going in each direction with dozens of rooms trailing off. The sergeant didn't even point out what was what, he just walked very fast. I was trying to keep up, carrying all my stuff. It was a very awkward long walk, in silence. We took multiple sets of stairs down when we arrived in a huge open area about three stories tall.

Sergeant Tillhammer said in his expressionless tone, "Here is your barracks—welcome to Texas."

All the barracks were named after US states. I don't know why either. Texas was the Flightline specialist maintainers' living quarters. It consisted of rows of rooms three stories tall that faced another set of rooms in a horseshoe shape with a courtyard in the middle. There were small walkways with a short rail fence outside the doors on the second and third levels. Some had chairs set up to see down to the courtyard. The courtyard had fake grass, picnic tables, and benches. This open area served as the place to meet up with others. Everyone had to walk through to get to their rooms to and from their work shift. The high ceiling that overlooked the courtyard had been painted with clouds and the Earth's sun. I supposed its intent was to make it feel like home. This area was intended for throwing a ball around or reading in an *outside* environment. However, in the Texas barracks we only used the courtyard for drinking and parties.

Tillhammer stopped at one of the rooms on the second floor and said, "I'm pairing you up with Specialist Dolphline. He's another Avionics troop. He'll get you squared away."

Tillhammer knocked on the door.

The specialist that answered looked as if he had just woken up. He gingerly cracked open the door with only enough room to expose his ragged head of hair. "Yeah, what do you want?!" he grumbled.

He then slowly looked up and his tired eyes opened wide fast when he saw the senior sergeant.

"Sorry, sir!" the frightened troop corrected as he opened the door more and tried to stand up straight, revealing a tall, lanky shirtless guy who had the expression of someone that was in a tremendous amount of trouble.

Tillhammer's tone had not changed. "I need you to take this Frank around and get him in-processed."

Dolphline's expression worsened. "Yes, but I—"

"I know, it's your night off. They can't afford to lose anyone on the Flightline."

"Yes, sir."

Tillhammer seemed to be in a hurry. While walking away he yelled, "Get him a room and Flightline gear! He'll be starting on your shift tomorrow. Make sure he knows where to go."

"Come on in," Dolphline said, exhausted. "Hey, Turtle, get up!"

His roommate sat up abruptly on the top bunk and said quickly in a squirrellish voice, "What's going on, Flip?!"

Dolphline turned to me. "Everyone calls me Flip." Then he yelled over to Turtle, "Tillhammer needs this new guy..." Flip turned to me, still sounding half-asleep. "What's your name?"

"Max."

"Max needs in-processed."

"Sounds like Flip got hammered," said Turtle as he lay back down.

Flip responded, "No, we both need to take him around." He gave me a smirk. "Besides you still know everywhere we need to go. So, we both got hammered."

"Oh, all right," Turtle said as he jumped down from his bed.

Flip wandered around his room trying to find clean clothes. I was surprised he found anything in this cramped bedroom whose closet looked like it had vomited all his clothes across the span of the floor. Turtle was surprisingly quick getting ready and stood right next to me. Turtle was a young specialist that didn't look old enough to drive, nor be part of this Space Military. He had short black hair and a large scar across his face. The scar was gruesome as it went up from the side of chin across his right cheek and almost to his eye. We continued to watch Flip try to find some clean clothes.

Standing next to me, without turning his head, Turtle stared straight ahead and said to me in a slow, plain voice, "Cougar."

"Cougar?" I questioned.

"You were about to ask me about my scar."

"No, I—I don't care."

"Flip! He doesn't care about me!"

Flip looked up after smelling one of his socks from the floor. "Doesn't surprise me, I don't care about you either."

Turtle then said to me, "His name is Samuel Dolphline. They used to call him Flipper, but now everyone just calls him Flip. You get it?"

"Not really."

"I don't get it either. He's not even from Florida, he's from Nebraska. I'm from Indiana. My name is Davy Michelangelo the Fourth, but everyone calls me Turtle. Do you get it?"

"Yeah, named after the—"

Turtle interrupted, "It's because nothing bothers me. I have a strong shell that deflects everything!"

Flip yelled from across the room, "No, we call you Turtle because you're short and you're slow!"

Turtle responded to me, "See, it doesn't bother me...the shell is strong with this one."

Flip finished getting ready and we were off.

The rest of the day seemed like a blur. I met the barracks manager, Sergeant Mast, who gave me the key card to my room. Room 209.

As we were leaving his office, Sergeant Mast said, "Hey, Flip, I heard there's going to be a room inspection tomorrow night. You may want to clean it up a bit."

"Thank you, good sir," replied Flip.

"Hey, you didn't hear it from me."

"Hear what?"

My room was only a few doors down from Flip and Turtle's. It looked clean, as if no one lived there. I only saw it for two seconds as I tossed my duffle bags in there. We then got a bite to eat at the chow hall, which was located very close to our barracks. The chow hall had a typical cafeteria style to it. Stand in line, tell the cook what you want, and watch the worker slop the food on your tray. Flip and I got omelets; Turtle went with the breakfast burrito. We found a small table to eat at.

I asked the guys, "So you're supposed to be off today?"

Flip shook his head. "We're not on the Flightline, so it's kind of our night off. Any appointments outside of work are considered not working. You have to schedule all your appointments after your shift or on your nights off. These include medical, dental, barracks problems, haircuts, pay issues, volunteering, you name it."

Turtle laughed, spitting out chunks of his burrito, and said sarcastically, "Volunteering."

Flip wiped the spit crumbs off his face. "Turtle! What the hell! Don't talk while you're eating! Max, you'll be lucky to have a real night off. At this point we expect to be screwed over. Besides, once we're done getting you squared away, we can relax. What's next on your in-processing list?"

My heart almost sank. "I didn't get a list. Tillhammer said you knew where to go."

"It should be on your tablet."

"Tablet?"

"Don't tell me you lost it! The tablet has your whole life on it. All your appointments, checklists, paycheck info. Hell, it's the main tool you use on the Flightline with all our technical data. You can't even work on ships without it. Think, Max, where did you see it last?"

"I never saw it. I never had it. I went straight from Medical to the barracks."

"Man, I am screwed. First day and you're losing things."

"It's not your fault. Can't we go back to Medical and see if they have it?"

"First of all, it doesn't matter. Hammer will find a way to blame it on me. Second of all, you can't just go to Medical—they won't let you in. You have to attempt to make an appointment, wait for a return message, and get a scheduled time. It's a whole process that will take most of a day, maybe five days."

My stomach was turning. I couldn't even eat. "Fine, show me how to make the appointment. Maybe I can get lucky."

"Sure, first step is to log into your tablet."

"Really?"

Flip put his head in his hands in defeat.

Turtle ever so slowly finished the last bite of his food, took a long drink of water, wiped his face with his napkin, set his napkin neatly down, and then spoke. "Medical doesn't have your tablet."

Flip and I looked at him with confusion.

Turtle continued in a slow, serious voice. "Medical doesn't give them out anymore. The IT team has it. They preload all newcomers' tablets and have them all waiting. All you need to do is give them your name and they'll give it to you."

Flip slugged Turtle hard in the arm. "Why didn't you say so? We've been freaking out over this?!"

"You told me not to talk while I was eating."

Turtle was right. The IT team had a tablet loaded with all my information. They showed me where to find the in-processing checklist and we were off. We went to the Training Office to ensure my on-the-job training was loaded. I got my picture taken for my Flightline area badge—hard to imagine, but my photo looked worse than my driver's license. We trekked all over the space station. I felt so lost as we went up and down stairs and across long corridors trying to find the offices on my checklist. Most of them only wanted to scan my ID card to get me in their system. There had to be an easier way to do this. We were in and out of some offices so fast I didn't even know what they were for. For some reason Turtle seemed to know where everything was. I understood why Flip dragged him along.

Our last stop on the list was to pick up my Flightline gear. This included gloves, unit patches, reflective vest, restraint harness, a helmet assembly with oxygen mask, and even a thin body liner to be worn under the coveralls that acted as a pressurization suit. By the time we got back to barracks and dropped off my gear, we were starving. It wasn't until our conversation at dinner that I came to a dark realization.

I asked Flip and Turtle, "Have you gone to any of the moons?"

Flip responded, "I went to Calidum, but Turtle never went."

Turtle said, "I'm waiting for the right deployment."

"How was Calidum?" I asked Flip.

"Hot and dirty. Same thing every day. Work on the ships, eat, sleep, and repeat."

"How long have you guys been here on station?"

Flip responded, "We've both been here almost two Earth years."

Turtle added, "We came across on the same transport and met each other in the Medical Bay."

I looked at Turtle. "That long ago? How did you know where all the places were on my checklist?"

"I was selected to drag a couple of Crew Chiefs about six weeks ago when they in-processed."

I was confused. "Six weeks ago? I thought they sent out the Space Bridge Transport every four months."

"They do. That last group left in August and arrived here in October."

My brain was hurting. "What day is it?"

Flip looked at his tablet. "It's day three hundred and twenty-five."

"Yeah, that's what they said in Medical. What does that mean?"

"It's the Julian Calendar based on the Earth year; we use that here on station. Each day of the year has a number from one to three hundred and sixty-five."

"Or three hundred and sixty-six," corrected Turtle.

"So, what does that translate to?" I asked in a panic.

Flip looked back at his tablet. "Three hundred and twenty-five is...November twenty-first."

I was feeling sick and couldn't eat. "I left Earth April first. I thought they said it takes two months to get here." I looked at his tablet to confirm the date and year. "That means I was in cryo-sleep for like seven months!"

Flip literally jumped out of his seat and stood up. "Outstanding! See, it *typically* takes about eight weeks, but there's nothing typical about it. Some guys get here in six weeks. I heard one group took almost a year. Space Bridge does some freaky shit!"

"How is this outstanding?!"

"To the Mountain!" shouted Turtle.

"This is truly outstanding indeed," expressed Flip. "Hurry and check your pay account on your tablet! While you were dreaming your life away, you continued to get paid for your service. Seven months of direct deposit without you spending a dirty dime. You won the freaking lottery."

"To the Mountain!" shouted Turtle again.

Flip looked at me with a sympathetic face. "It's the rules. New guy oversleeps, new guy pays for drinks."

"To the Mountain!" shouted Turtle for a third time.

We stopped by the barracks first to drop off my gear and to see the other maintainers returning from their shift. Flip caught up with another one of our Avionics troops in the courtyard.

Flip greeted her. "Sharyn, this is Max, our new Avionics troop. How was the shift?"

She spoke in a slow, tired voice. "Sharyn Brightly here. Nice to meet you. I hope you have the best of luck here. Welcome to the insanity." Then she pulled her black hair down out of a bun. "Tonight was boring and tedious. We didn't have much avionics work, so we were rented out to assist Crew Chiefs all night. Helping with refuels and chaining down ships. Then I got stuck helping Hydraulics out for a bit. I need a night off, only two more until mine."

Flip explained, "See, Max, since they have maintainers working the Flightline every single night, we switch off nights off. We usually get one night off every seven days."

I asked, "Do you only work at night?"

"No, it's just an expression. The time of the day is irrelevant here. The Space Station Prime is set in orbit in such a manner that the bottom of it always faces the Stella Star. They say there are a bunch of solar panels on the bottom. The top deck, which you'll see tomorrow, has the Flightline and runway. So, it's always night, doesn't matter what time you work."

"Okay."

Flip continued, "Sharyn, we're going to the Mountain and you're coming. Where's Big Marcus?"

"Marcus is stuck at work. Senior Tillhammer is going ballistic."

"What did Big Marcus do this time?"

"He missed a training appointment yesterday. Tillhammer's mad because he has to explain to the commander how it happened and how to prevent it from ever happening again. Listen, you guys go ahead—Marcus and I will join you later. I gotta get cleaned up, I smell like hydro." Then she trailed off to her room on the first floor of the far end of the barracks.

After she left, Flip tried to bring me up to speed. "I asked Sharyn about Big Marcus since they're usually walking together. Marcus is a large country boy and one of our most dedicated Crew Chiefs, but he does do some stupid crap. He's been in our barracks longer than anyone else. He's the only one here that has his own room."

Turtle added, "He's got the nice suite, the one with only one bed."

Flip continued, "Still, I know he'd rather rank up. Once you rank up to sergeant, you get to live in nicer quarters. Halfway across the station."

"How long's he been here?" I asked.

"I think we should ask him," responded Turtle. "Here he comes."

Running full speed down the courtyard came our Crew Chief, who stopped in front of us breathing hard. "You see Sharyn?"

Flip remarked, "Why are you running? Afraid you'll miss another appointment?"

"How do you know that? You had tonight off, probably sitting around doing nerd stuff."

"Hey, Marcus, this is Max, our new Avionics troop."

"Great, another lazy pointy-head."

"We were just discussing your current situation in the barracks. When are you moving up to the sergeant quarters?"

"I'm not gonna answer."

Turtle jumped in. "It's not his fault. The rank up test must be too hard for his tiny brain to handle."

"I'm a better maintainer than you, Turtle."

Turtle snickered. "Well, I'd sure hope you're a better maintainer. Anyone would be as long as you've been here."

"You're the worst. Why do you think they pulled you off the Flightline and made you work in Tool Counter?"

Flip responded, "How long have you been here, Marcus? Eight years?"

Turtle could barely get the next words out without laughing. "Marcus doesn't even know because he can't count that high."

Flip quickly asked, "So, what did Tillhammer want?"

Marcus was still staring angrily at Turtle. "Hammer said I have to come in early and stay late every night. I have to track down every- one that has an appointment and make sure they remember it."

Turtle couldn't wait to chime in. "Everyone with an appointment?"

"Everyone."

"I hope it's not more than eight."

Flip jumped in to stop Turtle from getting hurt. "Hey, Marcus, we're going to Mountain, our treat. Sharyn is getting ready in her room."

"Sounds good, thanks, guys." Then Marcus ran off in the direc- tion of Sharyn's room.

Flip said sincerely, "Great guy, Big Marcus, nicest pal in the world. I'd work with him any day."

Turtle agreed, "Yeah, good friend, sucks Hammer laid into him."

Flip, Turtle, and I went across Space Station Prime and up a few flights of stairs to what they'd been referring to as the Mountain. It was a little club that served finger foods and drinks. One side of this place was a small convenience store for buying alcohol to go;

the other part was a full bar. Walking into the Mountain felt like going back in time. The place had a long bar to sit at, as well as many tables around the main room. There was an old pool table in one corner and a few dart boards to the side. What really took me back was the number of pictures on the walls. They all depicted the aviation giants from Earth's airplane frontier era. Pictures included the Wright brothers, Earhart, Doolittle, and Tibbets, to name a few, along with their airplanes. There were also photos of C-130s, A-10s, and the truly legendary B-52. This place just felt right.

Once we got our drinks and found a table, Flip broke it down. "On a typical outing, we'll drink a couple beers here, then buy a case to bring back to the barracks."

I asked, "I take it the new guy carries the case of beer?"

Flip looked at me with a smirk and concern. "Heck no, we each carry our own case."

"I see. Also, Senior Sergeant Tillhammer referred to me as a Frank?"

"That's an acronym we use for the new guys around here—Fucking Rookie-Ass New Kid."

"Okay, then."

We were there for about an hour before Big Marcus and Sharyn arrived. The night was full of energy and fun as I learned more about Space Station Prime and Solar System Stella. Truthfully, I don't remember many details of the conversations that night. I know there were a lot of laughs, especially when Turtle got on Big Marcus's shoulders and was doing a fairly decent impersonation of Senior Tillhammer. We never did bring a case of beer back; we ended up staying at the Mountain until very late.

There were many things going through my spinning head that night; maybe it was the long day of running around with my in-processing scavenger hunt, or not having eaten much in the last few weeks, or perhaps it was the realization that I had lost seven months of my life. I suppose it was all these factors that led to me hurling everything from my stomach all over the fake grass of a neighboring barracks. At this point I had a sinking feeling inside. I *have to report for work on the Flightline in the morning.*

CHAPTER 3

Distant Neighbors

Max: Before we get the Flightline, I think we need some backstory.

Roger: Backstory...let's do it.

Max: Have you heard of Nikola Tesla?

Roger: Who hasn't? The great scientist, all his discoveries.

Max: Okay, so I won't go into it.

Roger: Whoa, hold on, I'd still like to hear your take on the story.

Max: Oh, all right...in the early 1900s, Nikola Tesla built this huge antenna called the Wardenclyff Tower in Long Island. This monstrous radio antenna was about two hundred feet tall. Locals panicked at the sight of this eyesore, with many speculations. Many thought this would electrocute anyone, or anything, in the area. Others thought it would stunt their children's growth and cause deformities. Still others were convinced Tesla was using the tower to sell secrets to the communists. The government claimed Tesla was using his technology to create a death ray that could destroy airplanes.

Tesla denied such claims but would not specify the tower's true purpose. He only stated it was for experiments to create more efficient energy for all. It was believed the government was seizing some of Tesla's assets. Tesla couldn't seem to get a break and was becoming deeper in debt. In 1917 the tower was destroyed.

Despite Tesla's setback, he continued to work tirelessly on his secret project. Although his enormous tower was destroyed, he continued to experiment with other radio towers of smaller scales. He became obsessed with his work, becoming a recluse to the world around him. In 1929, just before Tesla's mysterious disappearance, he wrote a letter to the New York Times. He even included a key to his current hotel residence, which contained all his new research. Nikola Tesla claimed he had discovered alien life in another galaxy and had been in communication with them for almost thirty years, over eight light-years away.

Roger: Has Tesla or his body ever been found?

Max: Not to my knowledge.

Roger: Why do you think he waited all that time to tell anyone about these aliens?

Max: There are different theories. Some think he was in grave danger and needed to expose the truth before his life was taken.

Roger: Why do you think he waited?

Max: I think he wanted to be absolutely sure. He figured no one would believe him unless he had concrete proof. I think the longer he communicated with the aliens, the more he discovered and more he became obsessed. I think he was afraid this discovery would put a target on him, so he ran off, changed his name and wanted to see this all unfold from a distance. Tesla probably wanted to show the world how great a scientist he was with one huge breakthrough. In the end I think he wanted to lay it all out on a table, as if he just dropped the mic, so to speak. One big F-you to the whole scientific community, especially Edison.

Roger: Good theory.

Max: Tesla did communicate with aliens. He learned to translate their languages, was intrigued by their culture, and learned a great deal about technological advancements. Volumes of schematics were discovered in Tesla's residence. Military and civilian scientists from around the world studied his work. These documents contained detailed diagrams of spaceships, the ion engine systems, and even how to freeze a living being in cryo-sleep over long periods of time. Another huge discovery was that of a natural wormhole within our solar system. This had unique properties that could link our star systems with his alien friends. In fact, that's how Tesla had been communicating with them. His radio waves sent through space would reflect off the so-called walls of this wormhole and could be received at the other end, light-years away.

It didn't take long for our engineers and scientists to transmit a message to the newly discovered distant star system, named Stella, to confirm the truth. They used Tesla's language guide and were in direct communication with people from the moon of Viridis. News was traveling expeditiously across our globe. People from every country were obsessed with learning all they could of our new distant neighbors as each new discovery brought on speculation, awe, and fear. Once Nikola Tesla's discovery had gone public, it forever changed the course of history as we all know it. This is when the reader thinks, oh, alternate timeline.

Roger: They say the aliens look just like us—that can't be right. You were there, did you see any ETs or Vulcans?

Max: *E.T.*? That was an outstanding movie! The title character, Elliot Taylor, a boy that loves D&D, meets a Jedi from a distant galaxy, runs from the authorities, and then gets real sick—great movie!

Roger: That's not how I remember it.

Max: To answer your question, no. The people of the Stella system are biologically exactly the same as us. Sorry to disappoint. I did see some from the moon of Viridis that looked like Vulcans, except for the ears, of course—they had Earth ears.

Roger: I heard there are three groups of aliens?

Max: Yes, each group lives on a separate moon orbiting the planet Centrum. The Stella system has one star and I believe twelve planets.

Roger: You believe twelve?

Max: There's debate about a couple of them. The people from the three moons don't always agree. None of the actual planets are able to withstand life. The planet Centrum is unique because it has three moons with intelligent life on them: Viridis, Nix, and Calidum. It's estimated that life originated on all of them millions of years ago. With different environments, they all formed their own unique languages, customs, traditions, religions, you name it. It was only about a thousand years ago that they discovered others existed within their own system.

The moon of Viridis is about eighty percent covered with water. Thousands of islands are spread across its vast oceans. Most of the islands have mass amounts of vegetation and gorgeous beaches. Viridis is a tropical paradise. They get tons of rain, but those warm sunny days make it worthwhile. Technologically, they have advanced quicker than the other two moons. We believe this is due to their islands. Their people were forced early to learn to travel by boat, then air. They learned many ways to communicate across the water, which led to radio transmissions. It wasn't long after that they were able to send messages out into space. Eventually, over some time, the moons Nix and Calidum picked up the transmissions. Then it was on. All three moons in communication. They were even able to develop a rudimentary fax machine to send pictures. They learned each other's languages, learned their customs and shared technology.

Roger: That's great that they shared.

Max: Well, Calidum is another story. Viridis and Nix mostly shared. Nix is—how should I put this? Nix is really, really, freaky cold. This frozen snowy moon is hard living. People can only live near the equator on the light side of the moon. The rest is too cold for anything to survive. It's the place no maintainer wants to deploy to. The Nix are survivors that lead decent lives and work hard. At the same time, you don't want to be on their bad side. They have some of the fiercest and toughest warriors.

Roger: I'd imagine so. With everything you're saying, I'm imagining fighters and hunters in a cold environment, similar to the Vikings.

Max: Well...I'd say more like Green Bay.

Roger: The third moon?

Max: Calidum is as opposite as you can get from Nix in all aspects. This planet is mostly desert and mountains. A very warm and dry place with not a lot of vegetation. The people on Calidum are farmers and miners. It's the place no one wants to deploy to, yet we all end up there.

Roger: Why is it so bad?

Max: The people of Calidum are set in their ways. They have strong ideals and don't want to compromise. Viridis and Nix share ideas and customs and have a general respect for each other, while those from

Calidum feel everyone should follow their rules.

Roger: Why do you think this is?

Max: Personally, I think the answer is simple. I think they need to have more fun.

Roger: Fun?

Max: Look at Viridis. Men and woman frolicking around half-naked on the beaches, some fully naked. They lay out in the sun. Drink wine all day. These people go out to parties. Their cities are full of life and entertainment. There's not a care in the world, or moon. I'm not sure what their saying is.

Roger: And the Nix?

Max: There's nothing more entertaining than watching the Nix Brawling Match. A huge stadium, two teams of fifty players on the field at the same time. I still don't understand all the rules, or lack of rules. Just imagine a rugby game with a hundred people on the field. Except there are no goal posts and no ball, just good old-fashioned carnage. The people of Nix know how to have fun. They work hard and play hard. The Calidums turn their heads at all these activities and believe they're righteous because of it. I think if they went out and had some real fun, they could enjoy life, and accept others.

Roger: They can't all be that way.

Max: Yeah, you're probably right. So anyways, back in the day the three moons continued communicating through radio. There was a huge push to develop space travel. With shared ideas between the Nix and Viridis, it didn't take long. Soon they ventured through space and connected face-to-face. Not long after that, the Viridis arrived on Calidum. For a while, things were good between all the moons. Then there were allegations the Calidums stole a spaceship from the Viridis. The ship was found eventually in a hangar on Calidum. It wasn't long after this that the Calidums engineered and developed their own spaceship.

Years went by, and space travel improved with many trade routes between the moons. There was always animosity against the Calidums from the other two moons. Which brings us to Centrum.

Roger: Centrum is the planet the three moons revolve around, correct?

Max: Yes, The massive planet Centrum. This place cannot sustain life, yet many have tried. Its temperature patterns are in constant flux, going to the extremes. Its acid rains eat though the toughest metals. But the main problem on Centrum is the wind, which rips through anything in its path. However, if the conditions are just right, one can land on Centrum safely and last a few hours.

Roger: Why would someone do that?

Max: Resources. Minerals as far as you can imagine, including platinum, iron and nickel. With the right mining equipment, the right weather monitoring systems and a whole lot of luck, mining is doable. Over time, people from all the moons figured it out and became rich, as they shuttled mining transports back and forth.

Roger: Sounds like they hit the jackpot.

Max: Let's not say that too fast. A scientist with the equivalent of a PhD from Viridis finally stood up to be heard. He alerted the entire Stella system to the apocalyptical problem they all face with mining Centrum.

Roger: What was his name?

Max: It doesn't matter.

Roger: Why would his name not matter?

Max: He's not part of the major story.

Roger: I think he seems important.

Max: Fine, his name is Peter.

Roger: Does Peter have a last name?

Max: Last name...Griffin, are you happy? No, wait, that's not right, I don't want to get sued. We'll just go with Jones. Before you ask, I don't know his first name. Anyways, Jones gets up and shows his complex formulas concerning the displacement of mass. Don't ask me to regurgitate it, I'm no scientist. The basic premise is that if you change the amount of matter from a planet or moon, it will eventually veer out of orbit.

Roger: That's not good.

Max: Nope. Then the debates came between the moons. Viridis wanted everyone to cease drilling, Calidum thought the scientist was dumb and made up false claims, and Nix had an idea that just might work. They could fill their transports with soil and rocks from their respective moons. Dump it off on Centrum, then mine the equivalent mass back home.

Roger: Did this work?

Max: In theory. Not in practice. Everyone assumed all others would follow these rules, so they thought, what would it matter if one or two mining transports didn't? No one wants to haul dirt across space. Many of these mining transports were random people with just enough money to buy a ship. They didn't see a need to follow the rules—let the others worry about this so-called weight displacement.

Roger: So now what?

Max: This is where Earth comes in. There was a call for help. They need a moderator. They need an enforcer that can regulate space travel. To act as a sort of customs for all ships coming and going between the moons and the planet. Over the years, they had also heard from Tesla of the number of battles we've endured. They learned about our World Wars and the technology we've discovered to better kill each other with. We're fortunate, or unfortunate, as it seems, to have a vast knowledge of military tactics. Our weapon systems have advanced far beyond their capabilities.

Roger: We do know how to destroy each other.

Max: True. A deal was made with Earth. Of course, the United States was the only country that agreed to all this. In return, the Viridis would continue to help us develop our space technology. They built the enormous transports used to ferry passengers and cargo to and from our distant systems across the Space Bridge wormhole. With the aid and resources of the Nix and Viridis, a few space stations were built, to include Space Station Prime. We brought men, women, supplies, and equipment, trying to maintain the peace. We also started shipping the BC-76s to the Stella system.

Roger: What's the BC-76?

Max: These are the main ships aboard Space Station Prime. Only the greatest line of spaceships ever built!

Roger: You say that with such confidence.

Max: Actually, if you ask any maintainer what the best spaceship is, they'll tell you it's the one they worked on first. The BC-76 is a truly impressive beast of a ship that can handle almost anything. Its eight powerful ion engines can support space travel or surface air travel in almost any environment. These ships can climb out of the moons' atmospheres with little trouble as their workhorse engines maintain an impressive thrust. The BC-76 can be configured as a bomber or cargo ship and is roughly two hundred feet long. The cargo bay can be configured for any combination of cargo or troop transfer, making this a versatile and essential transport. With its weapons loaded, it carries a destructive payload of guided munitions that can be delivered within a moon or a planet's atmosphere or even launched in space.

Roger: That sounded somewhat rehearsed.

Max: Well, I like that ship.

Roger: When was the first time you worked on one of these?

Max: To the Flightline...

CHAPTER 4

Night One

I woke up before my shift with my whole body aching. I got ready in my boots, pressurization liner and coveralls. Flip knocked on my door. We started walking down the corridors to get to work, carrying our backpacks with our helmet assemblies and gear. I was still feeling the pounding effects from last night but tried to hide it. Flip seemed perfectly fine.

I asked, "Where's Turtle?"

"He started an hour earlier than us since he works at the Tool Counter."

"I thought his job was Avionics like us?"

"He's still Avionics, just temporarily displaced. There's a bunch of miscellaneous jobs they have us maintainers do that aren't our primary job. It's called being *farmed out*. We have guys that debrief the pilots after each flight and record what's wrong with the ships. It's a full-time job because they process all the information and correctly submit it on each ship's computerized logs. Some of the sergeants are farmed out to the dark side and work in Quality Control. They come out and inspect our maintenance to ensure we're doing it correct and safe. Turtle will probably work at the Tool Counter for a year or two, then return to fixing ships again."

"That sounds horrible. Did he volunteer for that?"

"No one volunteers for these jobs. However, after being off the Flightline for a while, some get comfortable with it."

"What exactly is the Tool Counter?"

"You'll see it first thing tonight."

We walked up our last set of stairs and entered a large room with a bunch of maintainers in coveralls standing around, talking.

"This is it," said Flip. "We only have a few minutes—let me show you around quick. This is the roll call area. Next to it is the locker room. Put your bag down here for now. This other room is where they debrief the pilots. Over here down this hallway are all the senior sergeants' offices. That's where Tillhammer is. The very end of the hallway is where our chief and lieutenant are. Never go down there unless you've been summoned. Down this way is our auditorium for briefings. That other hallway leads you to the Tool Counter."

Flip stopped at one of the maintainers in the roll call area. "Max, this is Sergeant Jackson. He's our Avionics shift leader."

"It's good to meet you," I said as I shook his hand.

The sergeant smiled. "Welcome, Max. Tom Jackson, call me T.J. for short. I want to hear all about your trip over here and where you're from. However, it's gotta wait till later. We're forming up for roll call."

All the specialists and sergeants on our shift lined up in rows and columns. I stood between Flip and T.J. towards the back of the formation. Senior Sergeant Tillhammer stood in the front, reading off his tablet. He yelled out each of our names as we said, "Here," or "Present."

Tillhammer spoke in a slow monotone. "Make sure you wear your reflective vest every time you step foot on the Flightline. Last week Quality Control spotted a specialist just outside a ship, adjusting his harness. He wasn't wearing his reflective vest at the time, so now we have to explain to the commander why this happened and what steps we'll take to ensure it never happens again. Medical Bay is looking for volunteers to assist with its recurring blood drive. See Sergeant Diego for more details. The library is looking for volunteers to read to the children of Nix—don't worry, there'll be an interpreter. The kids will be here ten days from now for a field trip. See Senior Sergeant Fleming for more details. Chaplain McKinley wants to remind everyone that the Cookie Bus will be returning soon in full swing once every thirty days. He says not to be afraid to approach him. I need to see the following specialists after roll call to discuss your APRs..."

While he was reading off names, Flip whispered to me, "This is dragging on forever."

Tillhammer continued, "Now, Specialist Marcus York will give you a briefing. Front and center, York."

Big Marcus stepped out of the formation and went to the front, looking nervous. "Remember to always remember when your scheduled appointment is. It's not good to miss it, and if you do, it'll not be good for you or for anyone else. Also, I'm going to read off the people who have appointments tomorrow, so you need to remember that you have one tomorrow and not to miss it."

I could see maintainers trying not to laugh as Marcus was going through all the names.

Senior Tillhammer added, "Thank you, Specialist York. Everyone is dismissed to your expeditor."

Sergeant Peterson was our expeditor on shift. We grouped up around him as he was assigning work to all the different career fields.

After going through all the groups, he got to our team. "And for Avionics, I need Flip to ride the launch truck. Sergeant Jackson, go to Ship 222 to get turnover from the other shift. They're about halfway through a radar antenna change. Specialist Brightly, you take new Specialist Morgan to get tools and meet back at Triple Twos. Oh, Sharyn, make sure you train Max on the track system."

We went to the Tool Counter, along with many of the maintainers on shift.

Standing in the long line, Sharyn turned to me. "See, this is why I try to get tools before roll call—but, no, somebody dragged me to the Mountain last night, and I couldn't get here early enough."

"Hey, that was all Flip's idea."

"Oh, I know that. We had a blast. No harm done. Tomorrow, you get here before roll call and check out our standard tools. I'll show you how."

"Got it."

A number of maintainers were behind the counter handing out toolboxes and equipment to the rest of us. I saw Turtle back there as well, hurrying back and forth, getting the boxes or kits. Everyone had different tools depending on their career field, or the type of maintenance they were performing tonight. Once they took a good look at them, their tools were logged in to the computer under the individual's name. We got to the front and Sharyn asked Random Tool Counter Guy for an Avionics box.

We received the tools and Sharyn explained, "Every shift, we check out a toolbox and any other equipment we need, depending on what our work is. You have to look at every single tool and ensure all the tools are here."

The boxes had foam cutouts to let us easily see if a tool was missing. Each individual wrench or even small bit had a serial number lasered into it that matched the box number. There was also a checklist of all the contents.

Sharyn continued, "There better not be anything missing at the end of the shift. This will be checked in later, and if they find anything missing, our lives will come to an end fast. That's why we need to make sure it's all here before we check out. The entire Flightline shuts down if you lose a tool. They don't want that thing ending up in an engine or between the flight controls."

"Got it, don't lose a tool."

She looked at the Tool Counter worker. "We also need the radar checkout kit."

Random Tool Counter Guy responded, "I don't know what that is."

She yelled across the room, "Hey, Turtle, we're changing out an antenna and need that *special radar kit!*"

Turtle went to the far back of the room and brought us a small toolbox. I thought it was strange; all the kit had in it was a roll of aluminum foil and duct tape. I even looked at the checklist. Sure enough, it said the kit contained only those two items.

We headed to the locker room and put on our reflective vest, restraint harness, and helmet assembly that had an oxygen mask hanging down from it. Carrying our toolboxes, we arrived at a large door with a dozen warning signs on it. Sharyn hit the switch and sliding doors opened to reveal a tiny room. We stepped in and the door closed behind us.

Sharyn explained, "This is Entry Control Point One. There are five of them on the Flightline. There is absolutely no turning back now, only going forward from here. Just kidding, we can turn back. You just hit that button there. This entry point is where we hook up the other end of our harness to the track system in the floor like this. One final check of our tools—make sure your box is locked. Now hit the switch for the Flightline door."

I hit the big red button. The opposite door opened, and I was in extreme awe. I saw the expanse of stars beyond a massive clear dome that extended across the entire span of the Flightline and runway. Small lights zoomed across in the far distance beyond the dome. Those must be a few of our spaceships out there. On the ground in front of us were rows and rows of ships lined up as far as I could see. The atmosphere felt different. I could feel the cold, crisp air on my face. I heard the hum of power carts.

Sharyn spoke. "Taking it all in, I see. It's a trip. I remember my first time walking out here."

"This is crazy. We work out here every night?"

"Every night."

"Wow."

"Don't get too excited. After a while you'll learn to hate it. Let's practice this process right quick. Across the Flightline is the runway, and if you look up just at the edge of that far piece of dome, there's the giant space window above the runway. Every time a ship launches or lands, the alarms will go off and that window opens. When you hear the first alarm, you need to check your harness, secure your equipment, crouch down, put on your O2 mask and flip the switch. The switch activates your oxygen and pressure suit. Got it?"

"I think so. We practiced this in Tech School."

"Only this time there are no second chances. Do a quick practice run for me."

I quickly went through the motions, checking my equipment and crouching down with my mask on.

Sharyn corrected, "Good, but it's also a good idea to kneel or even sit on top of the toolbox, just to make sure it stays locked and in place. Let's go to work. Stay by my side. I'll help you out when we hear the first alarm. It's a bit challenging to navigate this track system, but you'll get it."

It was difficult to walk at first, dragging my harness chain behind with toolbox in hand. These tracks, embedded in the ground, spanned the distance of the Flightline. This maze of tracks reached every ship parking spot and even extended in front of the ships to allow the Crew Chiefs to marshall them out. Even the launch trucks drove on a rail system.

I felt a sense of enormous pride as we trudged past several BC-76s, ready to work on one of them. Of course, I suppressed my emotions. This was a typical night for everyone else. To me this was beyond anything I thought was possible. My heart was pounding. I tried to relish every second as I was so full of joy and awe. *I will never forget this moment*, I thought. *I'm in the US Space Military, about to work on a spaceship eight light-years from Earth. I finally made it to the Flightline.*

It was easy to spot Ship 222. Its nose radome was lifted in the air. The entire nose of the ship had a hinge assembly that allowed you to open it, pointing the thing upward and exposing a radar antenna. The antenna looked like a satellite dish. Only on Triple Twos, the defective antenna had already been removed and placed inside the cargo hold of the ship. There was also a large maintenance stand positioned under the radome, which was chained to the ground. Maintenance stands were platforms that could be extended high, with a ladder on one side.

Sergeant Jackson, or T.J., was there waiting for us. "Okay, team, the other shift removed the old one, so all we need do is install the new antenna and run it through an operational check."

I got on the stand and secured the toolbox to it. Sharyn and T.J. brought in the new antenna and joined me on the stand. They raised the antenna into position and told me where to install the bolts as they held it in place. We kept all the excess hardware in a bag secured inside the toolbox. As they held the antenna, I installed the bolts, and the antenna was up.

T.J. instructed, "Now connect the electrical plugs. Each one is labeled according to where it goes."

Fairly easy task, I thought as I connected all the plugs.

"Now's the tricky part," T.J. continued. "There's a waveguide tube that comes down that connects to the antenna assembly. Before we secure it, there's an O-ring that needs to be placed in its circular notch. It's tricky because if you put the O-ring in the waveguide, it'll easily fall out before you get a chance to connect it. Or worse, if it moves slightly out of the notch, it'll pinch and rip. This is our last O-ring, so don't rip it. I'm not sure if our Parts Supply has any more."

"That sounds bad. What if they don't?"

"Let's hope we don't need to find out. After years of doing this task, we've found the best way to make it stick is to get it nice and wet first. Here's the O-ring—you gotta put it in your mouth and get it real wet before sticking it up in there."

I did as I was told, but as soon as I got this small rubber O-ring in my mouth, a deafening alarm went off, the noise radiating across the Flightline.

"Alarm Yellow!" yelled T.J. "Max, close the toolbox. Lock it up! Make sure your harness is still connected to the stand!"

Sharyn screamed, "Put your mask on! Flip the switch!"

The three of us knelt on the stand when the Alarm Yellow tone changed to Alarm Red.

"You still have that O-ring?!" T.J. yelled through his mask.

I nodded yes.

"Good, don't swallow it!"

I felt the stand begin to shake; I felt my body being pulled as I hung on, trying to breathe through the mask with this O-ring in my mouth.

I heard Sharyn's muffled yelling. "This is awesome! Alarm Red on a maintenance stand!"

The suction died down and I heard the Alarm Green tone. T.J. patted my shoulder. I looked up and his mask was off. I took mine off as well and continued with the task. The O-ring stuck and I connected the tube.

"Next you need to install these tiny screws to secure the waveguide," instructed T.J.

There were eight tiny screws that had to be installed with a tiny Allen wrench. The problem with this was that they were above my head in a location that I couldn't see. I had to feel around for where these things went.

I had four of them installed when Sharyn screamed, "Vultures! Stop working!"

"What?!" I responded.

T.J. was in a panicked state as he turned on his tablet and quickly scrolled through the maintenance tasks.

"What step are we on, Sharyn?!"

"The last one, before the ops check!"

"I think I found it."

Just then a small flying drone, one foot wide, whizzed by our ship, slowing down to scan us with its camera.

"What's that?" I asked.

Sharyn answered, "Vulture drone. They're flown by Quality Control. They're checking up on our maintenance to see if we're doing anything wrong."

The drone zoomed off. T.J. sighed. "I think we're good. Hopefully it didn't see us with our tablet turned off. You know we need to be following our technical data step by step. Otherwise, we're dead."

I finish the last of the tiny screws. We unchained the stand, moved it to the side of the ship and rechained it. We then temporarily closed the nose radome and went to the ship's crew entry door. At this point we could detach our harnesses from the line and step in. Once inside the spaceship, we were able to take off our helmets as well. At this point Flip joined us after being dropped off by the expeditor truck. T.J., Sharyn, and Flip taught me how to turn on the radar system. They showed me all the bleeps, sweeps, and creeps.

T.J. then said, "Everything looks good, but we still need to check the close-range radar. We're only looking at the far end of the spectrum. We need to simulate a close radar signature. Flip, get Max prepped for the last check."

Flip looked at me. "Get out the radar kit. We need a target to be able to scan."

He then unrolled the aluminum foil and wrapped it around my torso around the harness connection point, securing it in place with duct tape.

Flip added, "Normally the radar won't pick this up, so we need to add more." He then wrapped the foil around my helmet and arms, attaching it with the tape.

Flip continued, "Now, walk out in front of the ship along the track. We'll see if we can pick you up on the radar."

I complied, not sure what to think of all this.

"We almost got you, now walk back and forth!" yelled Flip from the ship.

Just then Sergeant Peterson pulled up next to me in the truck along with a bunch of maintainers. They all pointed and laughed as I trudged back and forth wearing the shiny aluminum foil around me. I think some were taking pictures or videos with their tablets.

Flip yelled again, "Looking good! Now flap your arms up and down—I think we got you now!"

Sergeant Peterson, smiling, finally gave in and told me, "Okay, fun's over. Take that crap off and get back to the ship before that space window opens again."

I was embarrassed, yet very impressed at the same time. They were so convincing, with the so-called radar operation kit already prepared at the Tool Counter. These guys were good. We all had a good laugh, but I knew I'd have to be ready for anything.

Roger: That's great. How often does that window open and alarms go off?

Max: Too many times to count. All night, every night. Ships coming in, ships coming out. Flightline maintainers need to be ready. This is why they're constantly chained down, constantly aware of where their tools are at. We're trained to secure any loose equipment. Anything not secured will go flying. I saw a screwdriver fly right into the side of a ship once. It took the Sheet Metal team a whole shift to repair that panel. Extremely dangerous stuff, never a dull moment—you had to be focused.

Roger: Do you miss it?

Max: Only every single day.

Roger: Really?

Max: I miss being there, but I don't like the side effects.

Roger: Side effects? Explain?

Max: I was in a grocery store just last week. Walking down the soup aisle with my shopping cart. You know, the one with the wobbly wheels. I can never find one that works right. There was a guy walking behind me whose phone went off. No big deal, right? His phone's ringtone happened to be the same tone as Alarm Red. I heard that and immediately crouched down next to my shopping cart in a panic. I checked to see if my harness was secure, only to realize it wasn't there, and I wasn't on Space Station Prime. There was no threat of me being sucked out of this Wal-Mart on Earth.

Roger: Then what did you do?

Max: Nothing. I stood up and grabbed a can of chicken noodle soup like nothing happened. This is my life. This is a constant issue. You hear a sound that brings you right back in an instant. You know you're not in any danger, but you're still in a panicked state for that moment.

Roger: How do we fix that?

Max: I don't know yet. I thought you'd know.

CHAPTER 5

I Don't Have Three Arms

The next few weeks went by quickly. I met more of our maintenance team and was getting used to the process. On this night they were troubleshooting a problem that was affecting multiple avionics systems. I got there late because Tillhammer needed me to update my training records first. I got off the truck with my toolbox and tablet in hand. As I approached the ship, I saw Sharyn get off. She was hooked up to the harness system and started running away in the direction of the entry control point, about forty yards away.

"Sharyn where are you going?!" Sergeant Peterson, the expeditor, yelled at her from his truck.

"I don't have three arms!" she yelled back.

"Got it. Get in, I'll drive you!"

"Nope, it'll take too long. I'm almost there." By that time, she was a good distance away.

Confused, I climbed aboard the ship to see Flip sitting in the navigator seat, staring at the monitor, which had a list of numbers on it. He turned to me. "Hey, Max, don't worry about coming up. Leave yourself hooked to the Flightline. I need you to order a 5009 avionics junction box and pick it up from Parts Supply. They usually have them in stock."

He pointed to the monitor. "We got multiple avionics fails, which probably means that box is bad."

I placed the toolbox down and secured it just inside the door of the ship.

"Where did Sharyn go?" I asked.

In a calm voice and with a serious look on his face, Flip said, "Well, you know, Max, she doesn't have three arms."

"I know that, but where did she go?"

"She most likely went back to the barracks."

Sometimes it's better not to ask. I'd find out eventually. Standing outside the ship, I called for the Expeditor truck on the radio. As I waited, I opened my tablet and did a search for the 5009 junction box. According to the system, Parts Supply should have two in stock. Just because it said they had it didn't always mean they did. I put in an order just as the truck showed up. Sergeant Peterson picked me up and drove to Entry Control Point Four. It was the closest one to the lift that goes to the parts warehouse. I made my way through the entry point, disconnected my harness and headed to the elevator to go down a couple levels.

Walking past the Personnel Office, I saw them sitting back in their comfortable chairs with their feet up on their desks, laughing and talking to each other. I just shook my head and kept walking. Those that work in the Personnel Office work on all sorts of human relations programs, budgets and policies. They also deal with keeping records of all the people on station. We'd need to go there if there was anything wrong with our records, such as our rank not updated or medals weren't in the system. If you needed to reenlist or wanted to end your military career, this was where you went. They'd usually look upset when you walked in because then they'd have to pretend to work for a bit.

Roger: Sounds boring.

Max: You said it, not me. I passed by their drab office, and I finally arrived at the Parts Supply. They have a large section of the space station that acts as a sort of warehouse to hold the spare parts for the BC-76. The people at Parts Supply remind me of librarians.

Roger: Librarians? Why?

Max: You give them a number code and they go down the aisles and find your book. Only here they find your box. Numbers and boxes.

That's all they deal with all day long. Number, box, number, box. They typically don't even know what's in the box. Some are really good at their jobs and know where all the boxes are based on their number.

Roger: How big is this warehouse?

Max: You know the last scene of *Raiders of the Lost Ark*?

Roger: Never saw it.

Max: Well, it's that big. This warehouse has commonly changed parts that we may need. By commonly changed, I mean it's a random sample of the BC-76's entire inventory of parts. Sometimes they have something in stock. Sometimes they must message Earth to send it on the next transport. Who knows how long that'll take?

Roger: You can message Earth?

Max: Not really...

Every few months when the Space Bridge Transport returns to the Earth's solar system, they physically send multiple messages on it. The enormous transport carries a lengthy inventory list from all agencies on station: Parts Supply, the chow hall, the market, the Medical Bay, Security Police and even the Mountain. All agencies send their wish list in hopes of receiving what they ordered. You can even request special items to be delivered to the market. Turtle was always ordering comic books and other random stuff. Then we all waited for the next transport and hoped we'd get what we needed. Sometimes your wish list would come, sometimes not.

The majority of the food and supplies come from the moons. However, many unique items must be sent. We also sent some of our bad spaceship parts to what they call a backshop on station.

I never saw it, but I heard we had people from Earth and Viridis working there. They'll take our bad parts, take them apart and attempt to fix them. These are then put back into the warehouse. Parts that are beyond repair must come from Earth.

Most of our Avionics parts are fairly small, usually the size of a large shoebox or even a small carry-on luggage. I waited for the Parts Supply specialist to bring me the junction box. She wheels this thing out on a cart. The 5009 was about three feet by three feet by eight inches, and it was heavy. The box it came in was obviously bigger. I carry this huge box through the hallway to the lift. Telling myself, *One step at a time, you got this.*

I walk past the Personnel Office, and I hear a voice. "Looks like you're struggling. You want to get there quicker?!"

I responded, "Yes, please."

"Then walk faster."

No help ever came, I just heard laughing. I continue to the lift. I didn't want to set the box down because it was awkward to carry, and I already had a good grasp on it. After hitting the lift-up arrow with my elbow, I rested the box against the wall, still holding it as I waited for the elevator. I then continued to the entry control point, hooked my harness to the Flightline, called the truck and got a ride. While in the truck, I managed to get the part out of the box it came in. The truck stopped at Entry Control Point One, where Flip jumped in, holding a few boxes of food.

We finally made it back to the ship. Sharyn came down and helped me get the junction box into the cargo bay. Flip gave us each a food box and an energy drink. As we ate our sandwiches, trail mix and fruit cups, I told them about walking by the Personnel Office. They had a good laugh as they imagined me struggling with this huge box across the corridors with the others laughing.

Flip shook his head. "Fucking Nonners."

On the floor next to Sharyn, I noticed a metal beam about three feet long. I asked her, "Is that part of a bed?"

"Yeah, it's one of the posts that hold my bed together."

"Why?"

"Well, I don't have three arms. After we eat, I'll remove the bad 5009 and show you how it's done. Then you can install the new one." Sharyn then asked me, "Did you ever find out who your roommate is?"

"Yeah, it's a Weapons troop, Specialist Warren."

"What's he like?"

"I don't know. He works on the opposite shift as me and I barely see him. I only talked to him a couple times. Seems nice. The thing I like is that he keeps his side of the room very clean."

At that moment, Sharyn and I both stared at Flip.

Flip spoke with a mouth full of sandwich. "What?"

I asked, "What about your roommate, Sharyn?"

Sharyn answered, "Sherice Monroe—she's that Hydro troop I was talking to just before roll call. She's nice. We get along and share a lot of the same interests."

"Cool."

Sharyn got up. "Alright, I'm done. I'm heading into the Wine Cellar."

The 5009 junction box was located underneath the navigation station called the avionics bay. You had to open a panel and scurry down into a closed-in space. There was only enough room for one person to sit down surrounded by electrical equipment and bundles of wires running in every direction. One could barely move around. It was even hard to grab a tool without hitting something. One had to be extremely careful getting in and out, as to not pull out a wire or break a connection point on any of the equipment. Sharyn got herself seated in the avionics bay. Of course, there were other names for this enclosed space. Some called it the Wine Cellar, others called it the Hell Hole.

Once Sharyn got herself positioned, I lay down and tilted my head to watch her remove the 5009. The huge junction box was vertically bolted to the side wall in front of her. She showed me the multiple electrical plugs as she disconnected them. After that, there were four bolts on each corner of the box. She removed the two bottom ones first and then explained the tricky part. You had to hold this junction box up with two hands as you removed the last two bolts with the wrench. Impossible if you only had two arms, and there was definitely not enough room down there for two people. Sharyn asked for the bed rod. With this three-foot stick, she was able to sit on it and use it for leverage underneath the box to hold it in position as she removed the last two bolts.

I helped her hoist the old box out of the Wine Cellar. After she got out, it was my turn. Step one was to position myself in this cramped space. It was very hard to get comfortable, sitting down, trying to position my legs right without hitting anything. It took some time getting in right and I knew it would be hard getting out. As they lowered the new 5009, I had to be extra careful that it didn't snag itself on any of the wires. Getting this thing in position was no easy task. I lifted it up to see where the four corners aligned with the bolt holes, then had to set this heavy thing down. She was right, I needed three arms. It took some time, but I was able to get the box propped up against the wall using the bed rod as leverage under my leg. The first bolt was the hardest. Once I got the second bolt in, I was home free. Two more bolts, then the electrical plugs were all I had left. I then felt something next to my back.

"What are you doing?" I asked.

"Nothing, just checking on you," Flip responded.

Flip was able to squeeze his legs and lower half down in the Wine Cellar, squashed up against me. I looked behind me for a second and could only see the back lower half of his coveralls. Then without hesitation, he ripped one. Flip farted, right then and there. He just laughed as he climbed out.

"I hate you!" I yelled.

I was helpless. Stuck in the cell. Trapped with nothing but the chemical warfare fumes left by my own teammate. With my under-shirt pulled up over my nose, I had no choice but to finish hooking this thing up with the lingering odor. After the installation, I climbed out.

Flip let me know, "I hooked up the air cart—we should be ready to turn it on."

"Air cart?" I asked.

"Our avionics equipment gets warm over time and will overheat if they are not properly cooled during operation," Flip explained. "On the ground we need an air cart. It's similar to a generation unit parked next to the ship, only a lot bigger. It's got a long collapsible tube to bring in the air, about a foot in diameter and—"

Sharyn interrupted, "What color is it?"

"I don't know why I'm telling you this, we can all see out the window."

Sharyn laughed. "We were just gonna see how long you were going to go with this, thanks, Captain Obvious."

We powered it up and had no faults—we fixed the ship. Using that method to change the part is how they did it for years.

Roger: Did what for years, pass gas in the Hell Hole?

Max: I was talking about the bedpost method, but yes, farting in the Wine Cellar was a staple tradition for all the newcomers. It never got old. We're so immature. Whenever we replaced this junction box, someone would scream they don't have three arms and go running towards the barracks to get a bedpost. Then the Vultures came.

Roger: That's the Quality Control team, right?

Max: Correct. I'll never forget...

Inspector Sergeant James approached me. "Where did you get that bedpost?"

I answered, "From my bed."

"Why do you have it on the Flightline?"

"Because I don't have three arms."

"Why do you have it? It's not authorized on the Flightline."

"I can't change the part without it."

"Bullshit, show me."

We went as far as lowering Sergeant James into the Wine Cellar and pointing out how to change the junction box. We were tempted to gas him out but decided that wouldn't turn out good. James still didn't believe you couldn't change the part without it, claiming the technical directions on the tablet never mentioned additional tools other than the wrench for the bolts. We wanted him to change the part himself, but he came back saying he was an Engine troop, not qualified to change avionics parts. He thought we were trying to trap him.

This discussion went on for weeks. We had every Quality inspector looking into this method of part removal as well as countless discussions with our chief and commander. Flip had the *honor* of demonstrating the removal and install of the 5009 before an audience of eight inspectors. Each taking turns popping their heads down, watching the procedure. The final decision was for us to fill out a form that would be sent to the Major Command on Earth on the next Space Bridge Transport. The form would ask for a permanent change of direction in the technical data to instruct this new method to remove and install the 5009 junction box using a special leverage tool. We also had to fill out another form requesting a new tool to be engineered in the shape of a bedpost.

In the meantime, we were granted a special waiver to use our current bedpost method, but only after our station commander approved it, each and every time. We also had to have a bedpost labeled and put in the Tool Counter as an official tool, which had to be checked out each and every time we needed it. We never heard back from Major Command, nor did we see any changes in the technical data. I went for months sleeping in my bed that had been zip-tied at one end, since my bedpost resided in the Tool Counter room. We still don't have three arms.

CHAPTER 6

No-Show

Roger: Hey, Max, sorry I'm late. I had other matters that needed to be attended to.

Max: No problem at all. I'm not on any real schedule here.

Roger: Oh, I know, but I'm starting to enjoy these little talks. So, what do they do in the Space Military if you're late?

Max: Well, I can't speak for the whole Space Military, but in the maintenance world it's never a good thing. If you're late or absent they call it a no-show.

Roger: What's so bad about a no-show?

Max: Individual organizations like Finance, the Training Office, or Medical have certain expectations and timelines as to who or how many people show up for their appointments. If we abuse this and are late or absent it supposably puts a strain on them.

Roger: Supposably?

Max: I've walked past these offices multiple times. The Finance specialists are always sitting around. When you do go and ask them to help with your paycheck problems, they usually show you which site to go to on your tablet in order to fix the issue yourself. I'm not even sure why they brought them all the way out there. The Training Office, on the other hand, usually schedules each class into four- or eight-hour blocks. Then they speed through the lesson quickly.

We're usually done in half that time, only for them to dismiss us early. What do they do with the rest of that time? You can't tell me we've wasted their time.

Roger: What about Medical?

Max: Medical is just the opposite. They're always working. Waiting rooms packed with people, nonstop. One after the other, a never-ending line of customers. If anything, us being absent will give them a break for a minute so they can move on to the next three dozen patients.

Roger: What happens if you miss an appointment?

Max: Every time a maintainer misses an appointment, it goes on a status slideshow in front of the Maintenance commander in the daily morning briefing. The chief, lieutenant and all the senior sergeants attend these meetings. The senior sergeants and the no-shower's supervisor must stand up and explain why this person missed the appointment. Sometimes the shift expeditor will have to explain it as well. Then they need to explain what is being done to the individual, and what steps are being taken to prevent this from ever happening again in our unit. It's an agonizing drama to watch, and even worse to be the one standing up in front of the commander.

The statistics on the number of missed appointments are permanent and will remain on these slides until the end of time. They look at each month of stats as they compare them to the previous months. These numbers are tracked month to month, year to year, decade to decade. This is an obsessive futile effort to see a trend in missed appointments in hopes of stopping them forever. It'll never end. It doesn't matter what you do. We have brand-new specialists come in every few months. Individuals oversleep, lose track of time, get distracted by Flightline priorities, have actual emergencies, read their appointment time wrong, or are turned away from an appointment due to not having the correct items in their possession. For some reason that still counts as a no-show even if they showed up.

Roger: Wow, I guess it keeps you all paying attention to your personal schedules.

Max: I'll tell you what it does, it makes us freaking crazy...

This one instance I wanted to make sure I wasn't late to my training class, so I got to the Flightline early. We had all sorts of periodic training classes: fire extinguisher training, first aid to include CPR, small-arms training, cultural awareness to learn about the moons, and so forth.

On this particular occasion, I had the standard maintenance safety class. It was scheduled for four hours. It was more of a refresher that covered how to use the track system, the different alarms, tool usage and FOD control.

FOD is anything left on the Flightline or the ship that doesn't belong there. It's anything that has the potential to damage an engine if sucked in, or damage flight controls if it falls into the wrong area. We're constantly trying to prevent miscellaneous junk from being in the wrong place.

I secured my harness and started walking out to the spot. Sergeant Greenfield pulled up next to me in his Expeditor truck and asked, "What are you doing out here?"

"I was supposed to have my maintenance safety class. It says it's on Spot Two, but I don't see anyone else out here." I looked at my appointment reminder. "It's supposed to start in fifteen minutes."

"Are you serious?! That class is in the Training Wing, halfway across the station."

I read my appointment again. "But it says, *Bring your headset, reflective vest, and harness. Training at 1200 at S-2.*"

"That's S-2, not Spot two. It's the classroom number, in the Training Wing."

"What about all my Flightline equipment?"

"You still have to bring all that. They won't let you in if you don't have it. You won't actually use it in the classroom, but they need to verify that you have it. Now hurry."

"I can make it." I started to run toward the entry control point.

"Did you take the computer safety training course!" yelled Sarge as he drove next to me.

"Yeah, I did it last week."

"Did you print out your certificate?"

"Certificate?" I stopped, standing next to his driver's window. "I did the training. It's logged in the test database. Why do I need to print the certificate?"

"They won't let you in the class without that!"

"Can't they just look it up to see If I passed the computer training course?"

"They can, but they won't. They say they don't have the time to look up everyone's training. They won't do the in-person training unless you show that you did the computer training, and they won't let you in without that printout. I've been through this before with multiple specialists. It makes no sense, I know, but we have our hands tied. I hate to say this, but you'll never make it. By the time you log in to the computer and find a printer that actually works, you won't have time. We'll have to reschedule you for next week, but we're too close to the scheduled time. It's still going to count as a no-show against us. Shit, we can't get another no-show. I gotta think, gotta think..."

The expeditor then said to me, "I've got an idea that just might work. Get in the truck. We have less than ten minutes until your class starts."

Sarge then called our maintenance scheduler and put it on speaker. "Hey, Specialist Pechman, it's Sergeant Greenfield. Who else in our unit is scheduled for the maintenance safety class, besides Max Morgan?"

"Donar, sir."

"Okay, listen carefully—I need you to schedule a substitute. Put Donar's name under Max Morgan as a substitute."

"What? I can't do that."

"Yes, you can do that."

"Okay, I'll cancel Donar and put his name as Max's substitute."

"No, no, don't cancel Donar's original appointment. Just add him as a substitute for Max. Yes, I know. He'll be on there twice."

"Okay...if you say so..."

"Thanks, I gotta go."

"Five minutes left." Greenfield then called up Donar. "Hello, Donar."

"Hello, Sergeant Greenfield. I'm at the Training Office waiting to go in," answered Donar.

"Yes, I know you're at training. Listen, I need you to sign the class roster, then also sign next to Max Morgan's name."

"You want me to sign Max in?"

"No, don't sign his name, sign yours. You're his substitute tonight. Just cross off his name and write yours over it, then sign your name. I cleared it with Training—you're his substitute."

"So, I am going as Max?"

"No, you're still going as you. Let me start over. Next to your name on the sheet, sign in your name. Then go find Max's name and write your name next to it and sign your name. Yes, I know you'd be on the list twice. It's all good...are you good?"

"I think so."

"Okay, don't be late. We can't have a no-show. Oh, and you may have to take the quiz twice."

Sarge had a look of relief and pride as if he had just saved a flight from being canceled. He sighed. "See? That's how it's done. Those morons at the Training Office will scan all the names filled in on their roster. They'll only focus on the blank ones. Any blank name will be logged as a no-show. When they see your name crossed off and Donar in its place, they'll most likely check the substitute list on the Training database to confirm Donar was your substitute. No missed appointment. Genius at work."

Roger: Wow, I guess sometimes you just need to know how the system works.

Max: Almost.

Roger: Almost?

Max: I'd like to think it would have worked. However, Donar wasn't allowed in the class since he didn't know he had to bring his helmet and harness. He was turned away and prevented from attending. Sergeant Greenfield now has to stand up and explain to the commander why there were three no-shows for that class.

Roger: Three?

Max: Mine, Donar, and my substitute.

Roger: That doesn't make sense.

Max: Good, Roger, you're getting it now.

Roger: What happened to you next?

Max: I had to see the Hammer the next night.

I knocked on his office door. He said, "Enter."

"You wanted to see me, sir?"

"Actually, the chief wants to see you and he's not happy with you," Senior Sergeant Tillhammer said from his desk as I stood in front of him.

He continued, "Before you go into the chief's office, make sure you knock once on his door. Only open it when he tells you to, then slowly close the door behind you. Report in, and only call him Chief Rogowski. You will stand in front of his desk the entire time and maintain eye contact. Only talk when he asks you to. Answer everything with a 'Yes, Chief Rogowski.' Are you getting all this?"

"Yes, Senior Sergeant Tillhammer."

"Next time think twice about missing an appointment. You'll be going in alone. Come back and see me immediately after it is all done and over."

I walked down the long hallway, nervous and wondering what fate lay ahead of me. I approached the chief's office. The door was open. I could see the chief sitting at his desk, looking at his monitor. I timidly knocked on his door frame.

Chief Rogowski smiled and said, "Come in and have a seat." He pointed to a chair next to his desk. "Morgan. Max, correct?"

"Yes, Chief Rogowski." I sat down.

"It's just chief, or you call me Chief Bob. Where are you from, Max?"

"California, Chief." I tried to sit still without moving.

The chief talked slow in a sort of creepy deep voice. "That's a fine place, plenty of sunshine. I'm from its mirror image. Florida man myself. You go down the beach a lot?"

"I suppose, sometimes, Chief." My hands were sweaty as I tried to dry them on my pants.

"Why are you here? Something about a missed appointment?"

"Yes, Chief. I read the appointment slip and—"

"Let me stop you there," the chief interrupted. "Answer me this. Was it your *intent* to miss the said appointment? Did you wake up and say, 'You know, I'm just going to skip this one today'?"

"No, sir, I—"

"Let me tell you a story. I witnessed something in my youth. There were a couple of Hydro troops fixing a line going somewhere—it doesn't really matter where it was going. The specialist was working on getting the hydro line disconnected. He was a young pup—oh, I don't know, maybe eighteen, nineteen tops. This kid..." The chief stops and points to his head. "See my bald head? I can call him a kid. At my age, he was just a pup. So, the kid was green, and by green, I mean both very new and he came from farmland. Somewhere in Idaho, I suppose. Small town, low population. Next to the kid was his sergeant, his supervisor. He was a veteran, he was seasoned. Big fellow, muscular, from New York, looked like Mike Tyson. Do know of Mike Tyson?"

"Yes, Chief." I hated this; I just wanted his story to be over so I could go back to the Flightline. As he was talking, I looked around the room and saw various certificates and trophies of accomplishments. Looked like the chief was even a football star at one point.

The chief continued his story. "The sergeant stood towering behind the specialist, just watching, just waiting. The young specialist was struggling. He had the wrench on the bolt of the hydraulic line and just couldn't turn it. He had both his hands on it, pushing on the wrench, but he just didn't have the strength. Finally, the sergeant had enough. He told the specialist to lower his wrench. The sergeant then reached his huge arm over the shoulder of the specialist. He grabbed hold of the bolt with his bare hand and twisted it off with ease." The chief stopped for a second and asked, "You're following all this, right?"

"Yes, Chief."

"The young specialist was beside himself. He looked at his supervisor. Do you know what he said?"

"No, Chief. I don't." I was terrified at this moment.

"The young kid from the middle of nowhere looks up and says, 'Wow, you have gorilla hands.'"

I thought to myself, *I don't like where this story is going.*

The chief continued, "Can you believe that? Gorilla hands? That's what the kid said to his sergeant that looked like Mike Tyson. The sergeant's first instinct was to crush this kid's head in. But no, he took a second to look at the situation as a whole. *Intent.* This is a story about *intent*. The young specialist was from a small town in Idaho. He didn't know that was a bad thing to say to an individual like his supervisor. He was never taught that. The specialist saw a large hand and thought, *What else has a large hand?* You must look at the *intent* of what someone does or says. The sergeant realized there was no intent to offend him. It was meant to be a compliment. Does that make sense? Are you getting this?"

"Yes, Chief."

"You think on this. You can go now, Specialist Morgan."

I stood up fast. "Thank you, Chief." Then I headed right out of his office and went straight to Tillhammer. I knocked.

"Enter," the senior sergeant said. "No, stay standing. What did Chief Rogowski say?"

"I don't really know, sir."

"You don't know?"

"Sir, the chief—"

"*The* chief?"

"Chief Rogowski asked about the no-show. Since I didn't *intend* to miss an appointment, he sees no fault?"

"I still have to write you up. Do you have any questions or comments?"

"No, sir."

"You are dismissed. Don't miss another appointment."

CHAPTER 7

The Walk

Another night, another roll call. After Senior Sergeant Tillhammer went through the long list of names, he gave us updates. "Last week, a Quality Control drone caught someone not wearing eye protection while performing maintenance above their eyes. Those involved now know the penalty and the rest of us need to take steps necessary to ensure this will never happen again. There are several volunteer opportunities coming up in the next few weeks. Make sure you do a few of these so I have something to put on your APRs. One tomorrow involves helping the Finance Flight move furniture since they'll be moving their office to a different floor. See Sergeant Dorsey for more details."

Flip whispered to me, "Why can't they move their own crap?"

I shrugged my shoulders.

Tillhammer continued, "There will be a deployment to Nix in a few months. I need everyone to ensure your training is up to date."

Several members of the formation raised their hands.

Senior Tillhammer resumed. "No, you can't volunteer not to go. The Resource Office and the Production team will come up with the names. Remember, about thirty minutes from now, there will be a FOD walk for all. With that said and done, you are dismissed to the expeditor."

After getting the plan from Sergeant Peterson, most of us started walking out to the Flightline.

I walked with Flip. "Where are we going?"

Flip answered, "FOD walk. We gotta line up at the end of the Flightline."

"Aren't you going to hook in your harness?"

"No need right now. They gave the all clear. For the next couple hours, they'll keep the giant window closed. No ships coming in or out. You still need to wear the harness, just in case. Once everyone is here, we'll form one big line and all walk across the span of the Flightline looking for stuff."

"Looking for what?"

"Everything, anything that doesn't belong out here—hardware, trash, anything that has the potential to go flying in case the giant window opens. See? More people are coming out now."

"So why should there be anything at all out here if the giant window sucks it up?"

"It doesn't suck up everything. Stuff at the end of the Flightline near it, definitely. On the far end, it would suck up an entire four-foot-tall fire extinguisher if it wasn't chained down. The other stuff just gets tossed around or starts to fly towards the window, then falls once it closes."

"Who all is coming out for this?"

"Everyone associated with the Flightline: Fuels team, cargo loaders, Life Support, Ground Equipment, Weapons, even the flight crews."

"And Maintenance."

"Yes, always Maintenance. Quality Control runs the show for this one."

"Are they going to bring out the Vulture drones?"

"No, they'll come out here in person for these things. They like to do a head count of who's here."

"Looks like it's mainly Maintenance out here."

"What ratio of maintainers to the others do you think there is, Max?"

"Looks like about ninety percent Maintenance to ten percent all others."

"Really? Usually the number is lower."

"Lower than ninety percent?"

"No, lower than ten percent."

"Oh."

"See, Quality Control is out here now, doing the count."

We all spread out into this large line a few paces from each other. The Quality Control sergeant sounded a horn, and we all started walking.

As we walked, I scanned the ground. I asked Flip, "What do we do if we find anything?"

"You can put it in your pocket, put it in a bag, or just hold on to it."

"We didn't bring bags."

"I know—others did. You can just toss it their bags. See that guy? He brought a humungous garbage bag. What do you think he expects to find for that thing?"

"Who knows?" I started rambling. "FOD walk. FOD. FOD. What's FOD stand for again? Foreign Object...Debris?"

Flip answered, "No, Foreign Object Damage."

"Is it? You might be right. Then what are we looking for, damage?"

"Maybe it's both, I don't know. Yeah, I think it's both. I think it depends on the context."

"So, if a piece of hardware is just sitting there it's 'debris' and if it already caused harm it's 'damage' as in past tense?"

"Sounds about right. I found FOD on the ground or the bolt FODed the engine. Yeah, I guess it can be a noun or verb."

"What about an adjective?"

"What do you mean?"

"The FODed engine requires changing."

"Is that an adjective?"

"I don't know, I'm not an English major. The engine looks FODly today."

"I think you're making up words, but that sounds like an adverb, I believe."

"Where are we going with this, Flip?"

"I have no idea, Max. You started it, my good man."

"Hey, I think I found something. Yeah, it's a washer." Then in my best Stormtrooper voice, "Look, sir, droids."

"Yep."

"Really! All I get is a *yep*. That was funny."

"No, you're right, it was, but that's been like the tenth time I've heard that phrase since I've been on station."

"Well, sorry...I thought I was the first."

"Oh, don't be sorry. You said the right thing and at the right time, I might add. In fact, if you didn't say *the line* I would be concerned. Hey, there's some other stuff over here. I think these are some wire clippings and old splices."

"Which ship are we next to? I wonder who left that there."

"Oh, I almost forgot, Max. If you find a shiny golden bolt, that's extra special."

"Why, did you lose one?"

"No, Quality Control did. That is to say, they didn't lose it, but they usually put one out here somewhere to see if anyone finds it."

"So, you're telling me they purposely put a piece of FOD out here during a time when we're supposed to be preventing FOD from being out here?"

"You got it."

"What happens if we find it?"

"You get a prize. Usually, you get an extra night off work. That is, if our schedule can afford it."

"Sounds good, I'll take it."

"I'm not sure if I would."

"What do you mean?"

"If I found the golden bolt, I wouldn't tell anyone."

"Go on."

"I would put it in my pocket and act like nothing happened. At the end of the walk, Quality Control will see that no one turned it in, which to them means no one found it. Then they would go back to look for it and panic."

"That's insane, cruel, and ingenious. Go on."

"They would have to admit their mistake."

"Yeah, but then they'd shut down the whole Flightline and make all the maintainers go looking for it."

"It'd still be worth it. Hey, look down there."

"It looks like the tab off a soda can."

"Let me see that. No, that's definitely off a beer can."

"That's strange. So, what do we do with all this when we're done?"

"When we get to the end, we have to give it all to the Quality Control team. They take pictures of this trash and document everything. Then they put the pictures and numbers on a slide in front of the commander. They talk about it during the morning meetings and compare the numbers from this FOD walk to every single one ever conducted."

"So, are high numbers good or bad?"

"They're good. It shows how much stuff we found."

"I don't see it that way. I think high numbers are bad. We're the ones out here the most. If we were doing our regular jobs right, there wouldn't be anything out here to find."

"Wow, I think you just blew my mind. I think you're right, Max."

We handed over only *half* the FOD we found to Quality Control and found ourselves at the complete opposite side of the Flightline, away from our work center.

I asked Flip, "What do we do now?"

"We walk back. With the rest of the crowd."

"If we're all walking back to where we came from, wouldn't it make more sense to do another sweep of the Flightline in case anything was missed?"

"Nah, we're done. Look, Max, someone found the golden bolt."

"Looks like that one flight crew member that came out here."

"Great, he'll probably get a week off work."

We started the long trek back to our work center.

I asked Flip, "So what's your story? What'd you do before all this?"

"Who, me?"

"Yeah, what convinced Samuel Dolphline to sign up for this madness?"

"I was orphaned at a young age."

"Oh, I didn't know."

"My family's butler raised me. I would spend my days living the billionaire lifestyle and my nights as a masked vigilante fighting crime."

"Come on, Flip!"

"Okay, okay. I was adopted, so to speak. My birth mom got knocked up and had all sorts of problems with drugs and whatnot. I'd see her now and then, but it was really my grandparents that raised me. We lived in a small town in Nebraska. I almost dropped out of school a few times. I was held back a grade in seventh. It was always Grampa that forced me to continue. It wasn't that I didn't want to graduate. I just didn't want to be there. I wanted to be out doing other things. I guess I didn't see the point. Anything I wanted to know, I could just look up or ask someone that did know. Why do I need to know the life stages of insects? If I'm ever in the position where that info is relevant, I'll ask an expert."

"But you did graduate?"

"I did, just barely. After high school I had several jobs. I couldn't keep one for longer than a few weeks. I would just be bored or hate it. I had some weird starting jobs. I worked in a produce market, then cooked in a pizza place. I even spent a month setting floor tile. There was one job I had just before I joined the military that I really loved."

"What's that?"

"I worked as a cohost on a local radio show."

"No."

"Yes, it's true. I had a friend that already worked there, DJ Sammy Dee. I started hanging out with him and he got me aboard. Our show was so dumb. We would make prank phone calls and all sorts of stupid stuff. We did a lot of shenanigans on a live feed. I would go out and do something stupid as he talked about it live while he was video recording it. Then the videos would then be uploaded to the website. I'll show you if we ever make it back to Earth. That is, if the videos are still out there."

"Should be. Nothing truly dies on the Internet."

"Sammy Dee and I went to the city mall one day during his broadcast. You should have seen me. I was wearing a complete wetsuit, along with flippers, mask and snorkel."

"You walked around the mall with that?"

"Not only that, I swam in the fountain."

"Really, how long?"

"For eight and a half minutes. Then mall security came. He asked what I was doing there. I told him I was swimming. He then asked why. I told him I was looking for fish. I was escorted to a back room, and they actually called the real police to come get me."

"You got arrested?"

"Not really. The cop didn't even drive me to the station. It was almost worse; he drove me home! My grandpa opens the front door to find me standing there wearing a wetsuit with flippers with a cop standing next to me. I kid you not, no words were spoken. Grampa and the cop just looked at each other and gave each other the *disappointed dad* look as they shook their heads. I walked inside as the cop left."

"Was this the end of your radio days?"

"Oh no, Max, we were just getting started. Another time we went to the fast-food hamburger joint in the evening. I walked in wearing coveralls and had a clipboard. I asked to see who was in charge. The shift supervisor said he was in charge at the time. I explained I was from corporate and had already talked to their store manager, Mr. Kline. See, if you name-drop, it makes it more believable. I told the young shift supervisor I was here to exchange one of their obsolete tables for a new one due to the corporate agreement. I showed him which table we would be exchanging and had him sign the release form that I had pre-filled out on my clipboard. He even had a couple employees help me load it on our truck."

"You had a truck?"

"Sammy and I borrowed one from the radio station."

"Then what?"

"Then we went across the street to the taco place. I gave the taco shift leader the same spiel. I then gave the taco place the table we got from the hamburger joint. Then we went back and did the same for the hamburger joint. When we left, the hamburger joint had all red tables and one blue. The taco place had the reverse. It was glorious."

"Did they ever figure it out?"

"They did. Sammy Dee had a running bet on his radio show. People would call in and give the status of the table situation. It took twenty-three days before it was back to normal."

"You're insane. What's the craziest thing you guys did?"

"That would have to be the Great Detour. This took a whole team of friends. A bunch of us acquired some construction vests and traffic cones. We then started to divert traffic through the middle of town, making everyone turn right. At the same time, we had our other guys divert the cars through a neighborhood, blocking every way out, then back to the original main street. After all this was all said and done, these cars were driving in a continuous loop around and around. Most of them had their windows down, yelling and screaming. I just shrugged my shoulders and told them to talk to the next road worker, pointing them down the endless circle."

"How did it end?"

"Badly. It ended with the lot of us being hauled off by the police and sent to their station. My grampa was called. He actually pulled a few strings. I remember sitting in a cell when he stopped by. He said the police chief and him were pretty good friends. They were both in the Army Reserves together. He made a deal that could get me out of this, but I would have to make a decision."

"What's that?"

"If I joined the military, they would make this whole thing go away. I thought sure, I can spend two years away. No big deal. What's two years? I can do that."

"I think you're in for a bit more."

"That's the thing. I kept telling myself two years and I'm out. Then I went through boot camp and loved it. This is exciting. Something new every day. Meeting people from all over. I can do this; I want to do this. My granddad helped me. He told me if I followed three simple rules, I'd get through it."

"Only three rules?"

"Yep, he said start with these three. If I can last longer than a month, then I can start making up my own rules. Rule one, do exactly what you're told. If you're told to stand next to that green fence over there, you do it. Even if the fence looks brown to you, you pretend it's green and do whatever the sergeant tells you. Rule two, don't volunteer for anything. Rule three, keep your mouth shut. Rules two and three kind of go together. The first couple months are the hardest, but if you can get through being invisible, it'll be worth it in the long run."

"How'd that work out for you?"

"I took his advice seriously...and did the exact opposite. I questioned everything my drill sergeants asked the first two weeks. I was cocky and arrogant, I admit it. I talked constantly and was sure I wouldn't last more than another week. Then my drill sergeant said they needed to replace the current Dorm Chief and would consider volunteers. As a joke, I raised my hand and yelled, 'I'm your man, sir!' Would you believe they made me Dorm Chief?"

"You?!"

"Yeah, me. The crazy thing was that I loved it. I knew what needed to be done and I knew how to talk to people. It wasn't that hard. Just do what the drill instructors wanted to see. The rest could be faked. Even technical training was a blast. The point that I get to learn cool shit and they give me free food and a free place to live. This is a deal. Then I heard about this insane assignment of going to a distant galaxy. Maybe I was just crazy at the time, but I was all in. Of course, I didn't realize I'd be stuck working Flightline maintenance this whole time. It's not so bad."

"You're right, not so bad. It seems we made it back to our side of the Flightline. What do we have for the rest of the night?"

Flip pulled up his tablet. "We have that infrared sensor to change out."

"Really? I hate changing those. What's wrong with it?"

"It's got a cracked sensor screen and something on the inside is busted. Apparently upon landing they hit some FOD."

CHAPTER 8

Flying Beds

Roger: When did you see your first alien?

Max: I don't know.

Roger: How do you not know?

Flip and I were in the chow hall. After sitting down with our food, Flip asks me, "Max, you see that guy behind the counter that made you your omelet?"

"Yeah, what about him?"

"He's from Viridis."

"No way."

"It's true."

"I wouldn't have noticed. I didn't notice. I've seen him here for over a month, never even crossed my mind."

"I heard him talking with the other cook in a foreign language. Then I asked the cashier, Jaycee. She said they're both from Viridis."

"They seemed to understand English pretty good."

"Hard to tell, they only need to know a handful of food-related words. We normally just point to the food we want anyways."

"True."

"There's a bunch of them on station. Most people just don't see it. You may have already seen an alien and didn't know it. You know that guy with big gold bracelets in the barbershop?"

"Yeah."

"He's from Nix."

"What about the other one, with all the ear piercings and she's always jumping around talking crazy? I bet she's from one of these moons."

"No, she's one of ours. She's just really strange."

After our meal, we went back to the barracks.

Flip said, "Come with me. I need your help."

"What for?"

"It's been about a year since I pulled this one. I was going to fool you too, but I think you'll appreciate being in on it."

"Thanks…I think."

We went into Flip's room. He opened a desk drawer and grabbed a stack of papers. Here, take a look.

"This looks official," I said as I read the sheet. "'Attention all residents of Barracks Texas. We have recently received a shipment of new mattresses from the latest Space Transport from Earth. These will be delivered to your barracks on…'" I stopped. "The date is blank?"

"Yeah, we gotta fill those in. How about five days from now? That'll be…076 day."

"Okay… 'delivered to your barracks on 076 day. Each resident will need to bring their mattress down to the courtyard in order to receive their new one. These will need to be stacked neatly on the lawn in front of the Barracks Manager's Office. This will occur at 0700 and 1900 to accommodate both shifts.'"

"What do you think?"

I answered, "We work from 1800 to 0600. We won't make the 1900 time."

"You gotta put down two times for it to be believable, but truthfully the second time doesn't matter."

"Why is that?"

"Because everyone will realize it's a prank by the time the 0700 is over, believe me. News travels fast on station."

"What if Sergeant Mask finds out?"

"The barracks manager? He doesn't care."

"You said you've done this before?"

"Oh, yeah."

"So, won't they know it's a prank?"

"The guys that have been here awhile will just go along with it. Think of all the new people we've had since then."

"Why do we need to wait five days?"

"We need to put it in their heads, let it sink in, get them ready. It makes it more believable. Now we casually talk about this at work, get excited about getting a brand-new mattress to sleep on."

We added the dates and posted the flyers all around the barracks, then we sat in the courtyard watching. A few newcomers looked at the flyers and walked away. We saw some more experienced specialists laugh when they saw it and set a reminder on their tablets.

I asked Flip, "What other pranks do you have up your sleeve?"

"I'm working on a big one, but I don't have it all figured out yet."

"Well, what's it all about?"

"Let's just say it involves a disappearing room."

"In our barracks?"

"Yes, I'm going to make a room disappear."

"Go on."

"I'm still working out the details. I'll let you know."

A few days had passed. I was sitting in the cargo bay of Ship 3034 with a mess in front of me. One of our navigation components had a smashed plug on it. On an earlier flight the crew was loading some oversized cargo that wasn't secure. One of the boxes came off and crushed our component. The navigation box was easy to change, but its plug had to be replaced and many of its wires were severed. Each of these plugs have numerous wires going through them sending various signals to and from the component, which send commands to other instruments. This particular plug had twenty-eight individual wires running through it. Each wire had a pin on it that plugged into the other receptacle.

I had to solder new pins on many of the wires and double-check which wire went to which holes of the new plug. Any one wire put in the wrong position or not soldered correctly would cause a problem. I had to be careful. Like I said, it was a mess. We had a lot of avionics work on a couple other spaceships that night. Since this was really a one-person job, I was alone for most of this shift. My legs were getting cramped as I sat there trying to get into a more comfortable position to reach the wires. I looked at my tablet. The time just went from 2359 to 0000. It's now 076 day. Well, would you look at that, it's my birthday today. I wasn't going to make a big deal out of it. I doubted anyone knew anyways. I spent the whole night and early morning pushing through the mess. This was one of the most frustrating and tedious nights I'd had since I'd been here.

I finally finished the last wire, secured the rest of the plug and started cleaning up. Sergeant Banner and Specialist Jo-Leia Zwarc came aboard. They were on the Avionics team from our opposite shift.

"How's it going, Max?" asked Banner.

"I just finished the plug. All that's left is to push in the circuit breakers and run through the systems ops check. Hopefully I pinned it right."

"Great, we hope so too. We'll take it from here, thanks, Max."

Feeling exhausted from the work, I turned in my tools and met up with Flip. We headed straight to the barracks. Flip grabbed a cooler filled with beer and put it next to a bench in the courtyard. At about 0650, Flip starts yelling and knocking on doors. "Mattress exchange! Mattress exchange! Mattress exchange!"

I heard several others in the area join the chant from all three floors. "Mattress exchange! Mattress exchange!"

Turtle, Sharyn, and Big Marcus joined us at the bench. We passed them each a beer.

Flip said, "Sharyn, tell Max the news!"

Sharyn gave the news. "Marcus made sergeant. In fact, we both did. We'll start wearing the rank in a few months."

"Outstanding! Great for both of you," I said.

Flip pointed up to the third floor and patted my back rapidly as he jumped up and down. "There's one. Here we go, I'm so excited."

I look up to see a specialist carrying his mattress out of his room. He seemed to be struggling as he tried to carry it down the stairs. Three more came out doing the same thing. A crowd had gathered to watch in amusement, even the barracks manager, Sergeant Mast. News travels fast on Space Station Prime. People from other barracks came by as well. One from the second floor lost his grip on the mattress and it trampled down the stairs doing cartwheels all the way down the stairs. I looked over at the crowd of spectators.

I said to Flip, "Look, is that the cashier and cooks from the chow hall?"

"Holy crap, the two cooks from Viridis are here!"

Turtle counted a total of nineteen maintainers dragging their mattresses out. One from the third floor yelled, "Heads up!" as he tossed his down to the ground to the courtyard. Two more saw him do this and did the same thing.

"Flying beds!" yelled Turtle, then he ran and did a flying leap, landing with his body sprawled across one.

Big Marcus laughed so hard he spit out his beer.

Finally, someone yelled, "We've been had! There are no new mattresses coming!"

The look on their faces was priceless. Most looked confused. They were looking around with disbelief and started asking each other. It was obvious once they saw the mob of spectators laughing. Some of the crowd had their tablets raised as they were recording the whole thing. Even the Viridis cooks were laughing and pointing. The maintainers definitely knew it was a prank when they spotted our gang sitting back drinking some cold ones. The trio from the chow hall walked over to us.

Jaycee, the cashier, asked, "My friends want to know, did you orchestrate this?"

We stood up, and I responded, "Yes, but you have to give all the credit to Flip here." I patted his back.

She translated this to the cooks. They responded in their native tongue.

She repeated, "They are impressed and had a great moment to remember always. They wish you the best intentions in your future."

Flip responded, "Thank you, Jaycee. May I ask what their names are?"

"They are Bennold and Pawly."

"It's great you came out to join us, and we look forward to seeing you soon."

Jaycee translated the message. Bennold and Pawly smiled and bowed their heads. Then they put their fists out in front of them as if they were in a boxing stance. Flip and I smiled back and did the boxing fist gesture in return. They all smiled and walked off. Flip and I just looked at each other in awe.

I looked at my tablet after I heard a ding. "Hey, guys, I just got a message from Jo-Leia. Looks like 3034's nav system is good to go!"

"Yeah!" they all chimed in.

Sharyn laughed. "It keeps getting better. Now they have to drag these things back to their rooms." She couldn't contain herself as she snorted. "Look, they're trying to figure out which beds are theirs!"

Flip raised his beer and encouraged us to do the same. "Let us toast. Cheers. Happy birthday, Max!"

CHAPTER 9

Experience Points

Roger: Did you ever go to one of the Moons?

Max: I did, my first was Nix.

Roger: That's the cold place, right?

Max: Cold is an understatement, but yes. After the whole out-processing ordeal, I found myself on a BC-76 ready to depart.

Roger: Out-processing ordeal?

Max: It's always an ordeal. Basically, it consisted of a bunch of unnecessary steps and standing in lines all night.

Roger: Okay, then.

After the processing part, I found myself aboard one of our BC-76s for the first time as a passenger. My Avionics supervisor, T.J., was right by my side, helping me through this whole thing. We boarded the ship and sat in the cargo bay with the rest of our deployment group.

"I've always wondered this—why does the flight crew wear the specialized spacesuits and the rest of us don't on these journeys through space?" I asked T.J. "I mean, there's always a chance to lose oxygen, lose gravity or lose pressure, right?"

T.J. responded, "You know, that's a good question. We do have these little oxygen hoses that we can use. I think they're there just to make us feel better. I don't know, just another one of those things."

"It just doesn't feel right."

Before we knew it, we were taxiing across the Flightline. We felt abrupt acceleration as we roared down the runway through the giant window into space. Unlike leaving Earth, I didn't have the fear of us igniting boosters to leave the atmosphere. All the BC-76ers have gravity systems, so there was little chance we'd be floating around, as long as the systems kept working. Once in space, I moved towards the oval window on the side of the craft and peered through it. Nothing but the glory of open space. Even though I had been on station for some time, this was a new reminder of how far out in the vastness I really was. At one point we could make out the planet Centurium as we slowly creeped by it on the way to Nix.

Arriving on Nix was no easy task. We were told to secure ourselves in our seats. The rumble and pressure changes were insane as we entered their atmosphere and began our descent. The shaking was intense, and I kept wondering if it was normal or if we were being torn apart. I was so relieved once the shaking stopped. I looked out the window to see if I could make out the Nix landscape. All I could see was a dark layer of clouds. There were various lights beyond that, possibly some towns. It wasn't long before we landed.

Everything felt different here. As soon as I stepped outside the ship, I could feel the frozen crisp air stabbing my face with a hundred tiny needles of coldness. We moved quickly to unload the cargo from the ships and do the postflight inspections. Walking around felt strange. I felt out of shape, as it was difficult to walk, hard to breathe. Our bags felt heavier. Was this from being on the space station for so long? I found out later that the gravity on Nix had a slightly stronger force than on station. At least we weren't chained down to the Flightline. That was a huge change and mindset adjustment. I even went to chain the ship down and remembered it wouldn't be needed here. It was freeing not to have that constant fear of being exposed to space.

We couldn't do much that first day since it was pretty late. Our homes for the next six months were in a set of dwellings near the Flightline. Each dwelling had about twenty beds and that's it. At least our new temporary home was warm. The main issue was that the washrooms were in another building about thirty yards from where we were staying. It was horrible when you had to get up in the middle of your sleep to go outside to pee. Half-asleep, I would put on my unlaced boots and grab my large coat and run out in my underwear just to use the toilet.

That first morning on Nix, we all woke up to a surprise of three feet of snow. I squinted as I was trying to get used to the brightness. Everything was reflected off the frozen ground. I looked up and saw the bright glow of the sun just beyond the clouds. Then I remembered, *That's not our sun. That's the Stella Star and strangely this is the first time I've ever seen it.* The first day of my deployment, and I find myself standing on top of BC-76 with a shovel and broom. Harnessed to an attachment point, scooping off the layers of fresh snow, clearing it off the fuselage and wings. It felt like we were out here all day clearing snow and ice when the expeditor, Sergeant Greenfield, came by to pick up me and T.J. for lunch. He drove us off the Flightline a couple building away down to the chow hall.

Greenfield asked, "How you guys doing so far?"

I sat there in his truck covered with ice and snow, trying to get warm.

T.J. answered, "Good so far. When are we scheduled for our first launch?"

As Greenfield drove, he told us, "Hopefully tonight. Two are supposed to go up. We'll see if that happens with the snow and all. Did you hear about the Crew Chief, Sergeant Monty?"

We both answered, "No."

"He was up on a maintenance stand trying to remove the snow from 3034 and slipped. He tried to catch himself, but then he hit the ground real hard. He messed up his leg bad. I think it's broken. He's at Medical right now. I gotta check on him later."

"That's horrible," I said.

"What now? He's our best Crew Chief here," T.J. responded.

Greenfield answered, "I know, I know. First day and we're down one. We'll see what they want to do. Until then we'll all have to step it up."

T.J. and I got off the truck after it stopped.

Sergeant Greenfield told us, "You'll have to walk back when you're done eating. I gotta check on the rest."

T.J. and I learned the chow hall process. Seemed the same as everywhere—point to the food you want and watch them slop it on your tray. We got a table and ate fast.

I asked T.J., "This doesn't look too different than our food. There are a few things that look strange. Are the cooks from station?"

"No, they're all Nix. They just learned to cook some of our food."

"Nice. So, you've been here before?"

"I've been on Nix as a specialist, but not at this particular airfield."

"How different is this?"

"Last time we had a lot more people and a lot more ships. The building layout is way different. The only real similarities are our BC-76s and the cold and snow."

"There is plenty of that."

"On Nix, it seems we're snow and ice removers first and main-tainers second. You'll learn to drive the small snow loaders and even operate the deicers."

"Really?"

"Don't get too excited."

We finished up and headed outside. Bundled up, we start walking toward the Flightline.

I asked, "So, what's our mission here? I noticed none of our BC-76s are configured as bombers."

"From what I understand, we help transport goods across this moon. We're their main source for humanitarian relief. Anytime they need mass amounts of supplies or people sent somewhere, we can deliver. We also use these to transport the Nix Army troops and cargo here and there."

"I thought they had their own airplanes and ships."

"They do, but they're nothing like ours. With our radar capabilities and fast cargo loading, they aren't even close. Our ships can easily fly low-level just above their mountain ranges. Besides, we also have all those defensive countermeasures and infrared systems."

"What do we need defensive countermeasures out here for?"

"I'll tell you what, Max. I think I figured it out. It's all for practice."

"Practice?"

"That's right, practice. Why do we fly every single night on station? It's not like we transport stuff every time. Why are we flying every day here? It's all for practice. Think about it. On most of our missions, our cargo bay is empty. It's all to gain experience points."

"Experience points?"

"Everyone needs experience points. The pilots need to know how to get from here to there, how to put these ships through a gambit of options of defensive maneuvers, mountain flying, low-level approaches and so forth. The Load specialists need experience points in fast loading, multiple load configurations, and fast offloads. We as maintenance technicians and Crew Chiefs need experience launching and recovering ships. We need experience seeing what's broken and learning how to fix it. Think about it. If we sent a bunch of brand-new specialists in a real-life threatening situation where they had to do maintenance fast and accurate without fail, do you think they'd make it?"

"I see your point."

"It's all about practice, my man. Yes, we're here helping out the Nix move crap from here to there, but in the big picture we're training. We're gaining experience points in case the shit hits the fan and we need a crew of experts that can work together without fail in order to excel. Take it as you will, that's just my thoughts on why we do these things. The chiefs, officers and higher-ups may have another opinion, but this is how I see it."

"I think I'm getting it. Just answer me this. How does shoveling snow help me gain experience points? I was digging in a sandbox as a toddler."

"Perseverance, my friend. Learning to appreciate what you have, and what you're willing to do for the mission."

"Well, we're back to the Flightline. What's next on our list?"

"We unburied one ship from snow before lunch—looks like we have a few more to go."

"Can't they just run the engines up and take off? Won't the snow just fall off?"

"That's what I thought at first, but it's not the case. Too much ice and snow will weigh the ships down. There's an exact science to these craft. Extra weight will create a huge problem, causing a potential crash. Besides, any ice buildup within their flight controls can inhibit them, causing a lack of control. We need to fully clean them out—that's where the deicers come in."

The deicer is a huge truck with a lift that extends high in the air with a bucket of sorts on the end. It looks similar to an electrician's truck used to fix power lines. The truck is parked while a maintainer sits high above the ship. He then uses a combination of hot blowers and deicer fluid to break off the ice and prevent it from freezing again on the ship's surfaces. On Earth, these are fairly easy to use. The buckets are enclosed and heated where the maintainer sits in a chair with a couple of joysticks to maneuver around. They can also talk to the truck driver through a headset.

The problem was that we were not on Earth. The deicers we had were on loan from the people of Nix. All the instructions were written in Kereg, their native language. We had a guy from Nix try to explain to us how to operate it while a translator repeated. Even with the instructions, it seemed none of us really understood what he was saying. There were so many controls on this thing to heat the blowers and mix the fluid. Even driving it took a while to get used to. Nothing seemed natural. We used levers to turn. The acceleration and braking were done with hand controls. The Nix thought it was crazy that we use our feet to drive. The truth is no one really understood how to work these things. It was trial and error until we got it right.

The worst part about this hunk of junk was the bucket itself. This was not your enclosed comfortable boom. These Nix deicers only had a place to stand with some surrounding rails that came up to your waist. Totally exposed to the elements. There were a couple of hose blasters that you held up to shoot the hot air or fluid. You had to be careful with the air blaster, since it got hot very fast and could burn through your gloves if you weren't careful.

You could really feel the icy wind while being suspended high above the ground. The controls to move the boom back and forth were shaky and took some skill to move smoothly without allowing the whole basket from jerking around. After a while, the boom operator had to come down and swap positions with the truck driver in order not to freeze to death. I spent countless hours up in those things enduring the frozen wind.

Roger: What did you wear on Nix?

Max: I would wear underwear, thermal leggings, then the outer coveralls. I'd have two pairs of socks, one set being the thick insulated ones, with my winter boots. I would usually wear two T-shirts, then the long-sleeved thermal. Then heavy jacket over it all. I had a thin set of gloves, then heavy snow gloves over those. For my head, I usually wore what we called a head sock—a thick material that would cover my head, then come down over my ears and act as a scarf over my neck. You could adjust this so only a portion of your face was showing. I also had a set of ski goggles in case we were in blizzard conditions.

Roger: That's crazy. How'd you move around with all that?

Max: It was definitely a challenge.

Roger: What's the coldest temperature you experienced there?

Max: I believe it was negative forty.

Roger: Celsius or Fahrenheit?

Max: Does it really matter? Once it gets in the negative temperatures, it all feels like death. It's the wind chill that really gets you.

Roger: Why were you there again?

Max: I don't know, something about experience points.

CHAPTER 10

Heaters and Air Carts

One challenge on Nix was also a blessing. On shift we had to figure everything out on our own. With a small shift you really gain experience points fast because you're forced to. We were also constantly helping out the other career fields because they were short manned as well. Really a whole team effort out here. There were only four Avionics techs here. T.J. and me on one shift and Sergeant Banner and Specialist Ian on the other.

We were there for about a week and started to get a feel for things. T.J. and I had radio problems on Ship 1670 that we were trying to troubleshoot. We got called off that ship for a redball on another BC-76 getting ready to fly. We get to Ship 310 and see the problem. The satellite positioning system wasn't receiving any signals.

T.J. looked at me and said, "What do you think is causing that?"

"I don't know."

"You know the system. Think of the parts involved. What could cause it not to work?"

At this point I realized he knew the answer and was just testing me. "Probably the receiver or antenna."

"So, which one do we change?"

"The antenna?"

"Let's go with the receiver. Two reasons: the receivers break more often, and more importantly they're a lot faster to change. If it doesn't work, we'll look more into the system and as a last resort we'll change the antenna."

I run out to the expeditor truck and tell Sergeant Greenfield, "We need a satellite receiver."

He calls the Parts Supply on the radio. "See if we have a satellite positioning system receiver."

Even in a deployed location we still bring tons and tons of spare parts with us. Along with the parts, we bring a few Parts Supply personnel to manage it all. In a remote location like this, we're usually just renting out random buildings. We assign rooms for various offices, one to debrief the ships, one for Tool Counter. If there's a large warehouse we can use, we'll put all the spare parts in there and call it Parts Supply. I go with Sergeant Peterson to get the part. With part in hand, we arrive at the ship and get a call over the radio. Another scheduled flyer is having avionics issues.

Sergeant Greenfield tells me, "Give the receiver to T.J., then get back on the truck fast."

I ran out to the ship. It's easy to run without a harness strapped to my back, even though I have so many cold-weather layers on me. T.J. already had the old receiver removed.

I dropped off the new part. "I gotta go. We have another redball on a different ship."

"Good luck, you'll do fine!"

The expeditor drives me fast to Ship 3086. I ran off and headed to the flight deck. I was so nervous, I realized this was my first redball by myself. I could usually rely on others to troubleshot and make decisions. This one was all me. The pilots point to their screens and show me that almost none of their avionics are working right. I froze for a second, waiting for them to tell me what to do next. They just looked at me. I thought, *I gotta think of something quick.*

I told them, "We need to reset the system. Go ahead and shut down, then we'll bring it back up." It's like rebooting a computer. You'd be surprised, it works more often than you'd think. The problem is trying to explain it to the higher-ups. They'd ask, "How did you fix the ship?" "Oh, you know, I turned it off, then turned it back on. It's all good." Then they stare at you with concerned eyes, and you slowly walk away.

Anyways, today, luck was not on my side. Once the crew's systems returned, it still wasn't working right. I was breathing hard, sweating under all my clothes, almost in a panic state. Hopefully I wasn't showing it. I pulled up the maintenance page on their display screen and scrolled through to the faults page. Sure enough, I've seen these faults before.

I told them with confidence, "We need to change the avionics junction box."

The pilot asked, "How long? Do we need to shut down? What's the ETIC?"

"Um, I'll—I'll be right back."

I run out and tell Greenfield, "It's a bad 5009."

Sergeant Greenfield says, "Get in the truck." Then he called up Parts Supply to see if we had any, and he turned back to me. "How long will that take to change?"

"Maybe an hour if everything goes well."

Greenfield called the Production Superintendent in the building over his handheld radio. "Avionics needs to change the 5009 on Ship 3086. It'll take two hours."

The voice over radio responded, "Go to the spare."

Every day we have a number of ships that are scheduled to fly. The Crew Chiefs get them ready with all the preflight inspections, then they fuel the ships and ensure they're ready for flight. Along with the scheduled ships, we usually have a spare ship or two that are prepped for flight the same way. If there's any problem with the scheduled flyer that will take too long to alleviate, we'll transfer the crew to one of these spare spaceships.

The crew of 3086 grabbed their gear and went to the spare BC-76er, 0060. Their cargo load was transferred as well.

T.J. joined me on the truck. "The receiver fixed the other ship."

"That's great," I said.

"I see you ordered the junction box."

I explained the faults that I was seeing on the crew's monitor.

T.J. nodded in agreement. "Nice, I would have ordered the same thing. Since that's a one-man job, I'll let you do it. I'll head back to 1670 and see if I can figure out those radio issues. Let me know if you have any problems."

The expeditor truck dropped off T.J. at his ship, then he started to drive me to 3086.

"Sergeant Greenfield," I asked, "can we stop off next to the Tool Counter?"

"Sure, what additional tools do you need for that part?"

"I saw a wooden two-by-four lying on the ground near Tool Counter and I don't have three arms."

The spaceships had no heat while just sitting there. If we knew we'd be working on it for a while, we would drag out a heater cart. We had numerous heater units across the Flightline. These heaters here were similar to a power cart. Attached to the heater was a large collapsible hose about a foot in diameter. These hoses could be extended and placed inside the BC-76's crew entry door to heat the ship. Whenever we had work inside the ship, we'd have to bring these heaters out in order to survive out there for so long. Many of our components are in very tight places throughout the BC-76, like the Wine Cellar. It was hard enough to squeeze and contort our bodies to reach many of our parts. We'd have to get the heater hooked up, then start stripping layers of clothes off until we were down to a T-shirt, just to reach our maintenance.

Working on a component outside the ship was another story. It always took an extra maintainer or two. While one took the panel off or changed a part, the other maintainer had to stand right next to them, holding a heater hose and keeping them both warm. Without the heaters, frostbite and hypothermia would come fast. It didn't matter what we did, you could never get warm enough out there. Gloves were always a problem.

It's very difficult to do any type of maintenance wearing bulky gloves. You just need your bare fingers. This is especially true when you're working with small hardware and small tools, which is almost everything we do. The worst item to change in the cold is the radar antenna by far. Up on a maintenance stand, trying to keep warm. Aligning the antenna just right, then installing the bolts. It takes some practice to get it just right, but the worst part is using the small Allen wrench. These tiny screws are above your head, so you can't see them. It's impossible to hold a little Allen wrench with a glove on your hand. You'd have to take the gloves off. Something about the cold makes you lose feeling in your fingers. That's the challenge. Try to put screws in, that you can't see, nor can you feel where they go.

We pressed forward and kept trying until we got it. That's what all our maintainers did when facing something difficult. At that time there was no one else that knew our job. We couldn't just go to the Internet. We just pressed forward and worked our way through it until we fixed the issues. There were some issues that were hard to just push through. Other issues were the ones you thought you were doing right, but instead you found yourself fighting an uphill battle, to no avail.

Another day I was alone on the ship, loading the avionics program.

"What are you working on there?" said Sergeant Gray, a Quality Control inspector as he snuck up behind me.

He startled me and I almost jumped. It was a good thing I had my tablet out on the page displaying the steps of the procedure. Truth is I wasn't very familiar with the tasks and needed these steps to know the correct order of keystrokes.

"Just running through this program, sir."

"Can I see your tablet?"

"Sure."

Like I had a choice. While he was looking over the steps, I was in panic mode as I was running though questions in my head. Am I on the right step? Did I lock my toolbox? Did I document the ship's maintenance log correctly?

Sergeant Gray asked, "Where is your air cart?"

"My air cart?"

"It says you need to hook up an air-conditioning cart to cool down your avionics rack."

"It's like negative twelve outside."

"Are you arguing with me?"

"No, sir."

"Shut it down, then meet me in the building. I'll be in your superintendent's office."

I couldn't believe it, a Quality Control fail. I turned off the system and shut down the ship. All I was thinking was, *This can't be right.* Nothing about this seemed right. I looked around the Flightline. I didn't think we had an air-conditioning cart. I doubted one even existed on this frozen moon.

I wanted to find T.J. and let him know what was going on. Except he was on the opposite end of the Flightline, troubleshooting an autopilot issue. I arrived at the office of our Production Superintendent, Senior Sergeant Brooks. The door was closed. The door was never closed. Should I knock? I heard yelling—it was muffled, and I couldn't hear exactly what they were saying. It sounded like Senior Sergeant Brooks and Sergeant Gray were yelling. I sat on a chair near the office and waited. I felt like a kid going to see the school principal. I'd never really talked to the superintendent before. If he was yelling at the inspector like that, what was he going to do to me?

The door opened and Sergeant Gray stormed out of the office. He had a scowl on his face as he looked down at me and kept going. I guess he didn't want to talk to me.

I knocked on our superintendent's door frame. Senior Sergeant Brooks replied, "Come in, Specialist Morgan. I'm glad you're here, I was just going to send for you. Have a seat."

"How much trouble am I in?"

"You? Hell no! That inspector has no clue. You just worry about you. Let me handle Quality Control."

"So, what now?"

"This may go down as a failure on your part, but only because you should have let someone know about the requirement for an air cart. We could have fixed that before it escalated."

"I just figured—"

"I know, I know. It happens, not the end of world. I'll investigate this, and we'll have a solution soon. Hey, good job with that avionics redball the other day."

"But they went to the spare."

"That shouldn't be your concern. You immediately troubleshot the system and called out the correct fix. Our priority is to fix these ships—it doesn't matter how long that takes, as long as we're working smart. It's a good thing that problem came up before they launched."

"Thanks, sir."

"No, thank you. Good luck out there and try to stay warm."

I went from thinking my life was over to feeling pretty good.

Roger: What happened with the air cart situation?

Max: Idiocracy.

Roger: Really?

Max: Sergeant Gray contacted his supervisor on Space Station Prime. The next day they sent a BC-76 from the space station to Nix to deliver two air carts in its cargo hold.

Roger: It's twelve degrees and you still must hook up cold air conditioning?

Max: No, it was negative twelve, and yes. It keeps getting better. The step in the technical data says we need the air conditioning. We found out fast they weren't going to change that. Yet we'd freeze to death without a heater unit. So, there we were for the rest of the deployment, two hoses coming in the ship, one supplying cold air, the other warm air.

Roger: What about Sergeant Gray?

Max: We didn't see much of him. I think after his conversation with Senior Brooks, he was scared to come out to the Flightline.

CHAPTER 11

Field Trip

I had been on Nix for about a month or so when I was relaxing in the dwelling after working a full shift.

"To the Mountain!" bellowed a familiar voice.

"What?!" I looked behind me to see Big Marcus walking in carrying his bags.

"Big Marcus! What are you doing here?" I yelled. "Just passing through?"

"No, I'm here now. Just got in. I'll be here the rest of this deployment. They got me replacing Sergeant Monty. Something 'bout a broken leg?"

"Yeah, he fell hard. They sent him back to station."

"That sucks. Well, they knew you were all short-handed, so I'll be filling Monty's boots."

"That's great—I mean, not about Monty, but great to see you. Wait, I almost didn't notice your rank insignia. I guess I should be calling you Sergeant York now."

"No, you don't gotta do that."

"Looks good on you, Sergeant."

We went to the chow hall to catch up on what had been happening.

"I got good news, Max."

"What's that?"

"Sharyn and I are gonna get married."

"Wow, that's outstanding!"

"Right after I get back from here—we've been talkin' 'bout it."

"Perfect, I'm happy for you. You two are great. What else is new? How are the guys?"

"Not much is new with Flip. He's still up to lots of shenanigans. I'm not supposed to tell you about his latest one."

"Which means you're going to tell me."

"No, I promised."

"He's not going to prank me, is he? Then you have to tell me."

"No, nothing against you."

"Okay, okay, I won't dig. I don't want to get you in trouble. How's Turtle?"

"He's the same. They keep talking 'bout taking him out of Tool Counter and putting him back on the Flightline."

"Oh, yeah?"

"I don't think that'll be good. You didn't see him when he worked the line before. He was a mess."

"How so?"

"Getting Quality Control fails, losing tools, dropping parts."

"Well, maybe working in Tools has helped him. Wait, he dropped a part?"

"He dropped some avionics box during a redball—I dunno which one, all your boxes look the same. I was Crew Chief on that launch, and that was the last box in Parts Supply. They had to go to the spare. Then I heard he somehow dropped the infrared camera thing you got."

"Uh, I hate changing those."

"After that one, he was sent to Tools. That was before you came on station. Sharyn tells me everything."

The next few months were more of the same day in and day out. Snow removal, scheduled maintenance, unscheduled breaks, more snow removal and deicing. I did learn a lot more tasks. I was helping with refuels and ship recoveries. Big Marcus showed me how to marshall a ship out of its spot. Horrible process that is. I wished he never showed me the marshaling process.

When the flight crew is almost ready for launch, you walk out way in front of the ship. Then you wait, and wait, and wait. Then when you think they're just about ready to taxi, you wait some more. You almost start to go into a daze, just standing there staring straight ahead at this enormous ship as you keep telling it in your mind, *Anytime now.* The flight crew goes through their last-minute checks, waiting for the control tower to give them the clearance to start taxiing. Sometimes there's a problem with their checks, and they're just trying to figure it out. It's the worst when they open the crew entry door. That means they have a redball and need a technician to look at something. After that's resolved, you have to go through the whole waiting process again.

Eventually they shine their lights to indicate they're ready. That's when you snap out of your daze and tell yourself it's time. Wave the wands in a forward motion, then when they get to the right spot, you indicate a turn and watch them go. Lastly you give the ship a salute and they're off.

Did I mention we're on Nix? All that time standing and waiting in the extreme cold, freezing your butt off. There are no heaters out there in front of the ship. It's just you and the intense cold and wind. Horrible. After marshaling a couple ships in and out, they signed me off on the task. I was now fully qualified to do it anytime! Which meant whenever they needed someone, I was the guy. I told Marcus he should never have taught me. He just laughed.

We were coming up on our last week on Nix. T.J. signed up to go on some field trip when we all had a little time off. I signed up for it as well and tried to get Big Marcus to go.

I caught up with him after the shift. "Sergeant York!"

"Dude, it sounds weird coming from you. Just stick with Big Marcus."

"Okay, okay. Are you going on that trip?"

"Nah, what even is it?"

"No one knows. T.J. says it's a big secret, but we'll love it. Some sort of cool landmark or something."

"I dunno, maybe just stay in and write to Sharyn."

"No, man, you gotta come. It's the first time we actually have a full day off of maintenance. How often are you on a different planet, or moon, whatever, about to see something new? Besides, T.J. said he went to this place last time he deployed here. He seems really excited to show us."

"I'm not sure."

"He said they're even bringing a translator. We can talk to any Nix we see."

"But it's so cold out there."

"Okay, last try. Have you seen those big transports going up and down the roads?"

"The cool-looking green ones?"

"Yeah, T.J. says we're taking one of those."

"Okay, I'm in."

"Alright! I'll let him know. We'll leave the day after tomorrow."

The day of the trip, there were twelve of us maintainers going, to include T.J., Ian, Big Marcus, myself and others. The transport pulls up to where we were standing. This is going to be fun. The big green transport looked like a cross between a school bus and a snowmobile. We head on board. We were the last stop to pick up passengers. There were another thirty people with us from various career fields: Personnel, Medical, Security Police. Big Marcus and I sat next to each other.

The transport driver and tour guide were from Nix. The tour guide would point out things that we passed. We also had a translator named Marge from Earth that would, you know, translate. The transport roared its engines as we were off. This thing sped so fast I was a little nervous zooming across the road and even off the road, plowing through snowbanks.

The tour guide showed us various features, as Marge the translator told us what's going on. We passed a huge statue dedicated to the founder of the town. We passed several churches, including the oldest one. Then we passed other landmarks, to include an old radio tower that was the first one used to make contact with Viridis. After that we were cruising through nothing but a long, desolate stretch of land—looked like the salt flats in Utah. We get through that and head into an area with trees. Just then we saw something awesome. Two dozen actual dinosaurs were running. Marge tells us the Earth paleontologists would call these Gallimimus. A type of herbivore that almost runs like an ostrich. We watched these run alongside us in the transport as we glided across the snow. Instantly we start taking pictures with our tablets.

I turned to T.J. "Dinosaurs?! You never mentioned that."

Big Marcus was in awe and asked T.J., "Do they have the big ones or T. rexes?"

"Nah, but they did a long time ago. Most of those dangerous ones have been killed off."

Off in the distance, in the middle of nowhere, we see a huge structure. It looks almost as big as a football stadium.

Big Marcus looks at T.J. "Are we going to a game?"

T.J. answered, "No, it's more of a museum of sorts. It should be noted they just started allowing Earthlings to enter here. I was with the first-ever group two years ago."

"I was dragged out here for a museum?"

"Trust me, it'll be cool."

We park and our entire group heads in. It did look like a museum. We walked around and the tour guide showed us all sorts of artifacts and pictures of past explorers while Marge translated it all. It was somewhat interesting, but I didn't know who all these ancient people of Nix were, and I didn't really care what they did. I was glad T.J. was excited about this, and I was glad to see the dinosaurs. I spotted Big Marcus and felt bad—he looked so bored and out of his element. I felt horrible for dragging him along. We got to the end of the artifacts and pictures. Our group then stood before a large double door.

Marge translated, "They have asked that everyone leave your tablets and any other recording devices you have here on this table."

We placed our items on the table. Then a few Nix guards frisked each of us to ensure we complied. Marge continued. She told us if we want to proceed through the door, we must take an oath promising we will not tell anyone of what we see through the next room.

I look at T.J. and he gives me a nod of approval. We all agreed and repeated the words Marge gave us.

We stood there waiting. I was excited. *What is this? I know T.J. thought this was great—what could it be? Why so secretive?* The doors open and we step into a huge area as big as a baseball field. I stopped in my tracks. My body froze as I saw the structures. I was feeling light-headed as the blood seemed to escape my mind. I sat down fast right on the ground.

T.J. laughs as he comes to me. "You alright?"

I was almost crying. "It's—it's bloody Stonehenge!"

"Yeah, what do you think?"

"What do I think? It's fake, right? A copy? They copied us?"

"No, this is the real thing."

The stone pillars were in a circle shape. "It looks the same. This is Stonehenge. What's going on?"

"I honestly don't know. Nobody knows. They say theirs is about five thousand years old."

"Do you know what this means?"

"I know it's crazy."

"No, this is—this is more than crazy. This changes everything. We're connected—we're somehow—someone—this makes no sense. I need a moment."

"Dude, I didn't think you'd react like this."

"So, do they know what theirs is for? Did they figure out the mystery?"

"That's the funny thing. No, theirs is just as much of a mystery as ours."

"All I can say is thank you. This is cool, unbelievable."

I finally got up and joined up with Big Marcus. He thought it was great, but I know he didn't understand the significance of this. We spent a bit of time there, then we were escorted out and retrieved our tablets.

Roger: That is insane. We both have Stonehenge. What do you think it means?

Max: I'm still trying to wrap my head around it.

Roger: You said you took an oath? Not to tell anyone?

Max: Yeah, back then I kept it secret from my coworkers,. I didn't want to start an intergalactic incident. I did tell Flip and his reaction was similar to mine. Now, who cares who I tell? I'll never go back there. What are they going to do?

Roger: Your secret is safe with me.

Max: Besides, we all crossed our fingers.

Roger: You all crossed your fingers?

Max: We thought it'd be funny, the whole lot of us standing as we said the oath. We raised our hands and said the words, with our fingers crossed. Not even with the hand behind our back. We crossed the fingers of the hand that was raised right in front of them. They don't know our customs. They just thought that was the way we made a promise.

CHAPTER 12

Shenanigans

I finally returned from Nix and landed back on Space Station Prime without incident. I immediately met up with Flip and Turtle after their shift in the barracks courtyard.

Turtle yelled, "You survived the freezing!"

Flip said, "Welcome back. You look good. You look strong enough to pull the ears off a Gundark!"

I responded, "Thanks, Flip, I'm feeling good and glad I am finally back."

Turtle corrected, "That's Sergeant Dolphline to you."

"Sergeant?!"

Flip modestly grinned. "I'm no sergeant yet, but Turtle is indeed correct. I have been *selected* and will wear the prestigious rank of sergeant in a couple months."

"Well, great. I am happy for you. This is outstanding!"

"Let's talk. Turtle, will you do us the honors?"

Turtle exclaimed, "To the Mountain!"

Flip and I responded in unison, "To the Mountain!"

We got our drinks and found a table.

Turtle asked me, "You see anything different about that wall over there?"

After staring at it for a bit, I said, "Yeah, that picture is new. I think it used to be the Wright brothers."

Flip agreed, "Yes, indeed it was."

"Who's that new guy in the picture?"

"That, my pal, is the legendary Mr. Charles Taylor, with his epic mustache and all."

"Sorry, I've never heard of him."

"See, that's the problem, few people have. He was the mechanic for the Wright brothers. Charles Taylor is the world's first aircraft maintainer. He engineered and built their lightweight engine and fixed all their maintenance problems."

"How come I haven't heard of him?"

Turtle jumped in, "Pilots get all the credit."

Flip pointed out, "See, there's even a little plaque under his picture that explains all his accomplishments."

"That's really cool. Nice to see them put that up."

"Actually...we put it up."

"You put it up? When? How?"

"I know a girl that develops the photos that our navigators take from space. I sent her a picture of Charles Taylor that I pulled from my tablet. She was able to make it into this incredible photo. About a month ago, Turtle and I came here. While Turtle was distracting the staff, getting drinks, I snagged the Wright brothers from the wall. I went into the washroom stall, took apart the frame, and inserted Charles Taylor. Then I put it back on the wall without anyone seeing it."

"How long do you think it'll take before they realize it?"

"They probably already did. The staff just work here. They don't design what goes on the walls. They probably just assumed some higher-up wanted to change the picture."

"What did you do with the Wright brothers photo? Did you steal it?"

"I would never steal. It's still in the frame, behind Taylor."

"I missed you guys while on Nix. We had fun, but not to this level. It's great to have the three of us together again."

Turtle and Flip looked at each other.

Then Turtle looked at me. "We don't have long. I gotta go to Viridis next week. I'll be there for at least four months."

"Viridis!" I responded.

Flip turned to me. "You look upset."

"No, just thinking...I just know you'll be moving into the sergeants' quarters soon. Now Turtle is deploying. Both great things, but it's going to be strange with us all split up. At least I'll see you at work, Flip."

"Actually..."

"Actually what?"

"Actually, Senior Tillhammer split up all the shifts while you were away. You'll be on the other shift when you start back."

"Really?!"

Turtle jumped in, "So, anyone know where I can find a bathing suit and surfboard?"

I asked, "Tell me, Turtle, how did you get to go to Viridis? No one goes there. How'd you pull that off?"

Turtle ordered some more drinks. "Tell him, Flip."

Flip took a deep breath. "You know Random Tool Counter Guy?"

"Yeah, cool dude," I said.

"Well, he was selected to go with a bunch of maintainers and 76ers to Viridis. They needed him to keep track of the tools and equipment. Random Guy went through the entire deployment process. He was on the Viridis moon for three days until they sent him back."

"Sent him back? Back here? What did he do?"

"He didn't do anything. Well, not true, he did something, but that was years ago."

"I'm not following."

"Back on Earth, while he was still in high school, he was caught hacking into an elite college website."

Turtle interrupted, "He hit the various sites that handle admission, scholarships, and whatnot..."

Flip continued, "Apparently Random Guy, despite his poor grades, was all set to go. He gave himself a full scholarship, room and board and everything."

"How'd they catch him?" I asked.

"He was bragging."

"Bragging?"

"He was on some social media site bragging about what he did."

"Idiot."

"The FBI got involved. He was charged with computer hacking and fraud."

"So how was he able to get in the military?"

"That's the crazy part. Sometimes these agencies don't talk to each other. The FBI put Random Guy on a list. Which made it illegal for him to do two things. He wasn't allowed to log into the Internet, and he wasn't allowed to leave the country for ten years."

"We're in another solar system! He left the freaking country alright."

Turtle responded, "Technically not."

"We're not in space?"

"Oh, we're out here for sure, but he technically never left the country. See, Space Station Prime is still considered US territory. It's like leaving Washington and going to Alaska—still in the US."

"So how did he get caught at Viridis?"

Flip answered, "We have a computer system here that has an embedded FBI filing system."

"How do you know all this?"

"I was seeing a girl that works up there."

"Who? Are you still together?"

"No, that was like three girls ago."

"Was she hot? You still got her number?"

Turtle looked flustered. "Random Tool Guy!"

Flip responded, "Where were we? Oh yeah, the computer system with the FBI filing system. It's tied into the station's deployment records. The computers talk to each other. When Random Guy's living status changed from Station Prime to Viridis, it sent an alert to the FBI program. His file showed up and bam! He was sent back here in need of a replacement."

"So why did Turtle get selected? No offense, Turtle."

Turtle smiled. "I got skills."

Flip added, "They needed someone fast that knew the Tool system, and Turtle was the only one that had his training up to date."

"We're going to miss you. Good luck out there. I hear the beaches are wonderful."

Flip added, "Yeah, Turtle, they have nude beaches."

Turtle smiled big.

"You know," Flip added, "that means both women and *men* take their clothes off."

"What! I don't need to see that," said Turtle.

I laughed. "Don't stress him out. See? Turtle doesn't want to see the girls."

"That's not fair! Flip, tell Max about the room."

Flip answered, "Oh, you mean the disappearing room trick?"

I responded, "You actually pulled it off?"

"Yes, indeed, my good friend. This is going to be a long story."

"Hold on, let me get another round of drinks."

Flip started, "Once Big Marcus found out he was getting promoted to sergeant, I was close to having things figured out. Then when I saw your name on your deployment list to Nix, everything fell into place. Right after you deployed, our barracks manager, Mast, was replaced by Sergeant Belington. He came from the Personnel department—something to do with record keeping."

"That's too bad. Mast was cool."

"You can't be a barracks manager forever; I think he went back to working at the gym."

Turtle exclaimed, "There's a gym?!"

Flip continued, "The plan was in place. I had everything set. Maybe we shouldn't be drinking. This plan is complicated, and you must pay attention."

"Got it," I answered as I took another drink.

"Big Marcus had moved out of room 201 and was ready for his room to be inspected before a new specialist moved in. Sergeant Belington and Marcus arrived at his room, 201. Guess what they found?"

"I don't know."

"They found me!"

"They found you?"

"Yes, I was just getting out of bed."

"Marcus's bed?"

"No, he has a bunk bed."

"He never used to. He lived in that single room."

"Sergeant Belington didn't know that."

"Marcus was in on this as well. He told the barracks manager, 'Oh, that's just Flip, my roommate. I cleaned out my whole side of the room. I cleared out the closet here too.' Belington looked at his tablet. 'I don't see a Flip. What's your last name?'

"'Specialist Dolphline, at your service, sir!'

"'This says you're in room 200.'

"'No, I've been in 201 this whole time. Maybe Sergeant Mast put the wrong room number down.'

"'This also says you're supposed to be roomed with Specialist Michelangelo.'"

"Marcus turned to Flip. 'Who is Michael...something?'

"'That's Turtle,' I responded.

"Belington was looking confused. 'Yes, you should be with Michelangelo in room 200. He's the one with the scar, right?'

"I responded, 'He is, but, you know, I don't think this barracks has a room 200. I think the floor starts with 201.'

"Sergeant Belington took a step outside the room. 'Let's see. Room 202, 201. There's another room here on the end, but the door reads *equipment room*.'

"'I think they use that for overflow storage for some of the excess Flightline supplies. Do you have a master key?'

"'I think I do.' Sergeant Belington took out his master key card and opened the storage room, formerly room 200. It was packed from floor to ceiling with boxes.

"'Yep, that's definitely the excess Flightline supplies,' I said."

I asked Flip, "Excess Flightline supplies—what is that?"

"I made it up. Sergeant Belington worked in Personnel; he'd probably never been on the Flightline. So I went on, 'I think I know what happened with the roommate situation. I requested a room change to be paired up with Specialist Michelangelo, about six months ago. I bet Sergeant Mast changed it on the roster but never actually had us change rooms.'

"'Perhaps,' said Belington as he stared at his tablet."

"'Now that Marcus York left, can Michelangelo move in here like we were supposed to six months ago?'

"'Well, I don't see why not. We can ask him.' Belington looked back at his tablet with frustration. 'Where is Michelangelo at?'

"'Room 209, let's go see him.'"

"Hold on, Flip," I said, "209 is my room."

"Yeah, but you were deployed. Don't worry, let me continue. It all works out. So I led the trio down the hallway and knocked on 209. Turtle opened the door right away. 'May I help you?'

"Sergeant Belington asked, 'Are you still willing to move rooms to be paired up with Dolphline?'

"'I suppose. I could probably move my stuff out by...maybe tomorrow,' Turtle said, as he looked aroung the room looking at all Max's things.

"Sergeant Belington looked back at his tablet. 'This thing is so screwed up. Where are Specialists Max Morgan and Warren at? They should be here in 209.'

"Talking very rapidly, I responded, 'They're both deployed. Morgan is at Nix and Warren went to Calidum. Before Warren deployed, he was between rooms due to the last group leaving. Then, when they found out Morgan was going to Nix, Sergeant Mast put him in Morgan's room temporarily until he could per-manently assign him to the next available room. They should both be back from the deployment in a few months. With Michelangelo moving to my room, everything works out. Keep Warren and Morgan in the same room here at 209.'

"Sergeant Belington said, 'Let me get this straight. Dolphline and Michelangelo should be in room 201. Warren and Morgan are in room 209. There is no room 200, there never was.'

"I answered, 'I was really confused, but it sounds like you

understand it all. You seem more organized than Sergeant Mast. Thank you, Sergeant Belington, and welcome to Barracks Texas.'

"Belington looked flustered and muttered to himself, 'I need a drink.'

"Big Marcus raised his hands. 'To the Mountain!'

"I tried to stop him. 'No, Marcus, just—no.'"

The three of us got another round of drinks, and I had questions. "So basically, after everything was said and done, Turtle and you moved into Big Marcus's old room, leaving room 200 empty?"

"Precisely."

"You moved your bunk bed in there as well?"

"Correct."

"Where is Big Marcus's single bed?"

"In room 200. It was behind the boxes of the so-called Flightline supplies. I know a girl that works with Space Transport Receiving. She was able to give us a bunch of large empty boxes. I just had one row of them lined up in front of the door from floor to ceiling. Belington took one look at it and bought it."

Turtle yelled, "Room 200 has disappeared!"

"What is room 200 used for now?"

"We got rid of the boxes. Now this is our new living room. We have a couch in there as well. The hangout place—the place that only a few people know about. Turtle and I still have the keys to that room. I figure once I move out into the sergeants' quarters, I can still drop in from time to time and crash there."

"What about the key card for 201, where you've been living? You never had a key and Marcus had to turn his in, right?"

"Let's just say we were able to acquire a few blank key cards, and you know Turtle is good with a computer."

Turtle added in a deep voice, "I have a very particular set of skills."

I asked, "Last question, can I have the bedpost off of Big Marcus's old one?"

CHAPTER 13

Medical

Max: The next night I was running around with my in-processing checklist.

Roger: What are you talking about? Where are you going now?

Max: Nowhere. I came back to station. After being on Nix or any other deployment, I had to in-process back.

Roger: That makes no sense.

Max: I had a whole list of places to go. I had to go to Finance to fill out travel vouchers. Apparently, you get extra money when you leave, so that was a plus. I had to go to Family Support to ensure I was coping well with all the changes associated with coming back.

Roger: You experience change?

Max: I work on the Flightline—things are constantly changing. I get it. It's called Family Support for those that are married or have kids that they miss. I just don't see why they drag all the single specialists through this.

Roger: Well, maybe they don't know your status.

Max: Oh, they know. They have records on all of us.

Roger: I'm sure they're just there in case you need something or need to talk.

Max: I know, I know. I just like complaining sometimes. The worst of it all was going to Medical Bay. I must warn you, I'll probably do some more complaining.

Roger: That's what I'm here for.

Max: First of all, it's nothing but a big scavenger hunt.

Roger: Scavenger hunt?

Max: They give you a separate checklist of all the places in Medical you need to go to in order to in-process. I usually just run around and see which lines are the shortest and hope the long lines don't get any longer. You have to go to the lab to give blood. There's a stop at vaccinations to see if you're up to date. If not...more needles. Then there's dental to see if you're current or need to schedule any cleanings or work done. There's the optical center for contacts or glasses updates. The hearing lab is always fun.

Roger: Fun? I gotta hear this.

Max: What was that? Hard to hear you. It's the standard hearing test. They put you in a little soundproof cell and you're supposed to click a button every time you hear a faint ding over your headset. The dings get quieter and quieter as this program continues. In fact, the dings got quieter and quieter each time I took the test over the years. After a while in this booth, you start to hear faint dings left and right on your own. You start second-guessing yourself and hit the button at random times.

Then a computer voice comes on and says something to the effect of "Do not push the button when there is no sound."

Even after the test is complete, I still hear random beeps in my head for some time after.

Roger: What's next on your list?

Max: Usually, the last stop on the list is to go see the actual doctor. This process is so time consuming and I don't even know why. It starts with seeing the receptionist, who gives me a long form to fill out while I'm waiting for the doctor. Required items to fill out included full name, Social Security number, date of birth, gender...

Roger: You would think they already have that information on record.

Max: Yes, thank you! I cringe every time I fill out these forms. Here we are, a bunch of fools sitting in waiting rooms filling out redundant forms with information that's already on record. Each time I did this, I felt like either I was the butt of a practical joke or the people running this medical center couldn't come up with a better process. I should be able to walk in, scan my ID card and be done. Not only general information, but they also want a list of allergies, places I've been outside the station, past surgeries, past appointment dates. I can't remember all of this.

Roger: Did you have any serious health problems?

Max: Not really. Lucky for me, most of my issues came after my service.

Roger: Issues?

Max: Ringing in my ears, eyesight worsening, stomach issues, arthritis in my hands, backaches, undue stress, and I probably drink too much.

Roger: Did you drink before you joined?

Max: Not really.

Roger: So how much do you drink?

Max: You know those questionnaires I was talking about? They always ask the same question. "How much do you drink?"

Roger: How did you answer?

Max: Same as always, one or two a week.

Roger: How much do you drink now?

Max: One or two a week.

Roger: Mm-hmm.

I finally got called to see the doctor. Dr. Kim said, "I see you just got back from Nix, is that right?"

"Yes, just last night."

"How was it? Cold?"

"Well, yeah."

"Did you have any issues there? Any injuries, sicknesses, anything out of the ordinary?"

"Nope, all was fine."

"What about head injuries? Did you ever suffer any blow to your head?"

"Not that I remember."

"Did you see any combat?"

I thought to myself, there was a huge snowball fight where many of us suffered stinging ice blows, but I don't think that was what they were going for here.

I answered, "Nope."

"See anyone get shot or seriously injured?"

"No."

"Did you see anything that troubled you?"

I saw a man from Nix get out of the communal showers—that was troubling, but I'm sure that doesn't count. I told her, "Nope."

"Did you sexually harass anyone or did anyone sexually harass you?"

"No."

"Are you currently sexually harassing anyone or is anyone sexually harassing you?"

"No."

"Do you plan on sexually harassing anyone in the future?"

"No."

"Okay. It looks like you're in good shape. Do you have any questions about your health?"

"No, I think I'm good."

"Thank you, Specialist Morgan. Be sure to call if anything comes up."

Roger: Are these sessions always like this?

Max: Every time. Let's get back to the Flightline.

Roger: Let's.

CHAPTER 14

Compass Check

I arrived at the work center and saw so many new faces. Even though I was deployed for about half a year, a lot had changed in that time. Especially now, being on a different shift.

Senior Sergeant Fleming formed us up for roll call. "Good evening, everyone. Shift leads, let me know after roll call who's missing from your shop. The daily notes are in your email. If there are no questions, I'll be in my office if you need me. Dismissed to your expeditor."

Sergeant Diego, our Avionics lead, introduced me to the Avionics team. "Max, this is Specialist Galveston-Bergeson."

I shook his hand. "Galves...?"

He smiled. "Everyone just calls me G-17."

"Got it. Were you the only new Avionics troop we got this time?"

"Oh no, we got this dude on the other shift, Specialist Larry Alma. Ha, just be glad you're not working with him. He's real strange."

Sergeant Diego corrected, "Okay, be nice now. Max, I think you know Specialist Zwarc?"

"I've met Jo-Leia, but we haven't worked together."

"Let's get to work. G-17, did you get tools?"

G-17 responded, "Yessir, already got 'em."

"Great. Jo-Leia, take Gee to Ship 3086. Check out the infrared sensor. The flight crew said it would power up, but they didn't get a picture. Let me know where you are in a few hours. I may need you to ride the launch truck."

She replied, "Got it."

"Also, take your time. Go through the entire system with G-17. Just like I taught you."

"Will do."

"Max, you come with me. We need to check out Ship 1670."

It felt strange walking out to the station Flightline. Awkward to wear my gear again, the harness and helmet assembly. Seeing the hustle of maintainers walking to the ships, dragging their harness chain and toolboxes with them. Expeditor trucks driving in circles, directing the entire operation. It's hard to think the entire time I was deployed, this place continued to operate without skipping a beat. Maintenance never stops.

Walking to the ship, Sergeant Diego asked about my trip. He said he had been on Nix twice before and wouldn't hesitate to go back. We arrived at 1670, took off our gear and sat on the flight deck, up in the pilots' seats. We looked out the window across the Flightline.

He asked me, "Max, what do you know about avionics?"

I replied, "That's a broad question. Where should I start?"

"Exactly, too broad of a term for a simple answer. That's why you always need to break it down. Always break it down and isolate it into simple facts. Let's start with the navigation system. Do you understand how the nav system works as a whole?"

"Partially," I answered. "I know the system takes inputs from various systems to determine the most accurate location of the ship."

"So, what are those systems?"

"Let's see—there's the satellite positioning system that takes inputs from the satellites orbiting the various moons and above our Space Station Prime. There's also the internal nav system, and the compass system."

"Good so far. How does the compass system work?"

"Well, I know it doesn't do much on station here, or in space, but it can be used while in the moon's atmosphere."

"How is that?"

"I believe each moon has a magnetic north, so to speak, like Earth."

"Are they exactly like Earth?"

"No, each one is off by a certain number of degrees."

"You're on the right track. What is it called?"

"Great, now I'm trying to remember from tech school. I believe magnetic field versus geographic poles."

"Right, Max, but what does that mean for us? How does our BC-76 interpret that?"

"Okay, that I don't know."

"Our nav computer. Once the pilots select the atmosphere they're in, the computer translates the difference. If they're on Nix, the computer reads its magnetic field, then calculates the difference and gives the crew the actual geographic pole to orient, as long as those calculations are already pre-entered. Part of our job is to ensure these calculations are in the system before they depart to one of these moons."

Diego continues, "How about that satellite system? How does that work, Max?"

"That seems fairly straightforward. We bounce off a signal from any number of satellites. The computer calculates the distance, and it triangulates exactly where we are."

"There's a little more to it, but I believe you got the general picture. What about the internal navigational system?"

"I know there's an electron gyroscope involved, but I don't know exactly what it does."

"At least you're honest. The electron gyroscope senses movement. It's really that simple. It senses the acceleration the ship travels in any direction. It times how fast its lasers travel in relation to the movement."

"So how does it know where it is?"

"It doesn't."

"It doesn't?"

"No, it knows where it used to be. The only way to know where you are is to know where you used to be. See, it calculates its starting position and adds acceleration from different directions. Think of it as a chessboard. Have you played chess?"

"Of course."

"You have a knight, and you know where it started, then you

know it went forward two squares and left one. It should be easy to know where it is at now, right?"

"So basically, the internal nav records movement and places the ship in the new destination based on past movement?"

"See, you're getting it. All these inputs are sent to the mapping system and displayed on their monitors. This is another thing to check. Before a ship departs to one of the moons, we need to ensure a current map is loaded."

"So, the whole system takes all these calculations and determines the most accurate location of the ship and tracks it on the map. Makes sense. How do we check that?"

"See the screen here? Select preloaded destinations, then find the moon, hit select, and there you see it."

"So, if the entire nav system is off, how do we know which one is messing up?"

"That's where troubleshooting kicks in. You need to isolate the systems and see which one is off—we'll get to that. Here's another question. What's your best source to use to troubleshot? How you do know what each system is capable of?"

"Our tablets, the technical data. It has the whole description of our systems. There are even little troubleshooting trees, right?"

"That's a good place to start, but to really know your system, you need to look at the wiring diagrams, the schematics. These will show you everything about these systems. Every wire, every ground, every relay and how it's all connected to all the other systems. Learn these and you're home free."

"We went over these in technical school, but I still don't understand all the symbols."

"Looks like you got some homework. If you want to be lazy, learn these systems."

"Lazy? What do you mean?"

"I've seen maintainers spend countless hours running in circles over a fix when they could be done in minutes. The more you know, the easier this job is."

We finished going through the operation check again and I asked Diego, "We've gone through the whole checkout a dozen times—why haven't we seen any problems or errors? The crew wrote up the nav system as being intermittent."

"That's how it goes. Sometimes there's a problem that seems to go away. Maybe the system booted up bad with the crew, maybe they didn't go through the procedure correctly, maybe there were solar flares—who knows? It happens. As far as I can see, we went through this checkout thoroughly. I'm confident enough to sign it off as good."

"What will the expeditor say?"

"Sergeant Greenfield knows me; he'll agree with me. If it's not broke, don't fix it."

"Okay, then."

This wasn't the only learning session. Every night on shift, Diego would take me, G-17, or Jo-Leia through the process of each system. Sometimes separate, sometimes together. Then he'd give us homework. He would assign tasks. Diego would give me a week to look up the entire radar system. At the end of the week, I would have to give him a written report on where every part is in the system, how it's all connected, which circuit breakers are involved, what commonly fails on it, and how to fix each common fail.

It was frustrating at first but was fun after a while. I learned everything. By writing it all out, I could picture each system in my head. Since I had all these reports on my tablet, it became a helpful guide for me. I would be riding the launch truck and hear over the radio that the satellite positioning system was failing and could quickly pull it up on my tablet and see the whole system, giving me a good place to start. I was happy to see G-17 learn as well. I wished I had this when I first started.

There was one night in particular that resonates in my head. Sergeant Diego and I went to separate ships, which were parked next to each other, to do a satellite radio check. We would use the encrypted radio to bounce a signal off one of our space satellites, then back to the other ship. It allows the ships that are across the moons to still communicate. It seemed strange to communicate this way since we were in ships sitting next to each other, but it served its purpose. On the Flightline, we have various maintenance frequencies we use to perform these checks. They're reserved just for this purpose, to do radio calls ensuring all is heard loud and clear. On the ship by myself, I set the radio up and dialed in the maintenance frequency.

Then I made my radio call. "Triple Twos, this is Ship Balls Sixty for a radio check on satellite. How copy?"

I heard nothing. Not only did he not respond, I heard nothing. Usually I could hear the sidetone—that's when you hear your own voice over the headset. I looked over to Sergeant Diego's ship and saw him through the window. I pointed to my headset and raised my hands as if I didn't know. He gave a look that conveyed, *Figure it out.*

I went through the checkout again. I must be missing something. I checked the right frequency, the satellite configuration, the system looked like it was working. I thought to myself, *What would Diego do? Nothing, Diego always does these things right. I need to eliminate the variables.*

I turned on the local radio and called Station Tower. "Tower, this is Ship Zero-Zero-Sixty with a maintenance radio check. How copy?"

Still nothing, not even sidetone. Okay, now I was getting somewhere—it just wasn't the satellite radio. I looked back over to Diego; he was just sitting there patiently.

The regular ship's interphone was next. "Test, test."

Nothing. Was my headset bad? I looked down to where my headset cord connected to the ship. It was plugged in...but not plugged in. I was in such a hurry to get this check done that I didn't realize the plug wasn't completely secure in the receptacle. I snapped it in place.

"Test, test." *There it is.* I switched over to the satellite radio. "Ship Triple Twos, this is Balls Sixty for a radio check on satellite. How copy?"

"There you are. I copy you five by five," answered Sergeant Diego.

Five by five is radio talk, means *loud and clear* on a scale of one to five. If it's loud and not clear, they may say *five by one*. I was just relieved to hear Diego.

Still talking over the satellite frequency, he then added, "What was the issue? Looked like you were struggling."

"I was, but I figured it out. Stupid mistake, headset not plugged in all the way."

"Ahh, the old headset trick. What's important is that you figured it out and now you'll always know to check that."

"So, do we always use this frequency to do maintenance checks?"

"On the satellite radio we do. If we stay on long enough, we may hear from one of our maintainers on Viridis or Nix. Hey, look out there—the Cookie Bus just pulled up."

"What's the Cookie Bus?" I said as I saw a bus pull up outside my ship.

"It's how the chaplains give a little back. One comes out here periodically to hand out snacks and drinks. It's all good. Go ahead and shut down, grab some food and meet back up at my ship."

"Copy."

I shut down and departed the ship, hooked up my harness and headed to the bus. I saw that it was also on the track system like our expeditor trucks. I released my harness; enter the Cookie Bus and I was immediately greeted by Chaplain Christopher McKinley.

The chaplain greeted me. "How are you tonight, Specialist Morgan? I saw you departed that ship. Working on anything of interest?"

"Just checking the satellite radio."

"That's great, we sure appreciate all you do."

"Thanks. So how does this work? Do I have to transfer money to pay you or...?"

"No, no, It's all compliments of the chapel. Grab a few cookies and coffee, or juice if you prefer. Grab some for your buddies as well."

I grabbed a handful of cookies and two cups of coffee and started to head out. The chaplain saw me struggling to hold my drinks and secure my harness.

"Let me grab those drinks while you hook in," Chaplain McKinley offered.

"Thanks, sir, I appreciate it."

I arrive at the ship and make my way to the flight deck. Sergeant Diego greets me as I hand him a coffee and a couple cookies.

"Thanks, Max. I'm about finished updating the ship's maintenance log."

We both sat in the pilot seats, enjoying our cookies and coffee.

Diego then asked me, "What ship do we need to work on next?"

"Doesn't the expeditor tell us?"

"Oh, he does. In fact, he did; Sergeant Greenfield told me a list of things we need to do in order. However, I'm asking you. If you were in charge, what would your priorities be?"

"I'm not sure I'm following."

"Let me show you. Bring up your tablet. If you go to this screen, it shows you the flying schedule. These are the ships scheduled to launch in the next night or so. Now look at all the jobs assigned to our career field. See right here? This is all the avionics issues with our set of ships. It states the severity of each job. Level three indicates the ship can't fly until this is fixed. Two means it can fly, but only under limited situations. One shows it's just a minor problem."

"I didn't even know all this was out here."

"There's a lot to learn."

"Based on this, I think we should check out the radar glitch on 2046."

"That's a good guess. However, I know the engine shop is running up the engines on that one now."

"How about the autopilot on 3034?"

"Why's that?"

"Well, they're scheduled to depart to Viridis about fourteen hours from now, and I don't think the crew wants to fly manually there."

"Very good."

"Alarm Yellow!" I yelled as I jumped up and hurried to close the crew entry door in time.

I came back to the flight deck just in time for Alarm Red. The spaceship began to shake a little, but it was secure.

Diego pointed in front of us. "Look—look at the Cookie Bus!"

A few of the bus windows were left open. Coffee cups and napkins were being sucked out of the bus like a tornado had grabbed them. We could see Chaplain McKinley with his O2 mask on, frantically trying to close the windows. It was getting worse—now cookies were flying out as well as juice and coffee. I felt bad for laughing, I think we both did. The poor chaplain was getting covered with liquid, struggling to get the last window closed. Looking up, we could see an updrift of cookies, cups and napkins being hurled through the air towards the space window.

Alarm Green finally chimed. We received a radio call from Sergeant Greenfield to help with the cleanup effort. Everyone was to walk the Flightline to recover any leftover debris from the fiasco. I could see specialists running to pick up cookies. A few started eating the ones they found. Diego and I went to the Cookie Bus to help Chaplain McKinley clean up his mess. The chaplain looked exhausted and defeated as he sat on the floor of the bus, covered in coffee and juice, a handful of napkins in his hand.

Sergeant Diego looked at him and said, "Well, Chaplain, you came all the way out to the Flightline just to toss your cookies."

Then we all laughed and laughed, like it was the last scene of an '80s sitcom.

CHAPTER 15

Take Me to Church

Months flew by. I was able to see Flip, Sharyn, and Big Marcus, but our time together was limited. I'd see them at the shift turnover, or sometimes on our night off we'd meet for an hour or two. It's difficult being on different shifts. No one saw Turtle as he was probably living it up in Viridis. Part of this still felt right. I loved working with Jo-Leia and G-17. I was learning so much on shift with Sergeant Diego.

Then I received a special invitation message on my tablet. I was requested to attend the marriage of Sharyn Brightly and Marcus York. It looked so formal. I worked it out with Sergeant Diego and supervision to get part of that night off. In fact, so did Jo-Leia.

On the night of the wedding, Flip and I arrived at the chapel on station. The groomsmen were Flip and me, while the best man was Crew Chief Arthur Jordan. Along with Big Marcus, we all wore our military dress uniform. It didn't take much time for me to get it ready. I hadn't worn it since the short span right before I'd left Medical Bay with Tillhammer. I did have to loosen the belt a bit. I also had to help Flip with his uniform. He couldn't find half his stuff and we ended up borrowing pieces here and there from other maintainers.

The bridesmaids were Jo-Leia Zwarc and E&E's Beatrice Thatcher, the maid of honor being the Hydro troop Sherice Monroe. Sherice had been Sharyn's roommate in the barracks for years. When the bridesmaids walked out, we couldn't believe how gorgeous they looked. They wore strapless silver dresses that sparkled and had a long slit along their legs. They had ordered the dresses from Viridis. Night after night we usually only saw the girls in their maintenance coveralls with their hair tied back. It took us a second to even recognize them—they looked incredible. I was thinking, *I'm glad I got paired with Jo-Leia.*

I had to whisper to Flip, "Stop staring and close your mouth."

There was a pretty big group that showed up. Chaplain Christopher McKinley was presiding, while T.J. played the piano. I didn't even know he could play. It sounded great as we walked down the aisle with our partners arm in arm. Arthur and Sherice went first and Flip and Beatrice followed, while I walked in with Jo-Leia.

We stood at the sides of the altar. Big Marcus looked so nervous standing there waiting. The music changed and in walked Sharyn, beautiful white gown and all. Her supervisor, Sergeant Banner, handed her off to Marcus. The ceremony was wonderful. Everyone was smiling. Everyone was so happy for the young couple. Chaplain McKinley had a lot of great things to say about them and really focused on how big of a commitment marriage is.

They came to the part where the bride and groom would kneel, facing Chaplain McKinley and away from the audience.

Flip nudged my arm with his elbow and whispered, "Check this out."

The happy couple knelt, exposing the black soles of Marcus's shoes. In large white print read a word on each shoe, *HELP ME*.

You could hear chuckles from the audience.

I quietly asked Flip, "Does he know?"

"Marcus has no idea. Neither does Sharyn."

"She is going to kill you, you know that?"

"I know. Totally worth it."

The ceremony progressed. Chaplain McKinley gave the vows and pronounced them *man* and *wife*. We all clapped as Sharyn laid a big kiss on Marcus. After our wedding party departed the chapel, we stood around and talked for a bit. There was to be a big reception at the Mountain. They knew a few of us couldn't make it. I had to return to work. I said my congrats to Mr. and Mrs. York and started to head back to get ready for work.

Jo-Leia was right behind me and asked, "Care to escort me one more time back to the barracks?"

"Sure, are we walking arm in arm?"

"Not this time."

She took off her heels and walked barefoot with me across the huge space station. We got some very strange looks from others as we walked by their offices.

I said to Jo-Leia, "That was a great wedding. I'm so happy for them."

"It really was fun. I'm bummed we have to miss the reception."

"Yeah, me too."

"What did you think of Chaplain McKinley?"

"He gave a great speech at this event."

"Well, it's actually called a sermon, and the event is a ceremony."

"So, I learned something new. I take it you go to church?"

"Every Sunday. Well, when I can make it. The work schedule doesn't always allow it, but I try."

"That's great."

"You?"

"I went as a kid. I want to go. Part of me feels like I should, but for some reason I always find an excuse not to. Besides, it'd be weird going by myself."

"If you change your mind, you can always go with me. Sergeant Diego is always there as well."

"I may just do that."

We made it to the barracks. "Thanks for the walk, I'll see you at work."

"Oh, Jo-Leia...you look great tonight—I mean, the dress. You look...the dress is really pretty."

She rolled her eyes. "Thanks, Max. See you soon."

I changed back into my coveralls and headed to the Flightline, where I met up with Sergeant Diego and G-17. They were on Ship 1670, troubleshooting the radar system. The previous shift had already changed out the antenna, receiver-transmitter, and a couple other suspect parts, but the system still wouldn't scan properly. They were down to chasing wires. That's ensuring there were no opens or shorts on any of them throughout the system.

Sergeant Diego greeted me. "Welcome back, Max. Wanna pull up a wire diagram and see what you can figure out?"

"Always."

"G-17 is checking the wires at the antenna side...again. How was the wedding of the year?"

"Great, really good. Everything went perfect. I've never seen Sharyn and Marcus happier. Everyone agreed the chaplain did a did outstanding job."

"Chaplain McKinley, right?"

"It was."

"The chapel on station is a one-stop shop for all religions. Did Jo-Leia tell you about the big cross behind the altar?"

"No, what about it?"

"There's a huge cross for the Christian services. However, the cross can be swung to reveal a crucifix for a Catholic Mass. Then you can always close a giant curtain for any other service that doesn't want to see either of those."

"I was wondering about that."

"I think military chaplains have a difficult job."

"How's that?"

"Here's the thing. Everyone that goes to the chapel services or Mass loves the chaplains or priests. The people that go love the services. The problem occurs when the chaplain leaves the chapel."

"Problem?"

"A priest, minister, rabbi or monk are content being in their setting."

"This sounds like the start of a bad joke."

"It does, doesn't it? No, they're content in their element. They can stand up and have the freedom to say anything about their religion and everyone there will agree and applaud them for it. They can rejoice in the power of God or Abba. Give examples of Buddha's love or proclaim the gospels of Jesus Christ. It's all wonderful and has helped so many. However, a chaplain assigned to a military force seems to lose their power once they step outside their sacred area of worship. Hand me that multimeter, would you?"

"Here you go. Want me to disconnect the rest of these going to the RT?"

"Please and thank you." Diego continued, "When Chaplain McKinley is at Mass, he's comfortable and confident. I've seen it. When he comes out to the unit, he seems to be at a loss for words. Listen to him next time. You've seen him before commander's call or during your pre-deployment briefings. Everything is watered down and generic to try to appease every single military member in the audience. Bow your heads and meditate on your thoughts or your god, or spiritual well-being. Be kind to all, do unto others, and so forth."

"You're right."

"I know he means well, and I can't blame him. I can see the faces around the room. The religious that attend his Masses know he could do much better, while the nonbelievers are just rolling their eyes, wondering why they need to listen to a chaplain. No one is happy. I just feel bad for the chaplain. His prayers in these settings always ended the same—awkward silences and blank stares."

"What about the Cookie Bus? Everyone loves that."

"Everyone does love the Cookie Bus."

G-17 came back inside the cargo bay. "So, all the wires checked good. I still can't find anything wrong."

Diego said, "Look through the diagrams, see if you can find any other components running through this system that could cause those fails."

G-17 looked up. "Hey, Jo-Leia decided to join us."

She sure looked different coming back to work, I thought.

I said, "Welcome to the party."

She asked, "What's the radar system not doing?"

G-17 answered, "It's not scanning properly and we're getting these faults." He showed her on his tablet.

"Looks like an antenna. Did you swap out the antenna?"

"The other shift did," Diego answered. "It's the first thing they did."

"What if they got a bad one out of Parts Supply?"

We all stopped and just looked at her.

Sergeant Diego agreed and scratched his head. "Well, it's worth a shot. You and Max go get a new antenna, T.J. and I will keep looking this over."

Roger: So how could the antenna be bad? I thought it was new from Supply.

Max: The term "new" is a misnomer. Most of these parts are taken off the ship for a quick fix at the time. The part then goes to a backshop, where experts look into it and see if they can fix the problem that may be there. We have a backshop here on station. Any number of things can go wrong with these parts. Corroded internal parts, pieces disconnected, software that needs to be reloaded. Sometimes it just needs to be cleaned thoroughly. These backshops fix the problem, test it in their shop, and put the part back on the shelf in Parts Supply. Sometimes we get a part that still fails. Maybe it tested good, then something else failed. It may have been damaged when the Supply personnel were moving it around—who knows?

Roger: Sounds like it can be frustrating.

Max: Very. Once we got the new antenna, the change went smoothly and without issues. This goes fast when you have four people know-ing what they're doing. We then went to the flight deck and started to run through the ops checks.

Roger: Anyone heading out to wear aluminum foil this time?

Max: Nope, not this time...

As we were running up the check, crossing our fingers, Diego said to us, "I got a riddle for you all."

"All right, go ahead," I said.

"You're in a room. In front of you are three light switches. Each switch has a definite *off* and definite *on*."

"Okay."

"In the next room over, which you can't see from the first room, are three regular lightbulbs. Each lightbulb connects to one of the three switches. Starting in the first room, you can configure the three switches any way you want. Then you must go to the second room and tell me which switch goes to which light. This must be done without ever returning to the first room or using any special tools."

G-17 asked, "Can I bust open the walls and follow the wires?"

"No, you can't take anything apart. All you have is one shot at the switches and one time examining the bulbs. If you've heard it before or think you know the answer, tell me later or message me. I don't want you to spoil it for the others."

We ran through the rest of the checkout. Everything checked good. The scanning problem was gone along with the faults. We congratulated Jo-Leia and credited her for the fix.

CHAPTER 16

Turtle and the Cougar

It was a couple weeks after the wedding. I met up with Flip in the courtyard right after my shift. I knew he had the night off.

Flip ran up. "Guess what?"

"I don't know."

"Turtle comes back tonight with the gang from Viridis."

"How do you know these things?"

"I know a girl from the mobility unit."

"Of course you do."

"Turtle should be back in an hour or so. I already put a note on his door."

"What's the note say?"

"To the Mountain!"

Flip and I headed to the Mountain, and we started catching up on everything. After a bit I felt a tap on my right shoulder and immediately turned left to discover no one there. I turned to my right to see Turtle with a huge smile across his tan face.

He said, "Got you! Why'd you turn to your left?"

"Because you're always sneaking up on me and tapping my opposite shoulder."

"See, I knew that. That's why I stayed on your right this time."

I stood up and gave him a hug. "Welcome back, little man."

Flip joined in. "You look different. You look good—well, except for that huge scar of yours."

"Yeah, yeah, looking good and feeling good."

"Why's that?" I ask.

"I met a girl. I'm in love."

Flip and I looked at each other as if we both knew we had to squash this.

Flip started, "Turtle. You know what *deployment hot* means, right?"

Turtle responded, "Yes."

"Hold on," I said. "What's that?"

Flip seemed surprised, "Really? You were on Nix and never heard the term?"

"No."

"*Deployment hot* is the status of the opposite sex after you've been away for some time. After being somewhere that has tons of girls, you see things differently when you're away from that. Once you're working somewhere where your crew is limited, you start to lose your options. The girl that may have been a four or five here, over time, starts looking like an eight or nine. You deprive yourself of food for a long time, even the vegetables look like dessert."

"Got it."

"The problem is that people's brains stop working and they convivence themselves to settle for their options available."

Turtle jumped in, "That's not the case for me."

Flip responded, "I was on shift when you left. I saw who we sent to Viridis on those spaceships. Not the best lookers on there, and believe me, I was looking. I'm always looking."

"She's not from here."

Flip and I responded in unison, "What?!"

"She's a local girl from Viridis. She's a waitress at the food place right outside the airfield that we worked from."

Flip was puzzled. "You're dating an alien?"

"She is not! Technically, I was the alien there. She's perfect, and nice, and they're no different from us."

I said with sincerity, "Good for you. If you're both happy, that's great. What's her name?"

"Her name is Columbae."

Flip asked, "You got a picture?"

Turtle pouted. "I do, but I'll show you later, when I want to."

"Come on..."

"No."

"At least tell us about her. You said she works at a restaurant?"

"She works there part-time. The rest of her time, she works at the family business."

"What's that?"

"Don't laugh. Her dad makes dolls and other little toys for kids."

I jumped in, "That's great. Real good. We just want to make sure you've thought about how this is going to work. You can't just deploy there whenever you want."

Flip added, "Long-distance relations work sometimes, but that's rare. And when I say long-distance, this takes the cake."

Turtle was looking serious. It seemed his whole demeanor changed. "Can I tell you guys a story?"

"Sure," I said. "Let me get us another round first."

Turtle started, "Do you know how I got this scar on my face?"

Flip replied, "What are you, a joker now? No, you never told us. Something about an animal?"

I answered, "A cougar, right?"

Turtle took a long drink. "I've been meaning to tell you guys this for a long time, and this deployment really got me thinking. So here goes. My mom left me when I was very young. I was with my dad and two older sisters for a long time. Things weren't great. We lived in a small town in Indiana where everything was supposed to be perfect. The downtown would have its annual tree lighting in December. Everything looked like it was out of a storybook, lights and decorations everywhere. At least, it was perfect everywhere else. Not at my house. We never had money. My dad was always out doing what he called *side jobs*. My sisters seemed to care about me, but they were always out with their friends causing trouble or who knows what. I spent a lot of time alone in my room, playing video games, playing board games."

"Board games?" Flip asked.

"Yeah, I would be like four different characters and play each one with unique personalities and different strategy styles."

"Nothing wrong with that," I said.

"I would hear kids at school after Christmas break talk about all the cool gifts they got each year. My dad wasn't big on gifts. He wasn't big on anything. I'd see the kids playing ball outside, knowing I could never do that. I was never taught. Never shown how. As a kid, you can't just walk up to another and ask to learn how to throw or catch. I was teased—I was teased most of my life."

"Is that why you joined the military?"

"Partly. I joined because I had to get out. Had to get far, far away. My dad would date different women and bring them home. I hated every one of them. When I was seventeen, he started dating one and was getting very serious. I hated her the worst. I didn't understand what he saw in her. She was much older than him. She was always around the house, which meant I had to disappear. I would either walk the neighborhood or escape to my room. The worst part was that she didn't even live there. She had a huge house across town. They would drink. They would drink so much. I knew how much they were spending on it and how much he was spending on her."

"How did you know?" asked Flip.

"I saw the receipts; I saw the cash flow. My old man couldn't make it on his own. I was trying to help. I tried to manage his bank accounts. Hell, I even did his taxes for a couple years before I left. His woman was horrible. I knew every dime he spent on her was less for me and my sisters. She called me names. We would have screaming wars at each other throughout the house. It seemed my dad always took her side. He was never on my side. She was literally counting the days until I was eighteen so she could get rid of me."

Turtle continued, "Then there was the night of the huge mega ultra-fight. My dad was in the living room, drinking and watching TV. His old hag saw me going through my dad's bank accounts at our small wooden kitchen table. I was helping him. I was making sure we paid the rent on time. She started freaking out over it."

I asked, "What happened next?"

"She accused me of stealing his money. Then I accused her of being a money-hungry, sex whore, old ugly cougar. She then had the audacity to grab a kitchen knife and threaten me from across the table. I had enough. I snapped. I stood up and pushed the table with all my might, pinning her between it and the kitchen sink. With a fast movement, she reached over the table and slashed the knife across my face."

I was almost in tears. "Oh no, we didn't know."

"I fell to the ground, grabbing my bloody face. All I could hear was her screaming, 'I'm sorry. I'm sorry.' My dad came to my side and the rest was a blur. My dad stayed by my side at the hospital. Even through all the recoveries. This was the most time we'd spent together in years. It was great. We told stories, watched movies. I enjoyed every moment with him. I arrived back home, and things seemed better for a while. My sisters came by, and it seemed like things might be alright. They even gave me a birthday party. They raised enough to buy me a new computer. I'd never had a new computer. I was so excited. Everything was the best...until it wasn't."

Flip asked, "Until it wasn't?"

"The old cougar came back. She came back. Her and my dad were still together."

"What?!" we said.

"I was done. I left immediately. I left everything—my new computer, all my belongings, everything. I went and joined the military."

Flip asked, "Just like that? Straight from your house to the recruitment center?"

"I did make one stop. I stopped by the old cougar's house one last time. Literally one last time...I burned down her house."

I was in shock. "You did what?!"

Flip exclaimed, "Tell me you didn't!"

Turtle said in a serious voice, "I did. Her house, gone, burnt to the ground. It was gone so fast. I know they'll figure it out. Who else would have done it? I can't return."

I asked, "Can't return to Indiana?"

"Can't return to Earth. I'm done, nothing for me there."

"What about your sisters?"

"I miss them, but there's nothing there for me. It's settled. I'm going to move to Viridis and spend my days with Columbae."

Flip responded, "Have you thought this through? Will they even allow this? What will you do to earn a living?"

"I've thought everything through thoroughly. People from Earth have become residents of Viridis before. There's a process, but it's doable. I figure money will be no problem."

I responded, "Money is always a problem."

"I have backup plans."

"Backup plans?"

"There are many things on Viridis that they don't yet want, but I can give them a need to want it."

"Such as?"

"I have knowledge. I can give them the Rubik's Cube. I can give them video games such as Pac-Man or Tetris. I think they need to have Velcro. They will pay anything for our sports. I can *invent* the pool table, or bowling, or foosball. They have social media sites, but not like ones from Earth. I have a million ideas. I can be a god there."

Flip stopped him there. "You're crazy, you know that?"

I asked, "This is great and all, but what about your enlistment? Are you going to wait until you retire to try to find your way back to Viridis and make this happen?"

Turtle took another drink. "Have you seen my APRs? My numbers are low. They don't want me here. To tell you guys the truth, I don't know how much time I have left. I don't think they'll let me extend my enlistment. My time is almost up. I need this. I really do."

Flip stood up. "Turtle, we love you, man. We'll support you all the way. We just want to make sure you got this."

"As long as I have your support and Columbae, I got this."

CHAPTER 17

The Gravity of It All

I tossed and turned in my bed, thinking about the conversation we had just had with Turtle. That was the most I had ever heard Turtle talk at one time. It seemed this deployment had really changed him. I was worried. I finally dozed off...

Then I woke up suddenly in the dead of my sleep after hearing an explosion of noises. *What's going on? Everything is dark, I can't see,* I think to myself. *I'm trapped. I'm trapped under my bed. My leg is in extreme pain. Why are the fire alarms going off? Why is this bed on me? I can't move my leg. My foot is jammed under the side of my bed. Did the bunk collapse on me? No, that can't be right, I sleep on the top bunk. Where am I? I'm trapped with a bed on top of me. I feel pain all over. I need this thing off me.* With all my effort, I pushed the metal bunk bed over. It tipped over to its side. I heard a crash. I thought the bed had just destroyed my ceiling light. How was this possible? Then I realized I was lying on the ceiling of my barracks room.

There was only one possible explanation. The gravity generator was reversed. I need to get up. I need to check on the others. I need to find my stuff. I still can't see. It's pitch dark. My left ankle is in pain. The room suddenly shifts. Everything starts moving. I fall to the side, trying to grab onto anything I can. My hand! What happened? I think I sliced my finger on glass. My bed almost collapsed on me again. I was able to move in time. I'm against a wall. This is bad. Why does gravity keep shifting? I think my finger is bleeding.

I finally get my bearings. My room is skewed. I manage to stand up. I'm standing on my wall. I feel around and find my Flightline bag. Rummaging through it, I discover my tablet and turn it on. It gives me just enough light to see in front of me. My index finger on my right hand is sliced pretty bad. In my bag, I find some electrical tape.

This will have to do. I wrap my finger with the tape. Then I don my coveralls and even put on my restraint harness. The door to my room is at my feet. I carefully open it while standing on the wall to its side. The door swings out and opens fast. I look down to see a huge drop that spans the courtyard over to the other set of rooms.

Just outside the door is the railing that spans the walkway on this second floor. I carefully lower myself to the railing with its vertical slats and walk across it to Flip's extra room 200. Since we were out late, Flip stayed here last night. I'm freaked out each time I look down, hoping not to fall off this thing, hoping the gravity doesn't change again. I pound on the door above my head. Just in case there's another shift, I secure the other end of my harness to the railing. Flip pushes his door open as it swings down.

"Are you alright?!" I yelled.

"I am now!" Flip replied.

"Listen, Flip, you need to get your harness on. The gravity can shift at any given moment."

"I'm going to check on the others. Meet me in Turtle's room."

I made my way to Turtle's room and opened the door. I had to jump and grab into his door frame to lift myself in. Flip joined us as well and we sat on Turtle's wall with the floor to our backs. The fire alarms were still going off. Turtle was pale as he sat there, staring straight ahead.

"What now?! yelled Flip."

I answered, "Others might be hurt, or trapped, or unconscious, or worse. I think we need to help them."

Turtle started rambling. "What if it changes again? What if we fall? What if the beds fall again?!"

Flip looked at him. "Stay here and keep calm. You don't have to do anything."

I corrected, "No, Turtle, I need you to focus. Where is your tablet?" He pointed to the other side of the room. I went and got it. I continued, "Turtle, I need you to send a mass message to everyone in our unit. You have the recall roster, right?"

"Yeah, I can do that."

"Good. Tell them to report where they are and if they're okay. Even if they're at work right now. If anyone says they are hurt or trapped, put it on the message board."

"I can do that."

"While you do that, bring up the work schedule and start checking off who replied and who didn't. Flip and I will keep checking the messages. Let us know who's still missing from the barracks and we'll check on them first. Repeat what your job is."

"Mass message to all in our unit. Post if someone is hurt. Find out who didn't reply."

"Also, make sure you include all those from the Resource Office as well, to include Senior Tillhammer."

Just then we felt another shift. The room started to spin, and we grabbed onto each other and tried to remain safe as we slid down the wall to the ceiling. Then a loud booming noise resonated across our portion of the station. The noise stopped. The fire alarm stopped. Everything stopped. Then everything was in the air. There was no gravity at all.

We all just stared at each other as we found ourselves floating in midair along with everything else in Turtle's room.

I told them, "The plan doesn't change. Turtle, get on your tablet. Flip, come with me."

We pushed off the wall and floated to the door.

I said to Flip, "I have a plan. Go over near your room and hook up to the railing with your harness." I pushed off the door and headed to the opposite far end of the walkway using the railing as support as if it was a ladder. At the other end, I grabbed the long fire extinguisher hose from the wall. Then I made my way back to Flip with hose in hand, flying across the span of the barracks. We tied this end of the hose to the railing.

I instructed, "Flip, secure your harness to the hose. Now you can move freely along it. Check on all the doors on this level. If anyone is hurt, tell us on the Turtle's mass message board, and if possible, give them first aid. Also, whoever is able to help, have them hook onto the fire hose and start helping you. We need to check every room in the barracks."

He asked, "What are you going to do?"

"I'm going to the other floors to do the same."

I checked my tablet; Turtle had the mass messenger up and running. Senior Tillhammer was updating who was at our work center and who was unaccounted for. He said there was a space station maintenance team that was working on getting the gravity generators back online. He also added that they were having similar issues with the Flightline and trying to resolve those.

I looked over the second-floor railing to see the ground floor. I thought to myself, *I hope the gravity doesn't start working just yet.* I push off and fly to the ground floor. Pushing off anything I can find, I make my way to one of the first-floor fire extinguishers and span the hose across the ground-floor barracks. I met Jo-Leia at her room and told her the plan. I reminded her that we could regain gravity at any time, so always be hooked in—we don't know which way we might fall. She hooked her harness to the fire hose and started checking on everyone on the ground floor, getting anyone capable to help her with the effort.

Looking towards the third floor, I saw they had already spanned the fire hose across it. They also tied one hose from the third floor all the way to the ground level. I looked at my tablet again and saw a few maintainers with minor injuries, but nothing serious. I scrolled down and noticed Specialist Edwards from room 340 was unconscious and Mike Pechman had a broken arm in room 127.

After a couple minutes, a medical team arrived. I immediately told them about Edwards in room 340. Although they didn't have a harness on, they saw our fire hoses and were able to use them to guide themselves to Edwards. We checked on a few remaining rooms. With so many of us helping, we cleared the barracks fast.

Flip, Jo-Leia, and several others joined me at the ground level and asked, "Now what?"

I answered, "Texas is secure, let's go check on the other barracks."

A group of twelve of us headed to the other barracks. We found out only a small portion of the space station had lost gravity. There were two other full barracks that were affected. We split up into two groups and did what we could. The other residents in the other barracks all worked in other parts of station, so no one had harnesses except us. We did the same for these barracks, using the fire hoses and checking on all the rooms. We called for medical support if anyone was hurt. I found out later that four members from the Personnel and Services barracks perished that night. They were in the courtyard when the initial attack hit. Gravity reversed and they fell three stories toward the roof. In addition to that, there were a few broken bones, a couple concussions, lots of people freaking out. We helped some that were trapped under their beds or couldn't get their doors open. We reminded everyone to stay in a room or somewhere secure. Gravity could resume at any time.

Roger: Wow, that was intense. How long were you without gravity?

Max: A little over six hours. Once they got the generators working, it was chaos again with everything dropping to the floor. It was then that I was reminded of my hurt ankle. The places that lost gravity included three barracks and a bunch of random offices. The chow hall was hit bad. Food and kitchen supplies were everywhere. It would take a good while until that place was up and running again.

Roger: Where did you eat?

Max: We had the other chow hall, way across station, but most of us just ate the ration packs that were provided. Our Flightline was also affected.

Roger: It lost gravity as well?

Max: No, the giant space window opened and was seized. The controls to close the window wouldn't work. It took them about two hours to reset the system to get it to close.

Roger: Did this happen at the same time as the gravity loss?

Max: Almost instantaneous. No one was hurt from that. Everyone on the Flightline at the time was hooked in. They were all able to make it back to the entry control points without much incident.

Roger: Good thing.

CHAPTER 18

Preparations

For the next few nights or so, our work schedules were all screwed up. However, everyone worked when they could. My ankle still hurt as I continued to limp around. I'm not sure when the last time I slept was. We were at the barracks trying to do what we could to clean up the disaster. We all got a message. There was a mass recall and every maintainer needed to meet in the auditorium in one hour to receive a briefing from our commander. We found out quite a bit. I sat next to Turtle, Flip and T.J.

Colonel Fredrick gave the briefing. "There were several coordinated attacks the night our station lost gravity in one section and lost control of our Primary Runway Hatch."

Flip whispered, "So that's what the giant window is called."

The commander continued, "On Viridis, their largest airfield experienced sabotage at the same time as our attack. This caused dozens of their spaceships to be inactive as they found parts damaged and wires cut. Nix was hit the worst when four of their military posts were hit by many explosions, causing mass damage and casualties to thousands of their troops. We learned that two things were common to all these attacks. One, they were all inside jobs. Second, they were all performed by Calidums that were stationed at these locations as part of the Treaty Program. We believe, since these attacks took place at the same time as ours, that the Calidums are most likely responsible for ours as well. We still haven't found out who's responsible for the attacks on Space Station Prime. I'm not telling you this to scare you. We're letting you know that we all must remain vigilant. Report anything out of the ordinary. Those responsible are still out there."

Flip and I looked at each other with open eyes.

Colonel Fredrick continued, "We're going to Calidum. We're teaming up with the Viridis and Nix militaries, what little support they have. Many of you in this room will be deploying in three weeks' time. Many more may be on the next deployment. We will be sending both cargo and bomber ships there and setting up a base of operation. Nix has mostly a ground military to support us while Viridis will take to the skies with their limited air support. We will be on Calidum and use combined forces to take out the enemy's military capabilities. This coordinated attack was conjured up by the top US Space Military Intelligence Officers. I've seen their plan and it's an excellent one. It will be successful as long as we all do our jobs. As Flightline maintainers, I expect you to do the same jobs you do every night. Launch and recover spaceships, perform scheduled and unscheduled maintenance and do everything as accurate and safe as possible."

I turned to T.J. "Is this really happening?"

"It appears so," he said with a look of concern.

Colonel Fredrick finished up, "These next few weeks will be an all-out race to get things done. We will require many of the BC-76s to be converted over to bombers. For those of you going on this trip, your jobs will be extra tough. You will be tasked with helping with the Flightline as well as getting all your requirements complete to deploy in time. I have no doubt we can get this done. You have proven time and time again that you're the best. Let's prove it once again."

After the briefing, most of us ran straight to the Resource Office to see who was going to war. Twenty of us crowded the hall, peering in to see their fate. Sergeant Tillhammer looked flustered as he got up from behind his desk.

The senior sergeant yelled, "We're working on the deployment list! I can assure you we'll have the names as soon as we can. It's going to take all night. Until then, the Resource Office is closed! Any issues or problems you think you have will have to wait. Is this understood?!"

We replied with a disappointing, "Yes sir."

We split back to our regular shifts. Returning to work, we started the configuration process, reconfiguring a bunch of cargo ships over to a bomber configuration. This was a monstrous task. Over the next couple weeks, we were on full hands on deck, balls to the walls as Sergeant Peterson would say. We were doing everything we could to meet our deadlines. Each ship took an entire shift to configure and that was only if we had a dozen maintainers working the entire time with no unexpected issues.

All the seats and stanchions were disassembled and carried out. All the life support equipment was removed from the cargo bay. All the floorboards had to be unfastened and carefully hauled out. Removing the floorboards revealed a set of bomb bay doors that opened down and out. These doors had to be rigged and engaged to both the hydraulics system and our navigation system. The next step was call for the Titan. This enormous rotary launcher was trucked out and loaded into the ship. It was the device that would carry and launch all our guided bombs. The Titan spanned almost the entire length of the cargo hold, which we now called the bomb bay. Once it was in place and secured, all wires and components were hooked up. Lastly, an operation check was done to ensure we'd done everything right.

These operational checkouts were no easy task. We needed to ensure the bomb doors could open and close with ease. We also need to make sure all the components inside the Titan were talking to our navigation computers. This wasn't the old days of flying over a target and dropping a bomb, praying that it hit something it was supposed to. These present-day weapons will hit anything you tell them to, as long as you input the right coordinates and everything is working as planned. In order to operate these enormous bomb doors, we needed hydraulic power. This would require a full engine run to supply to the system its required 1.21 gigawatts.

Roger: What was that?

Max: Nothing, I was just seeing if you're paying attention...

Anyways, we would have an Engine crew running up the engines to provide the required hydraulic pressure for the doors. Crew Chiefs standing ground if any advanced rigged adjustments were needed. The Hydro team were there if there were any hydraulic problems. Lastly, of course, would be the Avionic techs to run through the nav computer to see if everything was synced right. I loved these checks, engines running, ship shaking. A bunch of maintainers on headsets talking and joking through it. Then if anything didn't work, we would all point fingers and blame the other groups. Most of these bomb door checks went well. We did have a few that needed adjustments to the door rigging, or hydraulic lines, cabling not secure, or parts being bad. I saw some of these checks take a couple nights just to weed out all the problems.

Roger: What about the Weapons troops? This is their system, right?

Max: I don't recall them being there. They load the bombs. We hadn't loaded anything yet, just running through the bomb door checks...

Once all our checks were run through, then we'd give the okay for the Weapons troops. Huge trucks carrying bombs sat on the sides of the Flightline. Then the Weapons team came out driving their jammers. Little forklift cars that would retrieve a bomb from the truck and carefully lift the weapon into place under the 76er. It looked like an orchestrated ballet of machines moving seamlessly across the Flightline. Maintainers make fun of Weapons troops, but you gotta hand it to them, they did know how to load the bombs. They were a professional and coordinated team, directing each other and hooking up all the components that attached the bomb assembly to the Titan. A truly impressive sight to see.

Roger: So, were you on the list?

Max: The deployment list? I was. Turtle had just returned from Viridis, so we knew he'd be out. Flip was really pulling to go on this one, but they needed him to stay here. He was told they needed to keep a few good troops on station to keep the process here going.

Roger: That's too bad.

Max: Yeah, he was really disappointed about this one.

It was a couple nights before my deployment when Senior Sergeant Fleming approached me after roll call and said, "Max, right before your shift is over, meet me in my office along with Sergeant Diego. I already let him know. Do not be late. You have a very important appointment at 1800."

"Yes, sir."

Why do they do this? Now I'll be stressing all night. Am I off the deployment? Did I screw up something? I hate this. I was racking my mind thinking what it could be. I asked Sergeant Diego, but he wouldn't say what it was about. This was a long night of doing radio checks, running up nav systems and helping with the bomber configs. At 1745 Sergeant Diego and I arrive at Senior Fleming's office. He wouldn't tell us what this was for. He just said wait here until 1800. We sat there in Senior Fleming's office as he was sitting at his desk working on APRs.

"Lightbulb," I finally said.

Diego questioned, "What's that?"

"It just came to me while sitting here. Your riddle about figuring out the switches and rooms."

"Go on."

"You turn two switches on. Then you wait a bit. Then you turn one of those off and check on the lights in the next room. One light will be on. The second will be off and cool. The third will be off, yet still warm after it had been turned on for some time."

"That's it. Good job. You see, you have to use all your other senses while troubleshooting, not just the obvious."

Right about 1800, Senior Fleming stood up fast at attention, we did the same. Colonel Fredrick and Chief Powers walked in.

Colonel Fredrick approached me and spoke loudly. "Specialist Max Morgan?!"

"Yes, sir." I was shaking.

"It looks like you're out of uniform!"

I looked down quickly and didn't understand.

The colonel reached into his pocket and took something out. "You should be wearing this sergeant rank. Congrats, Max. Effective immediately, you are Sergeant Morgan!"

He gave me the rank patch, shook my hand, then I saluted him.

I was beside myself; I didn't know what to say. "Thank you."

"Relax, Sergeant, what you did the night of that attack was truly impressive. You knew what had to be done and you took action without even being asked to. You may have saved the life of Specialist Edwards, allowing the medical team to get to him fast. That night, along with your hard work on Nix, is impressive. We've reviewed all your records and know you truly deserve this."

"Thank you, sir."

"Thank you, and good luck on Calidum. We all know you'll do great."

The colonel and chief left. I was still in shock as I stood there.

Sergeant Diego was smiling. "Great job, Sergeant."

I asked, "What now?"

"Now, you press forward. You earned this and deserve it. I don't know if you got a good look at the deployment list, but the only sergeant from Avionics is Sergeant Banner, and now you. You'll be running your own little team. I know you'll do just fine. Tomorrow, I need you to get those sergeant ranks sewn on your uniforms. It will probably take *all* night, so I don't expect to see you on shift."

"Oh, I don't think it'll take that long."

"It *will* take you all night. I don't want to see you."

"Oh, got it. Thank you!"

"Good luck, Max."

Roger: Good for you. Looks like they can spot real talent.

Max: Well, I don't know about that. It definitely got me a lot more responsibilities real fast.

Roger: Were you nervous about deploying?

Max: I was. I really was. I read about a lot of soldiers not being afraid of dying but being afraid to get hurt. For me, this was different. I was nervous about the unknown. From everything I heard, we should be perfectly safe. Our job was to stay on the Flightline and take care of our ships. We weren't out there on the roads or in the towns like the soldiers. There shouldn't be any fighting at our end, just doing our job. That's where I was the most nervous. Did I know my job well enough? I'd be running my own Avionics crew and making decisions, dealing with troubleshooting and redballs. I wasn't sure if I was ready for all that.

On the eve of my deployment, I needed to clear my head. Flip, Turtle, and I sat at our usual table at the Mountain.

Flip stood up, raised his mug, and said, "To Sergeant Max, the only maintainer in this history of all maintainers to be given a rank-up right there on the spot."

"Come on, I'm not the first."

"I'm telling you, Max, it's rare—like, extremely rare."

We talked about the attack on station. Wondered who was able to do it and why no one had been caught yet. Turtle was still going on and on about his Viridis girlfriend. They wished me luck on the deployment. I could tell Flip was still upset about not being able to go, although he never said anything.

I finally asked, "Are you two going to be alright here without me?"

Flip answered, "Always. You be careful out there. Remember about that deployment hot thing. They may look good, but that's just your other brain talking."

"I'll be careful."

"You better be. We can't lose you. Come back safe. Also, there's no Mountain there. No drinking at all. Their moon forbids it. So, you better drink up now. It's the last you'll get for a while."

For some reason, this whole night seemed different, and I felt something was missing. I was nervous about leaving. Flip was sad he had to stay. Turtle was evaluating his life on Viridis. We sat and we drank, then walked back to the barracks in almost silence. It was strange and we all felt it.

CHAPTER 19

Groundhogs Day One

The next night was spent standing in countless out-processing lines and sitting through endless briefings. It was a hurry-up-and-wait scenario as we were issued our gear. We wouldn't be wearing the basic maintenance coveralls for this trip. We all wore loose camouflage pants, T-shirts and military buttoned shirts over those. We were also supplied with protective helmets and flak vests, a type of near-bulletproof heavy outer vest. We would be issued rifles or handguns, but that would have to wait until we got to Calidum. We were almost ready to board the ships.

I was standing within a huge group of deployers. It wasn't only maintainers, but people from many different career fields across the station that were joining us. Our group went through the entry control point and stepped out to the Flightline. Many of them were in awe as they pointed up to the giant dome and gasped at the sight of it all. I was just wondering why I had to be part of this gaggle. It would have been so much easier if us maintainers just met them at the ship.

I look down at the line of ships. I'm sure to most, these all looked like the same BC-76s. I easily saw the subtle differences that marked the ones that were converted to bombers. We would be taking a group of ships to Calidum, half cargo, half bomber. Our group arrived at Ship 1670 and started to board. We were packed in. The entire ship was full. Shoulder to shoulder we sat, members of all ranks and career fields. I sat next to Avionics Specialist Ian and across from me was our new maintenance chief, Chief Powers. Not only were we squashed in this tight sitting formation, but we were also wearing flak vests and helmets. Our seats were sideways in relation to the ship. Those in seats facing in front of us were only an arm's length away. Our knees would overlap with the ones that we faced, so we had to sit with legs staggered. If anyone had to get up during the flight to use the urinal or toilet in the back, they would just have to climb over people and walk on their legs while supporting themselves with the stanchions.

In and out of sleep, we endured the trip. When the ship veered one way, we all veered together as if we were one element. We could all tell when we entered Calidum's atmosphere. The ship shook to what seemed like no end. Then a bright light shone through the windows, which was followed by a quiet stillness. After landing, we deboarded the ship and were greeted with intense starlight heat. This wasn't your "sweating on the porch in Georgia" heat. This was your "I just opened the oven and poked my head in" heat.

We were escorted off the Flightline and shown where to go to start our new in-processing steps. More lines to stand in. At the armory we were issued weapons. The specialists and sergeants received rifles while the seniors, chiefs, and officers were issued handguns. Each one of us had to verify the serial number on the weapon matched the one on the list next to our name. We were also issued a set number of rounds. By the end of this deployment, we would have to turn in our gun and the exact amount of ammo given. Anything lost would be a bad day for all of us.

On the Flightline we were almost never in the position to use our weapons. However, you never know. It's a precaution, just in case. If we did fire, we'd have to do an extensive report after it and account for our rounds. There's also that off chance someone mishandles their weapon, and it goes off. I don't even understand how someone could do that. We've all been trained. Always keep the safety on. Always. Until you're ready to shoot your intended target. With gun pointing towards the target, you flip the safety off. Even while cleaning the gun, you ensure all the ammo is removed…some people.

We were then sent to a briefing room to learn a few key issues concerning Calidum. A sergeant briefed us on the dangers associated with this place. The sergeant said something to this effect. "Due to recent events, there have had numerous attacks on this base of operation from random rocket attacks. The technology we put up here will sense an incoming rocket and send out an alarm across the base. When you hear this alarm, you need to immediately lie on the ground and cover your head. Most of these rockets or mortars that hit will explode up and out. Your best chance of survival will be to lie flat to avoid any shrapnel—after which you need to find a bunker close by to remain in until the all clear alarm is rung."

The sergeant played examples of the alarm tones and continued, "During this time, everyone in your unit will need to take account-ability to ensure everyone is safe."

When the briefing ended, our maintenance unit was told what time we needed to report to work, depending on which shift we were on. We were then assigned rooms. We headed out to find our clothing bags and gear. Lines and lines of identical bags from everyone on our flight lay on the ground. It took some time to find which ones were ours. Once we had located our stuff, a group of us headed towards our new living quarters.

We were almost there when an incoming alarm went off over the various load speakers. We all hit the ground fast. Lying there, I looked over to the other guys. We all had the same wide-eyed look of surprise. After almost a minute, we got up and ran to a nearby bunker. They have these bunkers all over this base. I couldn't believe we had only just gotten here and were already getting hit.

The Alarm Green tone went off and we made our way to our rooms. Hundreds of tiny buildings were lined up. We called these the huts. We found our hut numbers. Inside this small wooden shack was a short hallway with several rooms on each side. I found my room number. The tiny rooms were about six feet by six feet. Lying on the tiny bed, I was almost foot to head against each wall. Of course, the washrooms and shower were in a separate building. This was going to be fun.

It didn't feel like I slept much before my tablet's alarm went off. Time to get ready for work. The Flightline wasn't too far of a walk from the huts. I arrived at our new work center. On my shift for

Avionics were Specialist Jo-Leia Zwarc and Specialist Larry Alma. Opposite us on the other shift were Sergeant Banner, Ian, and G-17. My work shift was from noon to midnight.

We stayed on Space Station time as a twenty-four-hour day. Which was based on Earth's Greenwich Mean Time, we think. Who knows how they set the time after the whole Space Bridge trip? The time really screwed with you here, though. Calidum always faced the star, so it was always day here. Every day enduring the hot blaze of Stella.

We stood around the roll call area inside the building on our first day. We were then formed up and introduced to our maintenance leadership team. Chief Powers and Lieutenant Kirkland were in charge. They would be on a split overlapping schedule. After this first day we'd see them both for half our shift. Although not maintenance, Chaplain Christopher McKinley was on this deployment as well. The Production Superintendent on our shift was Senior Brickhouse with Sergeant Monty as our expeditor. He was the one that had broken his leg on Nix. All better now and he moved up to the position of expeditor. We also had that good old Senior Tillhammer on this deployment.

Senior Tillhammer took roll, then addressed us. "Here's how it's going to be. Any personnel issues or issues with your rooms, get with me. Any Flightline issues, get with your expeditor, who will answer directly to your pro super, Senior Brickhouse. You will need to carry your weapon and wear your armor to and from work and to and from the chow hall, or anywhere else you go on base. You can leave these items in this building when you work on the Flightline. You should have all received a locker to store your guns. I'm assuming you all know what to do if the alarms go off. After you drop to the ground, then reach a bunker, you will need to find someone with a radio to call in with your status for accountability."

Senior Brickhouse, our Production Superintendent, stepped up. "I understand this is the first deployment for some of you and it's the first time on Calidum for most of you. Once you get orientated, this is not much different than on station. All I ask is that you work hard and work together. We have a very robust flying schedule with limited people. We will be asking a lot of you. Many of you will be asked to help with other career fields. I don't want to hear anyone say, 'That's not my job.' We're all in this together and all on the same team. Most days, we won't have this long roll call. You will check in, get the daily notes from Senior Tillhammer, then report to your expeditor, Sergeant Monty. Some of you already know our LT and chief. They will handle most of the meetings with the top leadership and will handle any major issues. Here's Lieutenant Kirkland."

Lieutenant Kirkland looked young. He had short brown hair and wore old-style black-rimmed glasses as if he grew up in the 1950s.

Lieutenant Kirkland said, "Good afternoon, team. Like many of you, this is my first deployment. I just want you to know I am here to help with any issues. You have a really wonderful leadership team that cares. Like Senior Brickhouse said, we're all on the same team. Treat everyone with respect and we'll get through this together. Chief, anything to add?"

Chief Powers walked up slowly as if he was thinking. He took a deep breath, then spoke. "Twenty years ago I was in your very shoes, ready to launch every airplane we had on an airfield in the Middle East. Look at us now. Look at how far we've come. If you're not completely in awe at this...I don't know what. You are eight light-years from your hometowns. You are in the middle of an intergalactic war. I know, that sounds stupid when I hear it out loud. The truth is none of this really matters. No, really, we're not in this for the politics. We're not in this to take sides. We've signed up for one job. One job. We fix spaceships. They break, we fix them. Let the top leadership figure out if they want to blow something up or send troops here or there. Our mission is these BC-76s. We will give the flight crews a reliable ship every single time they go out. Look around the room. We are here for each other. We have each other's backs. All we can do is what we have been trained to do. All I ask is that you do your job with honest work."

Senior Tillhammer concluded, "You're dismissed to your expeditor."

I sent Specialist Alma to the Tool Counter to get our standard tools. Then I got with Sergeant Banner. He gave me the rundown on what we were doing. He showed me the flying schedule and explained which ones had avionics maintenance issues.

Then Banner said, "Good luck, Max, see you in a little less than twelve hours."

The first couple weeks on Calidum was a mind warp. The rocket alarms were going off all the time while we were here. We would find out later the enemy had no real targeting system. They were blindly lobbing rockets over, hoping to hit somewhere on the base. Sometimes buildings would be hit, and we would hear about it later. There were a few devastating times that they took out military members in other units. It was a game of hope and prayers for us. There was always a chance we could be next, but until then we just had to press forward with our jobs and take every alarm seriously.

It took some time getting oriented on the Flightline in the glaring heat. We would immediately take off our outer shirt and be down to our T-shirt, long pants, and boots every day. We quickly got into a routine of getting turnover, getting tools, working on the priority fixes and responding to redballs. We would help the load teams with the cargo. Other ships were loaded by the Weapons team with bombs. No matter what, these ships usually came back empty. Other times the ships were full of soldiers heading to one of the remote outposts. I saw cargo ships come back with Calidum prisoners, others with wounded soldiers. Day in and day out, go to breakfast, go to work, take a lunch, go to work, eat dinner, go to the hut. Next day repeat the process. Every day was the same thing, over and over again. They had a term for this: Groundhog Day.

CHAPTER 20

Llama

Larry Alma was the type of child picked last for kickball in school. The one that sat alone in the cafeteria. Flip worked directly with Specialist Alma for months before this deployment. He told me stories about this guy. People tried to be his friend. They tried to include him in their circles, but he just didn't fit in. Unfortunately, in Flightline maintenance, this usually doesn't end well for individuals that are like Larry Alma.

Flip had told me several stories involving Larry. On his first night on the Flightline, some of the other maintainers sent him to the Tool Counter to get the K9P. He kept asking for K9P and everyone in Tool Counter laughed at him. He came back furious and was stomping his feet, saying he hates it here and doesn't understand anything. Flip had to explain to him that he was asking for canine pee. It was a joke. When someone doesn't get a joke, or gets so frustrated by it, it usually only opens the floodgates for everyone to pick on them.

Another day Specialist Alma had a tear in one of his boots. He was told they were not suitable for the Flightline and needed to have an unserviceable tag on them until he was able to be issued new boots. These were the same tags we put on parts when they were discovered to be broken. Tags were filled out and attached to his boot. In order to get new boots, he was told to have a form signed off by various members in his chain of command. He had a checklist of people that would have to sign his form and initial the tag that hung from his left boot. He ran around going to all sorts of offices with a huge tag flapping around on his boot. His supervisor, the expeditor, and even the young lieutenant signed the form, acting as if this was a normal procedure. Getting to the Mobility

Section, they finally issued him a new set of boots. Everyone was secretly laughing, knowing this was one big prank.

Unfortunately, this deployment started no differently for Larry. I don't know how it got started or by whom, but someone called Specialist Larry Alma the Llama. Someone called him Llama, and it stuck. It stuck hard. This escalated fast. Larry the Llama spread within our unit. Within weeks this evolved into "Larry loves Llamas." Then I saw it written on the ceiling of launch trucks. They were written on the inside of porta potties. Larry Loves Llamas was written on top of the Fire Bottles, the huge four-foot fire extinguishers next to every spaceship. Bumper stickers were even made and put in random places. Even poorly drawn pictures were made depicting Larry loving Llamas. Use your imagination on that one. This was out of control.

He was fine with the name Llama, but only at first. Once they added the *love* part and he started seeing it everywhere, that's when he would get so mad. I tried to talk to him about it. I tried to help him. I felt it was my responsibility with him on my shift and all. The real problem was that every time I tried to talk to him about it, he seemed to get agitated and shun away.

Every day I had to remind Larry to get tools. How hard is it to remember? We do the same thing every day? I'd show him how to do a radio check. The next day he'd struggle with it. It wasn't bad that he struggled. It was bad that if he came across anything challenging, he would just give up without trying. I always got the impression he just didn't care. Other times he would skip important steps like not pulling a circuit breaker before removing a part. I was trying to be nice to him since he was teased so much, but at the same time I couldn't let these things slip. He had a job to do here and at this rate he was going to hurt someone or damage a ship.

At roll call one day, Senior Tillhammer addressed the issue. "We've all seen the llama writings in various places. This needs to stop now! Not only is this considered hazing, defacing government property is a violation. This will stop now! Those that are doing it know who you are. If you're caught doing this, you will pay! Not only will you be written up, you will pay to have all of these surfaces cleaned up or repainted. Then you will be sent back to the space station."

I believe Tillhammer's talk made things worse. Now it was a heightened challenge to people. The same day as this roll call, I had just sent Larry to get tools. I was standing around the Smoke Pit with a couple Crew Chiefs. Even if people didn't smoke, vape, or chew we all hung around this location. It was the central point between the building and the Tool Counter. It was the place where the expeditor trucks picked us up. I stood and listened as Crew Chiefs Janson and Caleb were talking.

Caleb said, "Look at Larry run, ever see someone run like that?"

Janson added, "He even runs like a damn llama."

I laughed along. He did run pretty funny. I knew I shouldn't laugh. I knew I should be standing up for Larry. At the same time, it was frustrating to work with someone that just doesn't get it.

Caleb looked perplexed. "What's a llama run like?"

Janson answered, "Oh, I don't know...like Larry."

They both laughed again.

Janson then said, "Can you believe Hammer?" He changed his voice deeper. "This needs to stop now, or you will pay."

Caleb responded in the Hammer voice, "If you're caught, you'll be written up."

"Notice that Hammer said *if* you are caught. I guess people are good to go if they just don't get caught."

"And what about being sent back to station? Oh no, don't send me back to the place where we can drink, get out of this blazing sun, and not be attacked by rockets."

I felt as if someone was listening to this conversation, because right after Caleb said the word *rockets*, the Incoming Alarm started to go off.

The three of us immediately dropped to the ground. It was at that point that I realized our mistake. Two seconds ago, the three of us were standing around the Smoke Pit. The place where cigarette ashes are dropped. The place where spit from chew is projected haphazardly onto the pavement. That same very spit and ash that was now seeping through our thin T-shirts.

After waiting on the ground for a minute or so, we ran to the building and did accountability. Then I tried to wipe as much of it off as I could with a paper towel and water. One thing was for sure. Every day after that, I brought an extra T-shirt with me to work.

Another day, Larry and I were in the bomb bay of a ship and we needed to reach the satellite positioning receiver that was well above our heads.

I looked at Larry. "See if you can find a ladder."

He came back a few minutes later and said, "Yep, found one."

"Where is it?"

"The Crew Chiefs are using it outside."

I tried to be patient. "Can we use it after they're done? How long will they be? If not, is there another one we can use?"

"I didn't ask them. You just asked me if I could find a ladder, and I did."

I tried everything with Larry. He couldn't do maintenance, had no clue how to troubleshoot. He was always wandering off. We'd be working on something and next thing you know he's walking across the Flightline, chasing those strange blue crickets they have here.

I would just have to keep him busy. This day I sent Larry to help the Crew Chiefs with a configuration. They were removing all the seats to allow room for a large cargo load. Jo-Leia and I were working on Ship 310. We had to change out the lower radio antenna. These things were always breaking out here on Calidum. These cargo ships were constantly landing on remote airfields out here and ending up getting smashed up from rocks.

The antennas could be fairly easy to change, as long as the connection point was still good. If not, we'd have to change that out as well, which could be a tedious task. The other big issue was that of the sealant. Once the new antenna was installed, we needed to mix an epoxy, then apply it around the edges to seal it up. It's more of an art than anything else. I've seen some people screw this up really bad when they end up with sealant all over themselves and smeared across the ship. It's really not difficult if you take your time. There was no way I was letting Larry do this.

As we worked, I asked Jo-Leia, "What do you think about all the Larry loves Llama crap?"

"Ha, I saw one the other day in the women's shower. There was a picture of a llama on a hoverboard, but this one said 'Llamas love Larry.'"

"So, you're laughing too."

"I know, I know. I can't help it. Just look at him sometimes."

"We gotta figure this out. I'm getting so frustrated with him. I don't know what to do at this point. I've tried helping him, but he doesn't seem to care. He screws up everything he touches."

Jo-Leia responded, "Listen, Max, Larry won't be the best maintainer, not by a long shot. Don't expect him to be. He must have skills in other areas. We just need to focus on what he can do and utilize his talents in that matter. Work on that for now until he gains confidence and more experience, then we can go from there."

"I know, but the problem is figuring out what he's good at. So far, I haven't seen much."

"He'll come around...I think...maybe?"

I was very impressed by Jo-Leia. I was surprised she hadn't made sergeant by now. She had been in longer than me and was a year older. I heard she received her bachelor's degree in aeronautics last year. She took classes on her off time through the space station's college program. She was great. She was more than great. She was smart, a hard worker, knew how to change parts, could troubleshoot...she was cute.

Roger: Cute?

Max: She was. Spending every single day with someone, over time you really get to know them. I found out a lot about Jo-Leia in these next few months. She was from the upper Midwest. Her mom served in the military as a pilot. Her goal was to become a pilot herself. After each shift, she'd get on her tablet and study all she could in order to become an officer. Jo-Leia was really out here for the experience. She wanted to get back to Earth and pursue her dream of flying. She was so easy to talk to and really got me. Even after work, I'd go to her hut and help her study.

Roger: Right.

Max: No, really, I would. Okay, yes, after a while, I admit things started to get pretty serious.

Roger: I thought so.

Max: It was great. We were happy and between the two of us we were doing great work on the Flightline. We would take turns babysitting Larry, trying to get him motivated to work. The only problem was our new relationship had to be on the down-low. These types of things can be frowned upon, with me being a sergeant and all.

Roger: Well, I guess sometimes you need to weigh the consequences.

CHAPTER 21

Franksgiving

Max: Ever have one of those days where everything and everyone around you irritated you to no end?

Roger: I think we all have. I also think you are about to tell me.

Max: This place was really getting to me. This starts the minute my alarm goes off to start my day and I open the door to the hut to make my way to the washrooms and showers. It's the blinding light and heat that attack me first. I have to close my eyes for half the walk as my eyes are trying to adjust to it. However, you can't walk blind due to the obstacles.

Roger: Obstacles?

Max: First of all, our entire base here is covered with rocks. Except the Flightline, of course. The rest of it has a layer of rocks everywhere you go. They say it prevents this place from becoming a huge mud bowl when it rains. I don't know, I haven't seen it rain yet. The second obstacle is these stupid little lizards that are running around everywhere.

Roger: Lizards—why are they stupid?

Max: Because they have no clue where they're going. Many times, they try to run right under my boots while I'm walking. I don't know if they're looking for shade or what. You end up tripping or hopping awkwardly to try not to squish them. Maybe I should just try to hit them, I don't know. Sometimes there's warm water in the showers, sometimes not—usually not. It's a guessing game each time. There definitely isn't any water pressure. I know, Roger, I should just be happy I can use a shower and not be stuck out on the field somewhere.

Roger: I'd say we're making progress if you know what I'm thinking.

Next stop for my day is the chow hall. More standing in long lines with my body armor and rifle to pick up a tray, point to the food I want and watch the worker slop it on my cardboard plate. I will admit, the food wasn't bad. They had some pretty good omelets. It was better than eating ration packs. I just wished the chow hall would change their menu a bit.

Then I'd get to work and have to hear Tillhammer ramble on about something we're doing wrong. At turnover, Sergeant Banner would give us priority jobs to do, then I'd get with Sergeant Monty and his list of priorities would be all different. You've already heard about the problems I had with Larry. I was trying to make our Avionics team look good, but I was always being taken two steps back with him.

There were times we needed to get on top of the BC-76s to reach an upper antenna or help Crew Chiefs with panels. There is a hatch you go up, then place your hands on top of the ship and lift yourself up. The first time I went up there, I burned my hands pretty good. Now I knew why those guys are always wearing gloves up there. The only time I felt cold here, besides the showers, was when I stepped out of a porta-potty and the temperature dropped about twenty degrees. The facilities near the Flightline consisted of a line of these things. Sitting, it was unbearable, as you felt like you were being cooked alive.

I'd say the worst part of this deployment, to this point in the story, was the attacks. It was a mind trip. Everywhere you walked, you were on high alert, always looking to see where the closest bunker was. Alarms would go off anytime. You would be walking and talking, then, bam, you were on the ground. Working on the ships, you have to get down, then shut off the entire system fast and head to a bunker. Sometimes we'd hear where they landed and were thankful it wasn't on us.

Roger: What did you do when you were sleeping in your hut?

Max: There was no point in running outside to a bunker. If there was a rocket attack near, you might get hit by shrapnel. The huts were the one place you did nothing. I'd hear the alarms and just lie there, hoping nothing hit us. The huts were so flimsy, if they were hit, we'd be goners. We all had the mentality of "if it's our time, it's our time."

Roger: Did the alarms and attacks resume the entire time you were on base?

Max: They did.

Roger: Did you ever leave the base?

Max: As maintainers, no. The Nix and Viridis had troops always heading off base. We also had our own soldiers, truck drivers, and other career fields out there as well. You gotta hand it to them, they were constantly out there enduring the madness to keep us safe on base. We were lucky and blessed to have such a great team protecting all of us. I could never thank them enough for what they did and what they sacrificed.

Roger: I take it you had walls or fences around this base.

Max: Of course.

Roger: So, let me get this straight. You are locked in a fenced-off area that you can't leave. You eat three meals a day, work an entire twelve-hour shift in the blazing heat, only to return to your tiny cell to sleep.

Max: That sounds about right.

Roger: You were in a maximum-security prison.

Max: I won't disagree with that. Even though every day felt like Groundhog Day, there were some exceptions. Celebrating a holiday away from home was always a mix of emotions to me. Not only were we light-years from Earth, but we were also deployed away from the friends we had come to call family on Space Station Prime. Thanksgiving was upon us.

Roger: I'm a little surprised you still celebrated holidays out there.

Max: It was their attempt to keep us sane.

Roger: How'd that work for you?

Max: I don't know, you tell me.

We had to arrive at work early that day while the opposite shift stayed late to take part in the festivities. The chief and lieutenant had a meal planned for us. Actually, I think it was the chief's idea and he let the LT do all the legwork. They had lots of tables set up in our roll call area, some tables even outside. They coordinated with the chow hall to have the meals delivered. We were waiting for the feast to start. Almost the entirety of both shifts crowded around. We looked over the buffet-type tables at the large spread of food, to include bread, fruits, potatoes, vegetables and an assortment of desserts. They even had plenty of turkey. Actually, it wasn't really turkey. It was some bird as big as an ostrich local to Calidum.

I stood next to Sergeant Banner, who told me, "Not much today—you have your regular launches. One goes up soon, so you may need to eat fast. Ship 2046 just landed and needs its satellite radio looked at."

I asked, "We still use our standard maintenance frequency for radio checks, right?"

"Yes, same on as on station. You'll need to look at 0060's infrared system. It wasn't rotating smoothly. It also has a lower antenna that may need to be changed, but that's the last priority."

"Got it."

"Room ten-hut!" bellowed Senior Tillhammer. We all stood at attention. Chaplain McKinley and Lieutenant Kirkland walked in.

"At ease!"

Lieutenant Kirkland started, "It's good to see everyone here at once. I normally only see a few at a time here or there. I just want to say you all are doing a fantastic job out there. This makes my job so much easier when I must explain it all to the general during the meetings. In fact, the chief is in one of those meetings right now. He sends his regards and wants everyone to enjoy this feast. Keep up the good work and don't hesitate to stop by my office if you ever need anything. My door is always open. Chaplain McKinley, would you do the honors?"

The chaplain stepped forward. "Bow your heads and join me. Dear almighty one, please bless this food and all who are here. We are so fortunate to spend this time together. Although we are far from home, we have made a new home with each other. We have endured so much together, we can easily look around to our new brothers and sisters. Thanksgiving is a time to reflect. It is a time to count our blessings. We have so much to thank our heavenly God, or your spiritual entities. Please give us all the strength not to dwell on the negatives but to look at the positives in everything around us. Amen."

The LT added, "Thank you, Chaplain. Time to get your food. We'll start with all the specialists and work our way up."

As the young specialists lined up for the food Sergeant Banner turned to me. "Ah, Franksgiving is upon us."

"Franksgiving?" I asked.

"You know, Fucking Rookie Ass New Kids. Every year they have a huge meal for the specialists to thank them and reward them for their service. Look at them all, laughing and enjoying every moment. Great to see all the Franks so happy."

I sat with the other sergeants and really enjoyed the meal. It's times like this you want to forget about being deployed, but it really only gets you thinking. Throughout the rest of the day, I was distracted. I was wondering about Flip and Turtle. Picturing them in the chow hall on station that always put out a big spread on Thanksgiving. I was wondering if Turtle was out of Tool Counter yet. If so, how was he doing back on the Flightline? I thought about his plans to go to Viridis and wondered how that would work for him.

After our shift, I walked back to the huts with Jo-Leia.

I said to her, "Less than a month to go."

"I'm excited. We should be back to station by Christmas."

"Then soon after that we'll find out if you made sergeant."

"Don't get my hopes up. Luck hasn't been by my side."

"Well, I'm at your side and I say you're going to make it."

"It would be nice to come clean about you and me."

"I know, it's weird acting all professional around you on the Flightline."

"You do act weird, that's for sure."

"What's your take on Turtle? You think he'll make it to Viridis?"

"Actually, no. I hate to say it. There's a whole background check involved to become a resident there. You need to have references. From what I've heard about Turtle's military records, I think he needs to make other plans. Besides, I heard how bad his maintenance was."

"I was thinking the same thing. I have a plan. I know he's not ready to go back to Earth just yet. I need to find a way to keep him in the military. I'm going to work with him every night on the

Flightline. Remember how Sergeant Diego would train us in detail, covering every system?"

"I remember his saying, *What do you know about Avionics?*"

"Yep. I'm going to do that. Turtle's smart—I don't think it'll take much to make him an outstanding troop. I know his thoughts on volunteering outside of work, but the higher-ups really eat that stuff up."

"School too. Ever since I started taking those college classes, Sergeant Tillhammer thought it was the best thing. I'm not saying that his opinion really matters, but an extra class here and there could really boost Turtle up."

"That settles it—only one more month. I'll start the same way with Turtle by saying, *What do you know about Avionics?*"

"Oh, one more thing, Max."

"What's that?"

"Happy Franksgiving!"

CHAPTER 22

The Road

The next day Jo-Leia and I were walking to work. I asked her, "Did you see Larry at breakfast?"

"Not today. Sometimes he skips it."

"I just don't want him to be late again. Tillhammer already wrote him up twice this month for it."

"There's only so much we can do."

"I know."

When we entered the work building, Sergeant Monty approached me. "Hey, Max, chief needs to see you in his office."

The door to the chief's office was closed. *It's never closed*, I thought. I knocked and they let me in, closing the door behind me. In the office were Chief Powers, Lieutenant Kirkland, Senior Sergeant Tillhammer and even Chaplain McKinley. *This can't be good*, I thought. They had me sit down.

The chief spoke very slowly. "Sergeant Morgan, there's no easy way to say this, and I'm sorry you must hear this from me. Specialist Michelangelo—Turtle, as we know him—is dead."

There are no words to describe what was going through my head. I was shaking, I felt sick, I had tears in my eyes and couldn't think straight.

I rambled, "No, this can't be! How? When? I don't...I can't..."

The chief continued, "We just received the news from the general. He received the message from the space station from the encrypted communicator. I understand you knew Turtle better than anyone here. I wanted to tell you first, before we deliver the news to the rest of the unit. We'll have a whole crew of counselors there when we do."

I was only hearing about half of what the chief was saying. However, this next part I heard loud and clear and it stung my heart worse than anything I could imagine.

The chief added, "We don't have all the details yet. They say it was suicide."

"No, not Turtle. Why?" Tears continued to slide down my face.

The chaplain addressed me. "We can't begin to imagine what you're feeling. This will take time. We're here to talk, to sort through this. We all take news of this nature differently. The important thing is to be able to comfort each other and reflect on how to help each other get through this."

Lieutenant Kirkland didn't say anything, but he put his hand on my shoulder and gave me a look that said he was here for me.

Senior Tillhammer just stood there and shook his head. His blank stare showed shock, pain, and remorse.

I looked around the room and uttered, "I need to talk to Flip."

The chief asked, "Who?"

The LT answered, "Flip is Sergeant Samuel Dolphline, Avionics troop, another close friend of Turtle. He is currently on the space station."

The chief replied, "Max, I don't know how that's possible. We're on the other side of Centrum. The only means of communication is through the encrypted communicator in the War Room. We can try, but it's only through text. You can't speak freely."

I repeated with tears in my eyes, "I need to talk to Flip."

Tillhammer blurted, "You heard the chief, it's not possible!"

I stood up and went for the door.

Hammer laid in. "Where are you going, Sergeant?!"

"I'm going to make a phone call."

Senior Tillhammer was about to say something when the chief interrupted. "Let him go. Chaplain McKinley, will you please go with Max? And don't leave his side."

"I'm on it," said the chaplain.

I made a beeline for the Flightline. My head was in a daze as I could barely focus on what was in front of me.

The chaplain ran behind me to catch up. "May I join you?"

"Sure."

"Where are we going? I'm not sure if I'm supposed to be out here."

I went to the closest BC-76 from the building. The power cart was sitting too far from the ship, and it would have to be pushed closer to hook up the cord. I released the brake and started to push it.

"Can you give me a hand?" I asked the chaplain.

Together we pushed it into position. He watched as I hooked it up and followed me onto the ship as I rapidly went through the power-up procedures.

In the flight deck, I sat in the pilot's seat. I pointed to the copilot position and told the chaplain, "Have a seat."

He asked, "Can I be doing all this?"

"You have no choice. You can't leave my side, can you? Besides, I may need you to talk to Flip."

I handed him a headset, plugged it in and showed him the volume controls. I turned on the satellite radio and tuned it to the standard maintenance frequency.

I called out, "Any station, any station, maintenance check, how copy?"

Nothing from the other end.

I repeated, "Maintenance check, how copy?"

This went on for a few minutes.

I saw the chaplain say something that I couldn't hear. I showed him the mic switch and how to talk over the interphone system.

He repeated through the interphone, "I said, how do you know anyone will answer?"

"Flip knows me. He'll figure it out. He knows I'll try to call. He has to. He just has to."

I continued trying, over and over again.

I told the chaplain, "Thoughts of Turtle are clouding my brain. Us hanging out in the barracks, all the shenanigans, all his one-liners. I just can't believe it."

"It's not going to be easy. We're never ready to lose someone."

"Why suicide? What was he thinking?"

"People usually aren't thinking clearly at that point."

Lieutenant Kirkland came up to the flight deck to check on us. The chaplain gave him a nod and a thumbs-up, then the LT left.

The chaplain continued, "Turtle was most likely struggling. Sometimes they bottle it up and there are no signs. People can't find the right answers and try to find a way out. All we can do is move forward. All we can do is pray for them and pray for ourselves. We can learn from these things. We will all mourn his loss, but we can't despair."

I continued the radio checks, to no avail. Every few minutes I'd try again. We continued to talk. I told Chaplain McKinley some of the stories. Our times at the Mountain, his Viridis girlfriend. I honestly don't know how much time we sat up there.

Then I heard a voice in my headset. "Maintenance check from Space Station Prime, anyone out there?"

I responded, "Loud and clear! Is this Flip?!"

"Max? It is."

"I got the news...I just can't believe it."

"I know."

"Are you okay? Talk to me, Flip."

"I'm not. I'm really not okay!"

"We got to get through this, man. We just have to."

"I talked with Turtle the night before. He was bummed about being rejected to live on Viridis. He'd been working on the Flightline since you left. He was working the opposite shift as me. He was actually doing fairly well. Not the best maintainer, but he was holding his own."

After a few minutes of me and Flip talking, the chaplain took off his headset and sat patiently. He looked over all the spaceship controls, then out the window across the Flightline. I was happy to have the time to sit with the chaplain prior to this. I felt in a better position to relay my thoughts to Flip. I talked with Flip for about an hour and we really got out what we were thinking. At one point Jo-Leia came up and gave me a long hug as she laid her head against my shoulder. I could tell she'd been crying as well.

She headed out and said, "I'll be right outside when you're done."

The chaplain went outside the ship with her. I continued to talk with Flip.

I finally had the courage to ask, "How did he do it? Were you there?"

Flip answered, "I wasn't there, but I heard. He did it at work, Max! On the Flightline! I still can't believe it." He was choking up and crying as he spoke. In fact, we both were. He continued, "Turtle went to the ship at the far end of the Flightline—the furthest away, the closest to the runway. He climbed up the hatch and stood on top of a ship and then jumped."

"I know the ships are tall, but how? That fall shouldn't have killed him!"

"No, Max. He jumped. He took off his harness and jumped during Alarm Red. He flew and was sucked out into fucking space."

"No!"

"A group of maintainers saw it happen. No one could believe it."

I asked Flip again, "Are you going to be alright?"

"I think so, yeah."

"Promise me two things."

"Anything."

"Promise me you won't hurt yourself. I really can't go through this again."

"I won't hurt myself."

"Also promise you'll go talk with a medical expert concerning all this."

"I already have, and I have a recurring appointment with someone from Medical."

"Great to hear."

"Your turn, Max."

"I'll be okay. I'll come back safe and sound, and I've got someone in mind to talk about all this."

"Is it the chaplain?"

"It is. One more thing. I know you said there were witnesses, but is any chance this was an accident? How do we know for sure?"

"I found a note."

"You found a note?"

"Just before I came out here to make the radio call, I stopped by his barracks room. Nothing was out of the ordinary. Then I checked room 200. There was a box and a note. The box had a bunch of miscellaneous stuff of Turtle's he had collected since he'd been here. Some old knickknacks, his comic books, some video games, his Rubik's Cube. Nothing too spectacular. The note was short and very dark and troubling."

"What did it say?"

"'To my best friends, I am truly sorry. Make sure my stuff finds a good home. I have enjoyed every moment with you, but my time is at an end. I feel this is my only way out. One last thing...why did the chicken cross the road?'"

CHAPTER 23

To Recovery

Roger: It pains me to know you went through all that. I understand how important Turtle was to you.

Max: I can't stop thinking about the times we had. Then I always wonder what I could have done differently to prevent this.

Roger: Were there warning signs?

Max: Nothing out of the ordinary. Even Flip said Turtle was upset about not being able to go to Viridis, but there weren't any other signs.

Roger: Experts will agree with me on this. Loved ones of the victims struggling can't blame themselves. You were there for him as much as possible. So was Flip. You had no fault in any of this. You must know this.

Max: I do. I know. Thanks.

I ended the radio call with Flip and shut the system down. The chaplain, Jo-Leia, and Larry were outside the ship. We talked a bit more and I even set up a time to meet with the chaplain in a couple days. Lieutenant Kirkland and Senior Sergeant Brickhouse stopped by as well.

The LT started, "We briefed the unit on it. Everyone is taking it hard. A few went with the counselors afterwards. We believe everyone will be alright, considering. I just want you to know we're all here for you. Anytime you need to talk, I'll be there."

"Thank you, sir."

Senior Brickhouse added, "We still need to launch a couple ships today, but we shouldn't need any Avionics work. The three of you need to take the rest of the day off. In fact, take as much time as you need, Max."

"What if there's a redball?"

"Prior to me being a pro super I was an Avionics troop. Worse comes to worst, I'll get some tools and figure it out."

"Got it, thank you."

Jo-Leia, Larry and I left work and headed to the chow hall. The LT and chaplain joined us, and we talked more during our meal. Afterwards they walked us all to the huts. I could see it in Jo-Leia's eyes—she wanted to comfort me but didn't want our relationship to be obvious. There was no way she could enter my hut with them there. I understood. I didn't sleep that much. I lay awake, taking it all in. Although sad, I felt much better. I felt better knowing how much support I had. I felt better talking with Flip and knew things were going to move forward.

The next day, I caught up with Jo-Leia and arrived at work for my regular shift.

Sergeant Banner stopped me. "Max, you don't need to be here. Take some time, Jo-Leia can handle it."

"No, this is where I need to be. Being around others is what's best for me."

"If that's what you want."

"You know what, go ahead and give the turnover to Jo-Leia."

"Where are you going?" She asked.

"I'm going to go with Larry to get tools."

I walked with Larry and asked him, "What do you know about Avionics?"

I knew I had to press forward. I felt it was the best way to get me through it all. I spent some quality time with Larry and learned more about him. Due to his hard upbringing, he really had trust issues. When people would try to help him, he would ignore most of it. In the past, anyone that he thought he respected ended up hurting him one way or another. He thought joining the military would be different. A way to start over, only in his mind, everyone was still out to get him.

On Larry's next day off, towards the end of roll call, I raised my hand.

Senior Tillhammer said, "Sergeant Morgan, what's on your mind?"

I walked to the front of the formation. "I just want everyone to know, anytime I see 'Larry loves Llamas' anywhere, I'm going to remove it. I know Turtle would agree with me."

Roger: How did that go?

Max: The room was very silent after roll call. From that point on, the llama situation was nonexistent.

Roger: Good to hear.

Max: The rest of the deployment went alright considering. Larry Alma was improving every week. I'd give him homework and he'd come back with full reports on the various systems. Jo-Leia was right—he wouldn't be the best Avionics troop, but I knew he'd be alright. I could see his confidence getting better and I could tell he appreciated all I did for him. I could see a real change in him.

I even started going to church each week with Jo-Leia. I found it soothing hearing Chaplain McKinley talk. Out of all the chaos of this place, the church was one place where it seemed time slowed down. I could just relax and focus. It was really nice but definitely different from the church I grew up with. For one thing, we were all in military uniforms and carried our armor and weapons in. A whole group of troops standing and singing hymns while carrying weapons. Such a sight to see. No kids, no older people. Just a group of soldiers taking a pause in this life to meditate and find peace. This was a good change. Jo-Leia liked the changes in me as well. We had made it to our last day of the deployment.

Roger: Last day—did you win the war?

Max: Who knows?

We sent cargo and troops here and there. Our bombers blew up a bunch of stuff. Another maintenance unit from the station came to replace us. We'll keep tag-teaming each other out for some time. Who knows how long this will last? I will say, we were lucky to have no one from our unit hit by rocket attacks, at least this time. On this last day, everyone cleared out their huts and started bringing their clothing bags out to the cargo yard to be loaded. Just as Jo-Leia and I started walking, it began to rain.

With bags in hand, she smiled. "This has been a wild deployment."

"You're telling me. Why did it have to wait till the last day to rain?"

"Last night was fun."

"What? The infrared scanner replacement?"

"You know what I mean."

"I know, and it was."

"So, what now?" she said playfully. "Is Sergeant Max Morgan going to ignore me when we get back to station?"

"What do you mean?"

"I just have a feeling, the minute we return, the whole deployment hot thing is going to wear off."

"No way, you're beautiful."

"I was talking about you."

"What?"

"Deployment hot works both ways, bub. What, you didn't think it works the same way for us girls?"

"That's harsh."

"I'm kidding."

"This rain is really coming down now."

"I know, all our stuff getting wet and muddy."

"How is there dirt in the rain?!"

"So, are you avoiding the question?"

I stopped walking and looked at Jo-Leia. "This was a tough deployment for sure. Senior Tillhammer, Larry and of course Turtle. There was one thing, one thing that always put a smile on my face and made me think, *Yeah, I got this.* It's been you. I see you and it just makes me happy. I'm lucky to be going through all this madness with someone that cares, someone that gets me. So of course I want this to continue."

"You're the best."

"You know I still have the first thing you ever texted me."

"I don't even remember."

"You told me that ship was good to go."

"Which ship?"

"It was 3034, the night I was on the opposite shift, repinning the nav system's wire connector. Sergeant Banner and you came to relieve me. I remember because it was my birthday and Flip did his big mattress exchange thing."

"That's right, I can't believe you remembered that text."

"Hard to forget, you're amazing."

We arrived at the cargo yard. Everyone had the same look of defeat as all our bags and uniforms were wet and muddy. We'd managed to get through the whole deployment without a drop of rain and now this. Another long day of standing in lines and waiting. The long flight home was cramped as we were squashed into another full BC-76.

As soon as we took off the runway from Calidum, many specialists and sergeants cheered as some were waving through the small portal windows on the sides of the ship. Of course, they were only waving with one finger, but I assume it's the thought that counts. Although we were all in great spirits going back to what we called *home*, there was still a lingering issue in the air.

Roger: What was that?

Max: The odor of an entire cargo ship full of wet and dirty maintainers who hadn't had a real hot shower in months.

CHAPTER 24

Dinner Guests

As soon as we arrived on Space Station Prime, I saw Flip standing there.

Jo-Leia said, "Go ahead, I'll catch up with you tomorrow."

Without words, Flip and I gave each other a long hug. He helped me find my bags and we made our way back to the barracks. For the first time ever, Flip seemed to be at a loss for words.

I started. "It'll be my last time coming to barracks, you know."

"Indeed. I'll help you move to the sergeants' quarters tomorrow. In fact, I already reserved you a nice suite. Not too far from mine."

"That sounds good. Real good."

"The nice thing is that all the sergeant quarters have a kitchenette."

"But I don't cook."

"Well, neither do I, but it's still cool to have one."

I continued, "Do you know what shift I'll be starting back on?

"You'll be on mine. I made sure of that—0600 to 1800."

"That's a good thing. Did we get any new troops?"

"We got a whole bunch of Franks. Looks like we'll be doing a lot of training."

"I'm okay with that."

We arrived at the Texas barracks.

I looked at Flip. "You know, I don't feel much like hitting the Mountain."

"Yeah, me neither. Why don't you get cleaned up and meet me in room 200?"

"I can do that."

The rest of the night was somber. We sat in room 200 and just talked. We talked about Turtle. We reminisced about all the times we had with him. I talked about the deployment with all its madness. I kept the parts about Jo-Leia out for now. I'd tell Flip eventually, but this was not the time. He told me all about the memorial service they had for Turtle.

Flip added, "It was so strange being in that chapel. You know, the last time I was there was for the York wedding."

I responded, "That's tough."

Flip continued, "That reminds me, Sharyn and Marcus invited us over to their place for a Christmas dinner."

"That sounds great."

"Yeah, I went over to their place a few times after...after Turtle. They really helped me sort things out."

"I was meaning to ask you something."

"What's that?"

"How did you know I would be on the satellite radio, on maintenance frequency?"

"I didn't know. I was in a state of shock and panic going through Turtle's old stuff when I got a message."

"What message?"

"Your LT, apparently. He figured out what you were up to. He used the encrypted communicator from your command center to text us the situation. He said you were trying to reach me on the satellite radio. He sent the message to our space station commander, then it was relayed all way down to me. Once I heard that, I knew to use the maintenance frequency."

I was almost in tears again, staring straight ahead.

Flip asked, "Are you okay, Max?"

"Yes, I just—I just never knew Lieutenant Kirkland went through all that, just for me, for us."

"I know, right?"

We continued to talk into the night. We agreed this would be our last night in room 200. We'd give the key cards to G-17 and Ian. The next morning, I felt like I had no time. I had to move into the sergeant quarters, go through the whole in-processing ordeal, get adjusted to my new schedule, and it was only a couple days before the holiday. I completed my tasks, but Christmas Day came fast. I felt bad since I was barely able to see Jo-Leia. Flip and I went to the sergeant chow hall for breakfast. We walked in and I saw the cooks.

I asked, "Is that...?"

"Indeed, it is. Bennold and Pawly from Viridis. They go back and forth between the sergeant chow hall and the specialist one."

As we were standing in line, I told Max all about Thanksgiving on Calidum. Then I asked him, "Ever heard of Franksgiving?"

"Franksgiving, no! That's too good."

We got our food and smiled at the cooks as we gave them one of those *fists in the air* hand gestures. They did the same as they recognized us from the mattress exchange.

We sat down, I asked Flip, "Do we need to bring anything to Sharyn and Marcus's tonight? It feels weird, like we're adults or something."

"I know, right? Let's stop by the market and see what they got."

As we were eating, we heard the cooks burst into song. One was playing a stringed instrument of some kind. They sang poorly with their broken accents, but it was a joy to see how much they were into it.

Bennold and Pawly sang to the tune of "Feliz Navidad," "We want to wish you American Christmas, we want to wish you American Christmas. We want to wish you American Christmas from the bottom of our hearts..."

I messaged Jo-Leia and she said she had other dinner plans but would try to see me late tonight. Flip and I arrived at the Yorks' with a cheese and meat tray in hand along with a couple cases of beer.

Marcus greeted us at the door. "Flip! Max!"

"Big Marcus!" we said in unison.

"Come on in."

The inside of their little home was all decorated and had the aroma of Christmas dinner. We heard holiday songs playing through their speakers.

Sharyn walked out of the kitchen with Jo-Leia and greeted us. "Welcome, so good to have you."

Jo-Leia said, "Nice to see you both. I trust Flip got you squared away in your new quarters."

I was surprised. "Jo-Leia, I didn't know you'd be here. It's great to see you, I just..."

Sharyn smiled. "Come on, Max, we all know about you two being a couple."

I looked at Jo-Leia. She responded, "Don't look at me. Somehow they knew and invited me for dinner."

Sharyn added, "Of course we know, all of maintenance knows. Word travels fast on the Flightline."

Big Marcus shook his head. "Don't blame me, I know nothing."

I said, "This is great. No, really. I'm glad you're here and we can all enjoy this together."

Dinner looked fabulous. For the first time in public, I could hold Jo-Leia's hand. We all sat at the table overlooking the feast.

Big Marcus then looked at Flip. "You're on."

Flip stood up and raised his glass, "Merry Christmas to our friends. Let us relish these moments and never forget them. Besides, how can we forget? We spend our nights chained to the top of a city flying endlessly through space. May we work hard and play even harder. To those we have grown with and are happy to call family. To family!"

We all raised our glasses and repeated, "To family!"

Flip continued, "To our brother Turtle..." Flip choked up with tears in his eyes and couldn't finish.

We all said in unison, "To Turtle."

We passed the food around and started to eat the grandiose meal. Flip was taking pictures of us and all the food. The song "Feliz Navidad" came on over their speakers, and Flip and I instantly started laughing. We had to tell the chow hall story.

Flip then said, "It's so great to see Max and Jo-Leia *finally* together."

I asked, "What do you mean *finally*?"

"What are you talking about? I saw the way you were looking at each other during turnover, months before you deployed. It was my idea to pair the two of you up during the wedding."

Sharyn added, "It's true."

"Really?!" I asked.

Jo-Leis looked as surprised as I was.

Flip added, "Well, yeah, that and with you two deploying together on the same shift. I would have real doubts about you if you didn't end up together."

Sharyn then asked Jo-Leia, "So...when was the first time you and Max knew you were a thing?"

"No," I protested.

Flip said, "Yes, give us all the enticing details."

Marcus joined in, "Too late now—our house, our rules. We gotta hear it."

Jo-Leia's face turned red.

Flip was smiling and shifting the palms of his hands together, awaiting a grand story.

"Alright, alright." I asked Jo-Leia, "You want me to tell it, or you got it?"

She took a long drink. "It's all you, bub."

"It had been a long day. I think Specialist Alma was out chasing crickets or something."

Jo-Leia corrected, "No, Larry was out helping Crew Chiefs with a tow."

"Okay, anyways, the first couple of months of the deployment, we really worked great together. I hate to say this, but I think it was our common frustration with Larry that helped us bond. We would joke all day on shift and just really got along. I felt like I could tell her everything, and she just got me."

Jo-Leia jumped in, "Get on with it, Max, you're embarrassing me."

"Okay, so Larry was away and the two of us were troubleshooting the bomb door integration."

Flip chimed in, "I hate that system. Too many wires going everywhere and then—"

Sharyn stopped him. "Shut up and let Max continue."

"We had the wiring schematics displayed on our tablets. Tools were everywhere. Parts disconnected. We knew there had to be an open in one of the wires. Jo-Leia was up on one ladder, checking the wires on a part high inside the bomb bay. I looked up and saw her. She was down to her tight T-shirt. She had the electrical plugs off and was checking every wire with the meter. Sweat was beading off her face. I could see she was having trouble reading the wire numbers. I got up on the other ladder and shined a light to where she was working. We were standing so close to each other high up on the ladders. Jo-Leia tried the last wire and we saw there was no continuity. I traced the wire down and found a break in the line. We had found the problem. Standing face-to-face, she just looked at me with a big smile. I don't know what came over me. I just leaned in and kissed her."

"Ohhh," said Flip.

Jo-Leia had her hands over her face.

Sharyn asked, "Then what?"

Jo-Leia responded, "My turn. So, Max decides to give me a kiss. I was like, okay, so this is happening. I really didn't expect it since he's a sergeant and all. Not that I didn't want it to happen. I just never thought it would. Was I happy? Yes. Was I surprised? You better believe it."

"Then what?" Big Marcus asked.

"Then out of the blue, would you believe the rocket alarms start going off? Max and I got down fast, then waited a few seconds and bolted to the closest bunker. We were already at the far end of the Flightline. Being at that far end, this bunker is rarely in use. Max used the handheld radio and called in our accountability. It was only the two of us in the bunker waiting for the Alarm Green."

Flip said with a smirk, "I like where this is going."

Jo-Leia continued, "Settle down now, Flip. Nothing major happened that day. Although we did make use of idle time in there and learned a great deal about how each other kissed."

Sharyn was so excited. "You two are so perfect."

Flip saved me. "Max, you're a gentleman and scholar. I won't press you anymore for details—for tonight, that is."

Sharyn then asked Flip, "So, who are you seeing this week? Is it one from Finance, or from Medical, or perhaps that Engine troop?"

Flip was taken aback. "Hey, just because I like to have options doesn't make me bad. To tell the truth, I'm currently between girls. On a break, so to speak."

Sharyn responded, "Yeah, yeah. I've just never seen you with one for more than a month."

Flip came back, "Okay, fair enough. Your turn, Sharyn and Big Marcus, you never mentioned this— do tell us how the honeymoon went?"

Big Marcus's face took to a blank stare. He shook his head and looked at Sharyn.

Sharyn took another drink and responded, "It was lovely. We spent it here in our humble abode. Our meals were catered by the finest chow hall we could find."

Flip responded, "That's it?"

Sharyn added, "I will say one thing, and one thing only."

"What's that?" Flip said, leaning in.

"I now know why they call him *Big* Marcus."

Flip yelled in disgust, "No, no, no, no! You've ruined it!"

Sharyn was laughing so hard. We all were.

Flip continued, "No! You know now what this means for us! From this point forward we will never be able to call him that again!"

CHAPTER 25

Commanders

The dinner party during that Christmas would never be forgotten. In January, Jo-Leia had in fact made sergeant. We continued to date. Midsummer, Flip ended up deploying to Calidum for six months. The next couple of years brought in many changes. We had a change of command where Colonel Fredrick would return to Earth and we received our new maintenance commander, Major Porter.

I continued to attend chapel every Sunday with Jo-Leia and enjoyed hearing Chaplain McKinley go on and on. I also continued to train Specialist Alma, and even took on the role of training most of the new Avionics troops. I really enjoyed this and could tell the more they knew, the easier the job would be for all of us. With the other sergeants running the show, we had plenty of time to train the new specialists. That is, when they weren't deploying left and right.

Other changes included that of the Resource Center. Senior Sergeant Tillhammer was retiring soon, and with Sergeant Diego becoming a senior sergeant, he ended up running the Resource Office. On the Flightline side of things, Sergeant Greenfield and Peterson both made senior and were moved up to Production Superintendents. This made more room for more Flightline expeditors. I was riding shotgun with our expeditor Sergeant Donar for the last month or so in the launch truck.

There's an interesting thing about launch trucks. When you put a bunch of maintainers in an enclosed space for hours on end, the conversations can get out of control, going from one extreme to another. I'm convinced the expression "What happens in Vegas stays in Vegas" originated in the military. You could be in a foxhole, an armored tank, or within the bowels of a submarine. Whenever two or more mission-critical military members are present for long periods of time is when the easily offended need to leave.

No language is censored. No subject is out of bounds. There are sex jokes, religious jokes, fat jokes, fart jokes, gay jokes and the classic "yo mama" jokes. The launch truck stories are never-ending. Stories of dating conquests in barracks or tales of grandiose adventures that may or may not have happened. Everyone rips on each other. No one is safe.

One common thing we all learn is how to censor ourselves. You throw one officer in the mix and you'd think this group just turned into a bunch of church mice. 'Yes, sir, no, ma'am, pleased to be here, may I show you around?' Once we're back with our people, it's game on. Even when a new sergeant or senior enters the picture, there's always a period where the others are trying to feel them out, seeing what they can get away with. One could write volumes and volumes of launch truck stories.

Roger: So, are you going to tell me a few?

Max: No way.

Roger: Really?

Max: I will respectfully maintain my innocence and protect those I know from any incriminating evidence.

Roger: ...

Max: Don't get your hopes up. This is the only clean launch truck story I could conjure up.

Sergeant Donar was driving, I was in the front passenger seat. Ian, Finch and a few other maintainers from Hydro, E&E, and Engines were in the back as we waited for this ship to go up. Specialist Finch was a fairly new Avionics troop that I had been training. He would always come up with the wildest stories and we loved him for that.

Donar watched the flight crew arrive at the ship. He turned around to the maintainers. "Hey, guys, listen up. This is an important launch. Our Commander Porter is flying this one, so nobody fuck it up."

Finch questioned, "I didn't know the commander flew?"

Donar answered, "Yeah, he was a pilot, still is. He has to fly every now and again to keep qualified. He don't fly a whole lot." After seeing the commander climb aboard, Sergeant Donar blurted out, "I miss football. Did you guys know I used to have a swimming pool?"

I asked, "What does that have to do with football?"

"Sunday. Me and my buddies would—"

Ian whispered, "My buddies and I."

"What? You know I can't hear too good, especially with all you in the launch truck. Anyways, on Sundays I'd have a bunch of friends over to my house—well, it was my dad's house. We'd sit outside and watch the game. My old man set up a TV outside, under the per-goalie."

Finch chimed in. "What the hell is a per-goalie?"

"You know, a per-goalie. That's what we called it. Like a roof outside to hide the shade."

Finch questioned, "Why are you hiding shade?"

Ian clarified, "I think he means pergola."

"You guys suck." Donar continued, "We'd watch the games outside and in between the commercials we'd jump in the pool. We'd also all run and do a cannonball whenever our team scored."

I asked him, "What was your team?"

"We had a bunch we liked, but living on the East Coast, we always rooted for the Redskins."

Ian whispered, "Does he know? Sarge left way before we did."

Finch called out, "Hey, Sarge, you hear? The Washington Redskins football team is no more?"

Sergeant Donar turned around. "What?! No Redskins?! Tell me."

Finch said, "It's a long story."

"Don't matter, we got lots of time before this ship goes up."

I turned around, trying to figure out what they were up to. "Ian! What's with your hands?"

Ian answered, "Finch and I have a bet. He safety-wired my wrists to this avionics part, and I'm seeing how long it'll take to get out of it using only items in the truck."

"I'm just going to turn around and pretend I never saw nor heard that. Continue with your football story, Finch."

Finch continued, "Alright, it starts in Texas."

"Why Tex-ass? Redskins are in D.C."

"Well, this story starts in Texas. Remember that big oil tycoon, Sam LaMarche?"

"Nope."

"Just think of a cross between Ross Perot and Boss Hog."

"I don't know no Ross whatever, but I loved them Duke boys."

"Sam LaMarche became governor of Texas and was a bit eccentric. He had these crazy ideas for Texas, such as the Great Oil Pipeline, the Great Monorail System, and the Great San Antonio Infrastructure Plan, to name a few. The weird thing was that all these plans worked and were making Texas tons of revenue. The craziest plan of his almost tore our country apart. This was the Great Texas Expanse Plan."

"I thought we were talking about football?"

"We'll get to it. Governor Sam LaMarche tried to make a deal with the Oklahoma governor, Elroy West. The deal was simple. LaMarche would buy Oklahoma for an insane amount of money. Every resident of Oklahoma would be given a huge amount of money—we're talking a few hundred thousand dollars each. These residents didn't have to move or anything, unless they wanted to. They could stay on the land, build a new house, buy a nice car, whatever. However, this land would now be part of Texas. Everywhere that Oklahoma is written, would be changed to Texas. Every Oklahoman would now be a Texan."

"The Oklahoma governor and his staff would all be out of a job, of course. Rumor had it they were to make even more money out of the deal. The country was in an uproar over this, demanding the federal government get involved, which they did. Memes were made, showing Oklahomans as sellouts, or showing Texas playing a Risk board game across America. I loved the one with the *Lord of the Rings* guy saying, 'One does not simply buy a state.'"

"So, did they make the deal?" asked Donar.

"I'll get to that. Of all the things going on, the one thing most people were concerned about was changing the American Flag. No one wanted to deal with us only having forty-nine stars. Fifty is such a nice round number. You would think people would be concerned about Texas getting larger, state takeovers, economic changes, and so forth. Nope, it was the forty-ninth star issue."

"So now we get to talk about the Redskins?"

"No, California."

"California?"

"Yes. California governor Don Blanche.

"Sounds like a gangster name."

"Well...he is a politician. Governor Blanche went to Washington to join in the Great Texas Expanse Plan discussions. Blanche's solution was to divide California into two states, Northern and Southern California. The truth of the manner is, most Californians have wanted this for a while. These discussions went on for a year until a deal was made and a contract was signed by all. California would be split into two states. Texas would now own the land formerly known as Oklahoma, the previous Oklahomans would be paid lots of dough, and most importantly, we would still have fifty states. Everyone wins, until—"

Donar interrupted, "Hey, we got a redball."

We heard over the radio that they were having problems with the radar system on 3034. The truck pulled up next to the ship.

I yelled to the back, "Ian and Finch, you got this one." Just as I turned around, I saw Ian's wrists still safely wired to that part, with a look of panic on his face. "Okay, it's Finch and me, then."

As we were running towards the ship with harness in tow, I said, "Finch, this one is yours. You figure out what's wrong."

He replied, "But the commander on there."

"No better time to learn than now. You got this!"

From the looks of it, the system was on, but there was no picture on their screen. No picture at all—this wasn't just a radar issue. Finch had the crew cycle through a couple different settings. It appeared nothing was coming up. He then quickly checked the circuit breakers to ensure none of them had popped. They all looked good. I was thinking this was a bad monitor. I was about to run an inquiry to see if we had one in stock, but I waited to see what Finch would do. He had the crew reset the system. It came back up with nothing displayed.

Finch asked me, "What do you think?"

"It's your redball," I told him.

"I think the monitor is bad. If we have the part, the whole process may take about fifteen to twenty minutes tops."

"Okay, run an inquiry and see if we got one. I'll let the expeditor know." We were about to leave when I thought, *Let me try something real quick.* I reached over the commander's shoulders and tried the monitor's dimmer knob. Instantly his monitor revealed everything. Major Porter looked pissed since he'd completely missed that part. No words were spoken as we departed the ship.

As we were heading back to the truck, I asked Finch, "Do you have all your tools? Did you bring anything up there with you?"

"Yep, just two tools." He showed me his hands. "Just these safety wire pliers and dykes."

"Why would you even need those for a redball?"

"I didn't want Ian to find them. We still got that bet going on."

"We have to talk, later."

I got back in the truck and Donar asked, "What's going on?"

I answered, "All good now. Pilot error."

Donar said, "Nice...oh!"

I told them all about the dimmer knob and the expression on the commander's face. We all had a good laugh.

Donar then said, "Okay, let's get back to the story. So, they made the deal and Oklahoma is gone?"

Finch continued, "Yes, well, most of it. Ever heard of the Chickasaw Nation of Oklahoma? The Native America tribal leaders of the various nations took to the courts. Their front-runner was Chief James Wolfe. Chief Wolfe brought it to everyone's attention that the Texas Expanse bill clearly states, and I'll say this slow, once the land becomes Texas territory, the Oklahomans will be paid the given amount. Well, once the land becomes Texas, the former Oklahomans are now Texans. They no longer have the title of Oklahomans, thus, there are no Oklahomans to be paid. Except, of course, those that live on the land that's protected from such deals, known as the Chickasaw Nation of Oklahoma, as well as the other tribal nations in the state. They're all still considered Oklahomans and are the only ones due that huge payout as stated in the bill. Chief Wolfe and all the tribal members of Oklahoma became millionaires overnight."

"So Chief Wolfe wanted to get rid of the Redskins name?"

"No, not quite. Let me close out what happened first. Sam LaMarche stayed fat and happy as he was able to expand Texas. He also started drilling for oil in the land formerly known as Oklahoma to expand his pipeline and make even more money. Elroy West went into hiding after losing his job, losing his state, and losing all credibility. Former Oklahomans were still in shock about not getting a dime out of it, and many left the state for Kansas or Arkansas. They couldn't stand being called Texans. Blanch took the position of governor of Northern California. They held a special election for a new Southern California governor. I remember this because some rich businessman from San Diego ran against that real popular singer, Gwen Stephanie. She just showed up, smiled, and ended up winning by a landslide."

"No doubt. What about the Redskins' name change?"

Ian shouted out, "Potato!"

"Shut up, Ian!" Finch responded.

Finch continued, "Chief Wolfe became famous quick. With his money and fame, he started becoming more and more involved in politics and decisions across the country. When the topic of changing the Washington Redskins' name came up, he was the first person the Washington team went to for advice. Chief Wolfe actually liked the Redskins' name. He thought it was an honor to have a team icon that represented Native Americans. However, he also knew some of his people found it offensive. So, Chief Wolfe met with various tribal leaders over a few months, and they came to a decision to kill the name."

"So, what's the name of team now?" questioned Donar.

"That, I do not know. They were in limbo for a while trying to figure out a name, then I left for space."

"Potato!" Ian chimed in again.

Sergeant Donar turned around. "Ian, why do you keep saying that?"

"It's simple. The Redskins didn't need to change their name. They can still be called Redskins. All they had to do was change their mascot and team logo to a potato."

CHAPTER 26

Tough Life

Flip asked, "Who's winning the game, by the way?"

I answered, "I think the Shirts have been winning; however, the Skins are about to score."

"Pass me another beer, would you, Max?"

"Why? Is the ice cooler too far from your arm?"

"Fine! I'll get it."

"Dude! You missed it, Jordan and Edwards ended up going for the same pass in the so-called end zone. They both jumped and ended up in the water just as a big wave came."

"Oh well."

"Hey, Flip, don't bury your feet in the sand, you'll get a weird tan line.

"Got it. Do you think the locals know we're from Earth?"

"Well, let me look around. We're the only ones on this beach drinking beer. The only ones wearing long shorts that go down to our knees. You're the only one out here taking pictures. We're speaking English, if that wasn't a dead giveaway. Also, I'm pretty sure none of the locals have seen American football."

"This is a tough life."

"Sure is."

"Cheers."

"Cheers."

Roger: Max, what's going on here?

Max: Oh, I just thought I'd skip ahead a bit to give you a taste, then I'll backtrack and show how we got there from here.

Roger: Why would you do that?

Max: I don't know, it always works in the movies. Let's go back about a month.

Roger: Okay?

I came in from the Flightline on station after working a long shift troubleshooting the bomb door system. I received a message to see Senior Sergeant Diego in the Resource Office.

"Congratulations on your rank and position," I greeted Diego. "I heard you took Senior Tillhammer's job."

"That's correct, Sergeant Morgan. Over the last few weeks, I've been getting turnover from him and learning all about this position."

"How did that go?"

"I learned a tremendous amount of how to conduct business around here, how to treat the troops, and how to run a schedule."

"Oh, well, that sounds great."

"I'll tell you what, Max. You can learn a lot from a good supervisor."

"I know that, for sure."

"However, you can learn *twice* as much from a bad supervisor."

"What do you mean by that?"

"You can always learn what not to do, or what you could do better."

"Oh? Did you learn *twice* as much from Tillhammer?"

"Is he gone yet?"

"No, I think he's got about six days left."

"Then I can't answer that yet."

"Okay, then."

Senior Diego continued, "You know how you were scheduled to go to Calidum next month?"

"Am I still going?"

"Well, I'm going to put this up to you. We just got word that we need to send a small crew to Viridis. I need to rearrange a few people to accommodate both deployments."

"Well, I haven't been to Viridis. I would love that opportunity."

"I thought so. Another thing. This will be a very small crew. You're only taking two 76ers in the cargo configurations. Let me get the maintenance crew list out: four Crew Chiefs, two on each shift. Only two of each other maintenance career fields: Engines, Hydro, E&E, Avionics and even a Sheet Metal troop."

"Sounds good."

"There will also be a senior sergeant on your crew. The chief hasn't selected one yet."

"You?"

"I wish. The chief is leaning towards someone from Production. It'll probably be Senior Sergeant Peterson. Any other career fields you can think of? What am I missing?"

"Will there be a parts warehouse there?"

"No, you'll take a small sample of parts—anything else will have to be ordered."

"So, will we need a Parts Supply person to help with the ordering process?"

"Yep, that wouldn't hurt. I'll add one to the list."

"What about Tool Counter or Debrief?"

"You know, I thought about that, but I think with this small crew you should be able to handle your own tools. You can assign someone to take charge of it. Same with Debrief—before the trip, get with the Debrief team and make sure you understand the whole process."

"Got it. What about a Quality Control inspector?"

"I'm going to pretend I didn't hear that."

"Hear what?"

"I need maintainers that are proficient to work a shift by themselves. I know you can handle it. Who else do you think we should bring from Avionics?"

I sat there thinking for a bit. A few names came to mind. I knew

Jo-Leia was out. She was still waiting to hear if she would be accepted to officer training.

On a whim, I said, "How about Sergeant Dolphline?"

"Flip? Come on, Max. You two on a deployment together? That could be trouble. Besides, haven't you two already been on a couple already?"

"Actually, no, never. It was always one or the other. Also, you said we'd be on separate shifts. It's not like we'll have much time to get in *trouble*, as you call it."

"Let me think on it."

The next night Senior Diego gave me the news towards the end of my shift. I was officially on the Viridis deployment. So was Flip, but he didn't know yet. I started walking to the sergeants' quarters with Flip.

"Guess what?" I asked.

"Let me guess, you're not deploying now?"

"No, I'm still deploying."

"That sucks. Calidum sucks."

"That's what I was going to tell you. You got picked up to deploy as well."

"Really?! I mean, it'll be cool to go with you, but I hate Calidum. I was just there last year."

"Diego is going to tell all the new deployers tomorrow. You are definitely going with me."

"Are we at least going to be on the same shift?"

"I'm afraid not."

"Man, this—"

"Alright, alright, here it is, Flip. We are deploying, but not to Calidum."

"What?"

"We're going to Nix!"

"Now you're really screwing with me. You're really enjoying this, aren't you?"

"Okay, okay. For real this time. You and I are going to Viridis."

"For real?!"

"Yes! Senior Diego said it's official. We're both deploying to Viridis with a couple BC-76ers."

"Outstanding!"

That night Jo-Leia met me in my quarters. She slowly walked into my small living quarters; her head was down. When she looked up, her face was redder than usual. I could see pain in her eyes.

I asked, "What happened? Did you find out about the officer training? You didn't get in?"

"No, actually, I did."

"That's great! Isn't it? You'll become a pilot."

"Yes, I got selected, but....by the time you get back from Viridis, I'll already be on my way to Earth. I don't want what we have together to be over. I just can't see any other way."

"I know this will be hard for both of us. I just know this is going to be great for you. It's what you always wanted. You have to do it. Besides, we never know. After my enlistment—"

"Max, we're talking another ten years or more. We can't hold each other to that, you know that."

"So now what?"

"I don't know...we leave on happy terms. We enjoy these next two weeks and be thankful for the time we had. We don't say good-bye, we say good luck."

"You're amazing."

The next couple weeks were a mix of emotions as I juggled my time with Jo-Leia and getting prepared for the deployment. She would be sent across the Space Bridge and start her officer train-ing. She was already set up to begin pilot training as well. I honestly had no idea when or if I'd ever see her again. Jo-Leia and I had one last night together and we felt things were going to be good for both of us. We wished each other the best of luck and I was on my way. I tried to remain calm about the situation, but deep down I was hurting. I was a mess with a mix of emotions. This was one of those things I'd have to work out internally.

It wasn't long before our small crew set off to Viridis in the two BC-76ers. It was so great being in the back of the cargo ships with all sorts of leg room. A few guys strung up hammocks across the span of the cargo bay. Flip and I were on separate BC-76s. In fact, all the career fields were split up just in case one ship ended up with any maintenance issues. The flight had no issues as we landed on this water moon that had a purple tint to its sky. As soon as we got off the ships, we quickly helped the Crew Chiefs with the postflight inspections. We walked to the building on this new airfield of ours that we were sharing with the people of Viridis. We joined our flight crews at the end of the Flightline, where they were waiting for us. Along with their bags, a couple of the pilots had drink coolers, and they each held a beer in their hands.

Flip turned to me and whispered, "Really? Don't bring 'em if you don't have enough for everyone."

Just then the pilot looked at us all and gave us each a beer. We could tell right then, this deployment was going to be different. There was a bus service that took us to the small village we would be living in. We would use this bus to go to and from work each time. This village had a few restaurants, stores, houses, and many hotels. We arrived at our hotel; Senior Sergeant Peterson distributed the room keys. There was a look of surprise when we realized we each got our own room.

Peterson then said, "Alright, team, find your rooms. Dump off your bags and meet back down in the lobby in twenty minutes."

We carried our bags upstairs to find our rooms. The hotel looked a bit run-down, but I'd take this any day after being on Nix or Calidum. I unlocked my door to find a small room with its own washroom. Looking around the room, I saw an extra set of doors to the rear of my room. Opening the doors was a glorious shock. We each had a small porch with a spectacular ocean view as the water reflected the purplish tint in the sky.

I stepped out onto the porch, then reached over the railing and knocked on my neighbor's back door. Flip opened it and was dumbfounded by the view.

"Holy crap!" he said.

"I know, right? Knock on the door next to you, keep it going."

Soon after, we had a whole row of maintainers standing on their porches, eyes wide open, staring at the majestic sight of endless blueish-purple water across to the horizon. We arrived back in the lobby to meet up with Senior Peterson. He led us into one of the business rooms along with all the flight crews.

Major Leroy Gatlin, our deployed commander, introduced himself and briefed us.

The commander said, "As you may have guessed, this is not your regular deployment. We will be flying the two BC-76ers and rotating our four flight crews. The pilots and Senior Sergeant Peterson have already been briefed on our mission. I won't go into more detail here, but I will once we're in a more secure location. While on idle time, I ask that no one leaves the surrounding area of this village. If you want to explore more of the island on your off days, you need to inform me first and we'll consider the situation. Maintainers will report to Senior Peterson for any of these trips. I don't think I need to tell anyone twice to be responsible. This trip is a blessing. I'm going to keep this simple. Don't do anything that will impact your career. Follow the rules and we'll enjoy every day here. Get in trouble, then you'll be heading back to station on the first shuttle or freighter I can find. Don't screw up this sweet deal here. I've given each flight crew the flying schedule as well as Senior Peterson. Don't be late."

Commander Gatlin continued, "One more thing. Some of the crews already brought it to my attention that your chargers for your tablets won't work on these electrical outlets. We're working on a solution, but don't be surprised if it takes a while. In the meantime, figure out how your room alarm clocks work. Our flying schedule is still on Zulu time here, and I honestly have no clue what the local time is. In fact, once someone figures out how to read these clocks, let me know. We also need to know what the conversion is. Let us all know. Our first launch is tomorrow at 0900. According to my tablet, that's just under fifteen hours from now. You are dismissed. Maintainers, report to Senior Peterson."

The air crew cleared out of the room and all the maintainers stayed. Senior Peterson briefed us.

"I've split us up in two groups. I'll have a set of each career field on team one and the rest of you on the second team. I'll jump back and forth between the two. Team one will show up three hours before each scheduled launch, get the ships ready and deal with any red-balls. You'll also have to stick around just in case the ships come back early for any reason. Team two will recover the ships and deal with any maintenance on the back side. Depending on how long these things are scheduled to fly, I'll adjust the schedule for all of us."

Peterson continued, "These missions are only going to be around eight hours long. So, we really won't have to be there around the clock. If nothing's broken, it'll be a short day. Otherwise, we'll work until it's fixed. We're just going to have to be flexible on this one. The other nice thing is they don't fly every day. By the looks of their schedule, they'll fly for about three or four days straight, then have a day or two off, then start the cycle again. Like Major Gatlin said, this could be a sweet deal out here. Let's not screw it up."

I was on the second shift. We would arrive each day and send the first shift home, then wait around for the ships to land. We knew as soon as we did the postflight inspections and resolved any maintenance issues, our shift was over. If E&E had work, I'd be right there at Specialist Fisher's side, helping him change a part or troubleshoot his system. Sergeant Matt F. Edwards, our Engine troop, would help Crew Chiefs Jordan and Young with all the postflight recoveries or maintenance issues. Other times, we'd assist Sergeant Pechman with any hydraulic leaks. I had Fisher and Pechman help me with a radar antenna change one day.

I loved this pace of work, as we all worked as a team, learning a little bit about each other's jobs. We did have some unexpected challenges. One was that of the tablet situation. The power outlets here were just not compatible. Our tablets died after the second day, and we had to rely on our experience to run through these systems or change the parts.

About two weeks in, I saw Specialist Fisher with his charger wire exposed as he was soldering a different connector and adapter to it.

I asked him, "What are you doing?"

Fisher responded, "If I can get this to work, I think we'll be able to use the Viridis electrical outlets to charge our tablets." Once he was done, we went to one of the buildings near the Flightline. We found an empty office room.

"Here goes nothing," he said as he plugged in his tablet with the modified charger. We heard a loud spark as the lights in the room went out. That wasn't the worst part. We could smell smoke emanating from his dead tablet.

He looked up with a look of surprise and frustration. "Now what?"

"I think we leave this room and never speak of this."

We walked back to the Flightline.

He was thinking and said, "That should have worked. There's got to be a way."

I asked, "What about our ship's power? We have those electrical outlets in the cargo bay. Can we make some sort of adapter for those?"

"Yeah, I think we can."

Specialist Fisher and I worked on rigging up another charger cable. I was reluctant to give him mine, but oh well. It wasn't working in our current state. We checked the new wire and were pretty sure this would work. Once Ship 3034 landed, we made our way on it.

I asked Fisher, "Alright, before we plug this thing in, tell me about this electrical outlet. What other systems does it go to? Is there any potential that this could cause damage?"

"No, it's just a straight shot to the circuit breaker, then to ship's power. Worst-case scenario is it'll pop a breaker."

"And fry my tablet?"

"Maybe, but I think I got it this time."

We crossed our fingers and plugged it in. We could see my tablet start to charge.

He yelled, "Yes!"

Sergeant Pechman was heading to the back of the ship. "What are you yelling at?"

"Fisher found a way to charge our tablets on the ship," I answered.

"Awesome! Let me know when yours is done. I'll plug mine in."

"What are you working on?" I asked.

Pechman answered, "The crew said there's a hydro leak down here at the far end. Look, there's all sorts of hydro fluid on the ground near the side rails."

"What's that coming from?"

"Well, there's always a little bit here, that's common, but it shouldn't be this much. I'll clean it up and check all the lines."

"Anything I can do to help?"

"If you could, get me some more absorbent pads."

"On it. Hey, Fisher, do you think you can make any more of those chargers?"

"Maybe. I'm not sure if we have another adapter—I'll look."

"If not, get with Sergeant Hayloft. He may be able to order a few through Parts Supply."

Once we knew for sure that the modified charger worked, we told Senior Peterson. He was thrilled and alerted the flight crews to the news. Fisher made a second charger adapter that we put on Ship Triple Twos. The flight crews would charge their tablets during the long flights, then we'd do what we could when the ships were on the ground. We even had to make a schedule of who got to use it and when.

Ship 3034 continued to have that hydraulic leak over the next few weeks. Pechman would go to the back of the ship on his hands and knees, cleaning up the fluid. He was swearing there were no leaks in the lines. I was in the cargo bay when Senior Peterson approached the back.

Pechman had fluid all over his hands and arms. "I can't find it. There's always a little residual, that's normal, but never this much.

I just can't find a leak. I've pressurized the lines and can't find anything."

Senior Peterson replied, "Then why is there a pool of liquid down here every time the ship comes back?! This has been going on for a month now! We need to figure this out. Is there anything we can do to help?"

"No, I'll keep looking."

"What exactly did the flight crew say?"

"Same as always. They go back here to use the urinal and see the hydro fluid on the ground."

Peterson looked around. "Max, hand me your water bottle."

He then poured it into the urinal. The three of us looked down and could see water leaking through an unforeseen crack in the small tube, forming a puddle of water mixed with the residual hydro. Apparently, all it takes is a tiny amount of residual hydraulic fluid to turn any liquid red. The look on Pechman's face was priceless. He had been up to his elbows cleaning up piss for the last month. It didn't take long for the Crew Chiefs to repair the line. Jordan showed Young how to do it.

We had a couple days off and our entire maintenance team headed down to the beach.

Flip and I sat in a couple beach chairs, taking in the sun as the others played football.

Flip said, "This is a tough life."

"Sure is."

"Cheers."

"Cheers."

"Look, Sergeant Pechman decided to join us."

Flip yelled, "Hey, Pechman! You might want to jump in the ocean to get cleaned up. We heard about your battle with the urinal."

I added, "But be careful—one drop of hydro fluid could turn this whole area into the Red Sea!"

CHAPTER 27

Island-Hopping

A few weeks went by, and I went to Senior Peterson with a question. "I noticed next week we have a break of three days before we fly again. I have a request."

"What's that?"

"I want to take a trip to a nearby island. The Island of Flos. I can easily make it back in two days' time."

"I don't think we can risk that. Too many factors involved. You traveling on a foreign moon and all. What's the reason for this?"

"Sir, you remember Turtle, right?"

"Of course."

"It was his girlfriend, his fiancée. I know she lives on that island. I don't know if she knows...if she knows what happened to Turtle. I want to—I need to find her. I need to tell her about Turtle."

"I see. This is too dangerous for you to go...alone. You'll need to take someone with you."

"What about Flip?"

"No, can't do that. I can't lose both Avionics troops. Not that you'll get lost, but we can't risk it."

"How about Fisher?"

"That'll work. I'll need to see your travel plans. I want to know where and when you'll be at each stop."

"Yes, sir. I will. Thank you."

I met up with Fisher. "You want to go on a trip? Pack your overnight bag—next week we're going on an adventure!"

A week went by. The two of us with our backpacks waited at the docks, ready to set sail on a local transport boat with tickets in our hands.

Fisher turned to me. "Are you sure we'll find her?"

"Who knows? We have her name and the village she's from. How hard can that be?"

"Have you seen the population of these places? She could be a needle in a haystack. All we have is her first name, and you said you never saw a picture of her."

"Alright, have a little faith. Besides, worse comes to worst, we backpack across this moon and come up empty-handed. At least we have a cool story to tell. Who else do you know that island-jumps on foreign moons?"

"You do have high hopes."

"I wonder if that's our ship coming in?"

"Maybe."

We showed our tickets and boarded the small vessel. The trip took about five hours across the open waters. We were on the main deck looking over the expanse of the ocean. We were in awe of it all with the purplish sky and water. We also saw something strange. They were about two feet long. These crazy creatures looked like small dolphins but also had wings. They would fly overhead, then swoop down into the water and swim for some time. Some would come up out of the water carrying fish in their mouths, then another one would swoop by and try to steal it. We spent hours on the deck, just watching these weird things swim, fly, and fight each other. About halfway through the voyage, I looked over at Fisher. He was extremely pale and shaking.

"You okay, man?" I asked.

"I think I'll be alright, just feeling a bit sick."

"What's wrong? Never been on the ocean before?"

"I'm from Colorado, so, no."

We made it to the port at Flos and departed the boat. It was a long trip, and I could tell Fisher was relieved to be back on solid ground. We took some time to recover by going to a local market and getting some food. We ate some bread and fruit and Fisher said he was feeling a little better.

He asked me, "Now what?"

I reached into my pocket and brought out a piece of paper with poorly drawn markings.

"What's that?"

"A map."

"Why don't you use your tablet?"

"Because the battery is low and I have no way to charge it. We may need it for emergencies."

"When did you draw that thing?"

"I brought up the map system on the ship, zoomed in on Flos and drew it the best I could. According to this, the airfield is about six miles away. Turtle said Columbae worked at a restaurant or something not too far from the airfield. We can make our way there and scout out the neighboring towns."

"Sounds good. Is there a taxi or do we walk it?"

"Your guess is as good as mine. Do you speak Viridis?"

"Well, if I hadn't fried my tablet, we would have the translator, so no."

"Well, for now, I say we just start walking. If we see some sort of transportation on the way, we'll take it."

We start walking down the side of the road on this unknown island. Vehicles that looked like hovercrafts sped pass us as we made our journey.

Fisher asked me, "Max, what's your story?"

"What do you mean?"

"I don't know, just trying to pass the time. I'm sure you have a backstory. We all do. What's yours?"

"I think I'm just lucky."

"Lucky?"

"Lucky for the lot I was given. I don't have a wild past, nothing out of the ordinary. I grew up in an average home. Only child. Two loving parents. We weren't poor, but we weren't rich either. Average. I was just there. Doing normal stuff, living a regular life. I was fortunate. We'd take vacations. In Southern California you could do anything any given day. Go to the beach, go to the snowy mountains, go to any number of theme parks, go to concerts. I had a good childhood. I really did. I can't complain. I see everyone else and hear all these elaborate stories of struggling families. I feel bad sometimes because mine was good. Real good. I look back and am just thankful for how lucky I was. I know it would sound cooler to have real drama growing up, but it just wasn't the case."

"No, that's cool. Why did you join the Space Military and volunteer for this remote assignment, then?"

"Well, both my dad and my grandfather were in the military. It just felt like the right thing to do. I thought, if I don't do this, I'll be forever wondering to myself what it would have been like. I told myself at first, why not just try it out? If I hate it, then I'll get out, then I'll know. At least I tried, at least I did something to be proud of. If I end up liking it, I'll stick around, then I'll know I made the right decision."

"I hear you."

"When I first heard about the interstellar assignment, I immediately called my dad. I wanted to take it. To go to space, who doesn't want that? However, I knew it would be ages before I saw them again. He said it's my decision. He said to follow my dreams. No matter what, they'd support me. For some reason this just felt right."

"That's cool."

"And now we're lost, backpacking across a distant moon, on a remote island, on an unnamed highway, looking for a place with no name and a girl with no picture. All is right with the universe."

"Hear, hear."

We continued to walk for some time until we approached a town.

Fisher asked, "Okay, so we need to find any eating establishment and ask if they know a Columbae, right?"

"Right. Also, her father works in some sort of toy shop. Let me know if you see one of those."

"So, restaurant or toy shop."

We stopped at a few food places and asked for Columbae. We only received blank stares back. We found a store with an assortment of goods. I found a large map of the island that they were selling, but it was very plain and without details.

I approached the salesman, pointed to it and asked him, "Do you have a map? A smaller map, map of town?"

I showed him the large map and pointed to where their town was while using a hand gesture as created an exploded view to show a more detailed area.

He finally responded, "Ah, oppidum, ya, ya." He went to the back. Fisher and I just stared at each other, thinking this was going nowhere. To our surprise, he came back and unfolded a large map of the local area. It was very detailed, and each building had words inscribed on top of it.

"How much?" I asked. I grabbed some Viridis cash I had exchanged before the trip. Taking out a bunch of bills, I showed him. He pointed to one of the bills and showed two fingers. I gave him three.

I then pointed at the map and pointed at the ground and all around the room. "Where are we on this map?"

It took him a minute, then he pointed to a place on it.

"Thank you," I said. I smiled and bowed my head.

We headed outside and were trying to figure this thing out. Fisher noticed something. "Look, according to that man, we're here. Across the street is that restaurant that had never heard of Columbae."

"Right."

"See that symbol, the weird squiggle?"

"Yeah."

"I think that means food. See, there's another one down the street where we bought that fish."

"I think you're right, and that looks that looks like the airfield."

"Near it are three more of the food squiggles."

"Let's check them out."

We walked another two miles or so to a restaurant near the airfield as indicated on the map. We sat at a table and a very attractive waitress approached us. She said something we didn't understand.

I asked her, "Columbae? Do you know Columbae?"

In broken English, she responded, "Yes, yes, I know. Who you?"

"Max and Fisher, we're looking for Columbae."

"I know, but why you look?"

"I'm friends with Turtle."

She looked confused.

I repeated, "Turtle—Davy Michelangelo?"

Her face lit up. "Davy? Davy?!" She then took a picture out of her apron and showed us. Sure enough it was a great picture of her and Turtle standing and smiling with the open ocean in the background.

I responded, "Yes! Davy. We know Davy, you're Columbae!"

"Yes, yes. I am learning Earth language for Davy. Where is Davy? Is he here? Can I see Davy?"

"Can we talk? Do you have a minute? Can you sit with us?"

She walked away and talked with another waitress. She then untied her apron, set it down, and joined us at the table.

I started, "I don't know how to tell you this. Davy is no longer with us, he passed away...he's dead."

She burst into tears. The other waitress came by to comfort her.

Columbae asked, "Dead? How he die?"

I answered, "He...there was an accident at work. I wanted to find you—I wanted to tell you."

"You came out here to tell me?"

"We came a long way. Davy would have wanted that."

"I'm sorry I cry."

"No, that's fine. We all cried."

"I will miss Davy."

"Yes, we all will."

"Thank you. Thank you for coming far to tell me."

We sat there for some time, trying to comfort Columbae the best we could.

After some time, I finally asked, "I have a question—do you still work in a shop for kids?"

She looked confused.

"Your dad's shop. Dolls, toys?"

"Yes, my dad, toy store."

I reached into my backpack and handed her something. "Here, give this to your dad. He can take it apart and figure out how to make a thousand of them. It's a toy of sorts. It's a puzzle. See, it's a cube with colors on each of the nine squares on every side. You can rotate all the sides like this. The goal is to make each side one solid color. See, I started it—only got the green side done."

"That looks good. What is it named?"

"Let's just call it the Davy Cube—or better yet, the Columbae Cube. Yeah, that sounds better."

"Thank you."

"Sure. Or name it whatever you want. It's yours. I have a feeling it will sell very good out here."

CHAPTER 28

Birds of a Feather

After talking with Columbae, we asked her where a good place to stay for the night would be. She offered up her house, but we politely declined. The awkwardness of it all. She pointed us to the location of a local inn. The next morning, we made our way back to the docks and took the long trip back. Fisher and I got back to the air base without much of a problem except a little seasickness on Fisher's part. Overall, I felt so much better after speaking with Columbae. As if I had closed the loop, so to speak. I told Flip all about the trip. He was relieved he didn't go after hearing how sick Fisher got on the boat. Apparently, Flip had trouble on open waters as well.

It was back to work on the Flightline. We arrived at work in surprise that one of our ships had already landed on the previous shift.

Senior Peterson briefed us. "Ship 3034 came down early with multiple bird strikes."

Let me give you a brief overview of bird strikes. Hitting a bird at the speeds these ships go can be anywhere between a nonissue to catastrophic. The flight crew usually knows when they hit one. Without seeing the extent of the damage, they need to land so we can evaluate the problem. Not only is the damage looked at, but we evaluate the type of animal that the ship hit.

Well, we don't, but others do. Here on Viridis, we give a sample to the Viridis Airfield Management. It's then sent to a lab to determine what type of fowl it was. They'll take this information to try to determine trends or migration habits. Sometimes they can predict where they'll be so our crews can change their flight plan accordingly. The other option is to find a way to relocate these birds somewhere else. They take birds seriously here. We found out that all birds are sacred here on Viridis. They don't even eat them.

We collect the feathers or snarge and put it in a bag. Snarge is whatever else is left, besides the feathers. Just scope up the innards or swab the blood and put it in a baggie for others to deal with. We always hoped the strike was a nonissue. If this was the case, we'd collect the sample and look for damage. Today that was not the case. As soon as we got to the ship, Edwards grabbed a ladder and was looking at each of the eight ion engines.

I heard Edwards yell from the top of his ladder, "Son of a bitch!"

Senior Peterson asked, "What is it?"

"Dammit! There's damage all through these. Both engines—three and four look like garbage. I gotta take a closer look."

At the same time, our Crew Chief, Jordan, and our Sheet Metal troop, Rose Caron, were up looking at the left wing's leading edge. These are panels that extend across the front of the wings. I could already see from the ground there were multiple hits along it.

Jordan yelled down to the senior, "Leading edge has to come off, then we can see if there's any damage behind it."

Peterson looked up at Rose. "Do you think you can repair it?"

She replied, "I know I don't have enough metal here for this fix. I'll see if the Viridis Airfield here has anything I can use."

"Good. Max, go with Sergeant Caron and see what you two can find out."

I walked with Rose across the Flightline to another building. Rose was—how should I say this? So, before we left for Viridis, I saw the deployment roster. I knew Marcus had worked with a bunch of Sheet Metal troops before. I asked him about Rose Caron. Marcus sat back and said, 'Well...she's cool but looks like a cross between Ronald McDonald and Chewbacca.' I know, I know, it's a bit harsh. I didn't even believe Marcus at the time. However, after meeting Rose for the first time, I thought, yeah, I can see that. Other than that, she was great—very nice, just not really my type.

I asked Rose, "Will any type of metal work for the fix?"

"Have you heard that story about that Sheet Metal dude during Vietnam?"

"Can't say that I have."

Rose told me, "In the Vietnam War, the US had airplanes called Voodoos. One of them landed with its engine, wing and tail totally shredded by enemy fire. The maintenance guys had absolutely no aluminum or other metal to fix the shit. So, the Sheet Metal master sergeant looks over to his assistant, who was drinking a beer. He just stared at him. The assistant apologizes and starts to put his drink down. The master sergeant says, 'No, drink up, and after that one drink another.' Confused, the assistant asked what was going on. The master sergeant said, 'Go out and find as many empty beer cans as you can. Get others to help. Check all the trash bins—we're going to repair this plane.'"

"Really?" I asked.

"That's how I heard the story. The master sergeant sliced open all the cans, flattened them out and riveted them in place, creating panels to cover the airplane's surfaces."

"Did it work? Did it fly?"

"It did—it was flown all the way from Vietnam to Taiwan like this." Rose continued, "That's not all. Just to brag about his accomplishment, the Sheet Metal guy decided to display the metal with all the beer labels prominently on the outside of the plane for all to see upon landing."

"So, do you need me to start drinking a beer?"

"If you do, get me one, but that won't help our situation."

"No?"

"Cool story, but for space travel we're going to need a special graphite-epoxy titanium composite. I doubt they have the correct alloy here. We'll most likely have to order the materials from the space station. Worse comes to worst, we'll have to replace the entire leading edge. I'll know more once they remove it and I can take a closer look."

We took a look at the local supply of metal alloys. Rose couldn't find anything suitable. We then met with Sergeant Hayloft, the Parts Supply guy, to start the process to order the correct material.

I asked Hayloft, "So how does this work? This is coming from the space station, right?"

Hayloft answered as he was quickly typing on his computer device, "Not necessarily. I'm the main supply system now. It's bouncing this request all over various channels. Ideally, we'll find a supplier here on Viridis and can have it here soon via spaceship, airplane, or even boat. Other times a part could come from Nix, but that's rare. Most of the time it'll come from station. If that's the case, they'll send it from one of our BC-76s or a local space freighter or shuttle. I'm searching the database now for the best options based on where we can get if from and transportation routes."

"How'd you learn all this?"

"What'd you think, we only dealt with boxes and numbers?"

I looked at Rose. She just gave me a shrug.

Hayloft continued, "Got one. There's the right metal material on a nearby island. They can fly it via airplane, and it should be here in about thirty Earth hours."

"Great. Rose, let's go tell Peterson. Thanks, Hayloft."

Just then, Edwards ran in. "Hayloft, I need two engines."

It turns out we had one engine here and had to get the other one from the space station. It would be sent on a commercial freighter and might get here in three or four days. Edwards was out getting everything he needed to start the first engine change. Senior Peterson was away working with Viridis Airfield Management to secure a crane to be used for the engine changes. The rest of us continued to help Jordan with the leading edge. This seemed like a hundred screws going across the whole thing. With the maintenance stands under the wing, we worked at it from all sides. At this point we had all the hardware off and were starting to pull it off the ship. It wasn't budging.

I looked up while standing on top of the ship and said, "Is that Triple Twos that just landed? Why is it down early, and why are there fire trucks heading out?"

Jordan responded, "I don't know—who's got the handheld radio?!"

I said, "Senior Peterson should have one radio. Who has the other one?"

Jordan turned to Pechman. "You got the radio?!"

Pechman replied, "Sorry, the volume was down."

He turned it up and we all listened. "Emergency crews are responding to possible smoke in the flight deck..."

We tried to radio Senior Peterson, but there was no answer. At this point, Ship 222 stopped right after it entered the Flightline from the runway taxiway. Several Viridis fire trucks gathered around it. Sergeant Jordan ran out to meet the fire chief.

The rest of us continued to listen to the radio of the emergency team traffic. We could hear the ship's engines shut down and then saw the cargo door open as the flight crew ran out, after which a few firefighters entered the ship. After a few minutes, they walked out calmly and talked to Sergeant Jordan. The flight crew went back on the ship and retrieved their flight bags. Then they got on a bus that took them towards the building.

I told Pechman, "Senior Peterson still isn't here. Run to the building and debrief the crew, see what they wrote up."

"On it," he said.

Jordan started walking back towards us to 3034 as all the emergency vehicles drove back to their sections.

I asked Jordan, "What's going on?"

"The pilot said the flight crew heard a boom, then smelled something like burnt electrical components somewhere behind them. They couldn't figure out where it was coming from. The loadmaster in the cargo bay said he never smelled anything."

"What now?"

"The fire chief's English was a little broken, but I got the gist. He said they didn't see anything and the ship is turned back to maintenance. We'll need to tow it back to its parking spot and figure out which system caused the smoke."

"Fun."

"I'm going to get a tow vehicle. Have Specialist Young get the tow bar ready and start assembling a tow team."

"Got it."

Just then Sergeant Pechman came back after talking with the flight crew of 222.

He read off his tablet, "Multiple issues: radar won't display an image, interphone in the left rear cargo bay is out, the air conditioning wasn't heating, number seven engine showed low power, something about the satellite positioning not doing something, their cargo ramp is sticking, and to top it all off we have that smoke smell in the flight deck."

"Is that all?!" asked Edwards.

I asked, "What wasn't the satellite radio doing?"

Pechman answered, "I don't know."

"Did you ask?"

"Dude, I know nothing of your stuff, I wouldn't even know where to begin."

"Okay, no problem, I'll take a look."

Senior Peterson came back a couple minutes later, oblivious to what had just transpired. "I have great news. I found a crane we can use for the engine changes!"

We all just looked at him with faces of defeat.

I asked, "Is your radio dead?"

"Hey, would you look at that? It is. I'll get a new battery. Why are you all looking at me like that?"

We casually looked over our shoulders to Ship 222 parked off in the distance near the runway.

Senior Peterson was shocked. "What did I miss?!"

Peterson took a long look at all the write-ups, then he addressed us. "With 3034 out for a few days with that bird strike, our focus needs to be Triple Twos. It's scheduled to launch first thing in the morning. We need to get it towed to the spot first. Where's Jordan?"

I answered, "Getting a tow vehicle."

"Great, and Edwards?"

"He was getting the engine and change kit for 3034."

"Alright, I'll get with him and tell him to look at Triple Twos' engine first. Everyone else will help with the tow. Once it's on the spot, we'll need to work smart. The first thing is to figure out the smoke smell. Start with just applying power. After that, we need to turn on only one system at a time to try to isolate where it's coming from. Be ready to shut down the moment you sense anything. Once we isolate the issue, it'll be business as usual. Max, look at the radar, satellite positioning, and interphone. Fisher, run up the AC. Edwards will check out the number seven engine, and Jordan and I will take a look at the cargo ramp. Any questions?"

Fisher asked, "Sir, did you say you were going to look that the ramp?"

"Yeah, I did my share of Crew Chief work. Did you think I was born an expeditor?"

Peterson continued, "Since we're already down one ship, we're definitely going to need this one fixed for tomorrow's critical mission. We'll need to work balls to the walls until then. We got this. Oh, where did I say to tow it?"

"You said back on its spot."

"Actually, we need to tow it to the engine run spot. That's the last one at the end of the Flightline. I'll call Tower and get the clearance."

We get the tow vehicle hooked up and the tow team guided Triple Twos towards its spot. The team consisted of one to drive the tow vehicle pulling the ship. There was another sitting in the flight deck working the ship's brake system. Another was walking next to the tow vehicle, watching everything around him and talking on a headset talking to the driver. Others are walking alongside each wingtip and tail to ensure the ship didn't hit anything. Our job was to blow a whistle and wave our arms all around if we got close to anything. Most of the time there's no threat. This is mainly a concern when going into a hangar or close to other vehicles.

Jordan towed the 76er to the engine run spot and we started to troubleshoot this apparent smoke. There was no electrical smell during the tow. Even with power applied, we still didn't smell anything. In the flight deck was Fisher, Pechman, Edwards, and me. I started turning on each system one at a time. Specialist Young came up, doing his postflights.

He said, "Smells like chicken and dumplings up here."

Edwards responded, "What are you talking about?"

"Chicken and dumplings. My nana used to make it."

"Really, you can smell that over everything else in the air? Do you smell any electrical smoke?"

"Nope."

Young started to empty the crew's trash out. He stopped and pulled a box out of the trash bag.

"See! I was right." Young held up the empty food container and read it. "Mr. Moe's chicken and dumpling meal in a box."

"Does the box state how to fix this ship?" snickered Edwards.

"Let's see, nutritional info...fifteen ounces...remove from foil bag...transfer to microwave-safe dish...two minutes..."

I interrupted, "What was that last part?"

"Two minutes..."

"No. Young, do me a favor and open the microwave in the galley."

"Okay...oh my! You guys got to see this!"

We looked in the tiny galley behind the flight deck. Sure enough, there was a burnt-up chicken meal in a foil type of bag. The entire rear of the microwave was black. We called Senior Peterson to take a look as well.

He responded, "That was easy. Good job finding the electrical smoke smell. Make sure the microwave's circuit breaker is pulled out, if not already popped. Edwards and Jordan, get ready for the engine run. Young, you're on ground. Fisher and Max, stay up here and troubleshoot your systems."

Edwards and Jordan were in the pilot seats. Young was in front of the ship, standing ground with a headset, monitoring the outside of the ship. We were all plugged into the interphone system. Fisher and I were sitting behind the pilot seats, getting ready to run up our systems. One by one, Sergeant Edwards ran up the powerful ion engines until all eight were trying to pull this ship off the ground. We sat there with headsets on, feeling the vibrations of the ship.

In the navigator's seat, I started to run up the radar system. At the same time I had the satellite positioning system doing a search for reliable satellites to link to. I looked over to Fisher. He had the AC system going, checking the heat. While my systems were still warming up, so to speak, I headed to the back of the cargo bay. Using the connected headset in the back right, I did a quick inter-phone check to see if the system back here is working.

"Check, check, Marco...?"

"Polo," chimed in Jordan. "Is that Max?"

"Yep, checking the cargo bay interphone. Hold on, let me check the left headset unit."

From the left one, I checked again. "Do-be-do-be-do...anyone there?"

Nothing. I quickly looked down to see the loadmaster headset not plugged in all the way. I thought to myself, *Ah, the old headset trick.*

Snapping it into place, I reached out again. "Check, baby, check, baby..."

"One, two, three," replied Jordan.

"Good, loud and clear."

"Same here."

I headed back to see how the radar was doing. Still no picture. I'd have to wait until Young was away from the front of the ship before I could transmit, but with no picture at all, there was no point in checking that now. I had Jordan and Edwards bring up the radar picture on the pilot monitors. No luck there as well. I check the faults page and see a familiar fault code. It points to a bad video circuit card inside the receiver-transmitter. *Great, I'll have to change the RT.*

I took a look at the satellite position system and it seemed to be a bad receiver. I radioed Peterson and told him which parts I would need. I then checked on Fisher. *Where is Fisher?* I think.

I got back on interphone. "Where's Fisher?"

Edwards answered, "I thought it was your turn to watch him. How do you lose a whole person? No one left the ship."

"Hold on." I came back, "He's here, just in the Wine Cellar."

I looked down and he was in the cramped-up space, banging on one of the heater valves with a wrench.

Edwards made a few adjustments to the number seven engine and the second engine run was a success. This took forever and we were closing in on the time this ship had to launch again. By the time we finished with the engine runs, our other shift had already been back to work for an hour or so. They had everything ready to tow the ship back to its regular spot. The rest of us got with Senior Peterson, Flip, and the other shift's E&E troop, Beatrice Thatcher.

Peterson radioed the other shift Crew Chief. "Hold off on the tow. I got with the flight crew—they can taxi out of that engine run spot. That'll save us some time. I need you to look at that cargo ramp. Check the rigging, see if it's misaligned. I'll be there soon to assist."

Fisher told Senior Peterson and Beatrice, "Looks like a bad heater valve. I got it to open, but it's jammed up pretty good. Probably need to replace the assembly."

Peterson said, "Okay. Thatcher, go see if we have any or need to order one. Ship 222 is scheduled to launch in less than two hours. Can we replace it by then?"

Beatrice replied, "No, that'll take at least three or four hours to change, but I should be able to do a temp fix, then we can replace the assembly when it lands again."

"Flip, did you inquire about those parts?"

"Indeed. The satellite receiver and the radar RT are no bueno. They'll have to come from station. Crazy thing, we don't have those common parts, yet we had a spare microwave in the kits."

"Okay, we'll have to cann those from Ship 3034."

Cann is short for cannibalization. If it'll take too long to get a part, we can take one from another ship that isn't flying. It's good when needed, but it takes a lot more work. We need to go through the whole removal process from one ship, then install it on the other. Then wait for the new part to come in and install it back on the one we canned it from. The worst part is dealing with all the maintenance logs and the ordering process, since we ordered it for 222, yet the part will go to 3034 when it comes in.

Peterson turned to Flip. "What's the ETIC. How long will it take to cann them?"

Flip answered, "The satellite receiver will be no problem. Change and ops check, about an hour."

"Great."

"Not great. The radar RT will take two or three hours."

I quickly said, "I'll stay over and help."

Flip asked Peterson, "You want me to tell the Crew Chiefs we have a microwave in stock?"

"No. That's our last priority. They can fly all day without that. Maybe fly all week. That'll teach 'em to break our ship."

Flip laughed, then asked me, "What were the radar fault codes?"

I told him.

Flip looked at his tablet. "Hold on. This may just be a bad video card. We should be able to pop open the good RT and just swap those cards around."

The senior asked, "You can do that?"

"Yeah, the procedure isn't in the regular maintenance steps. However, if you go to the backshop tasks, it shows how to do it."

"Great thinking."

We quickly started the process of canning these parts. I worked on the satellite receiver as Flip grabbed the RT video card. Definitely a quicker fix than changing out the entire RT. The Crew Chiefs and Senior Peterson were able to rig the cargo ramp. Beatrice temp-fixed the heater valve. The flight crew had its engines running while Flip and I finished signing off the maintenance logs. We gave the okay, Peterson signed off his part, and the ship was good to go.

"Sorry, Flip."

"Why's that?"

"Sorry we couldn't do the entire radar check. I was going to have you run around wearing aluminum foil."

"Ha! I think the flight crew used the rest of it to cook their meal."

CHAPTER 29

Flock Together

It would be almost another week until we had both ships operational. We worked together to get the leading edge off and gave it to Rose. She got all the material in and was able to repair it. It looked good but would have to be repainted once we made it back to station. The bright yellow patches gave the ship a unique personality.

We all helped Sergeant Edwards replace the engine. Since none of us were Engine troops, Edwards ran around directing us. Take this part off, disconnect these, that goes there. We worked hard to get this removed. Even the senior helped by operating the enormous crane to lift the old engine off. Installing the new engine was difficult as well, but we all worked together. The second engine was replaced by the other shift.

Being one ship down, we flew the heck out of Triple Twos by rotating the flight crews in and out. Once we had 3034 back in business, it was flying as usual. Things were going well, which meant we were back to getting a couple days off here and there. On one of our days off, a whole group of us went into town, which included Flip, Beatrice, Rose, Edwards, Pechman, Fisher, and me. We walked down by the beach.

I pointed to the ocean. "Hey, Fisher, should we take a boat out for the day?"

He just groaned. We then found ourselves in the middle of downtown. There are many little cafés, and we saw so many Viridis folks just sitting outside at tables, drinking wine.

Flip asked, "Don't these people have jobs?"

Beatrice answered, "Who knows? Doesn't look like it."

We found rows and rows of local shops and explored each one. The salespeople would instantly greet us. We stuck out here. It was obvious to almost everyone that we were from Earth. The shop-keepers would point out the knickknacks or clothes to try to get a sale. What we found surprising was that every store we entered, they would offer up free alcohol. They gave us shots of some weird liquor. I guess they figured the more we had, the more we'd spend. Apparently, this worked. We were amassing all sorts of useless crap. At one point, we were leaving a store and had to cross a busy street.

Pechman said, "You guys go ahead, I'm going to buy these grapes."

We crossed the busy street and waited for him.

Flip turned to me. "Do you think he'll figure out the traffic lights?"

"No way. The triangles, circles, and squares—not a chance."

We were all taking bets on how this would turn out. Yet no one would predict what happened next. One of the symbols changed. The cross traffic stopped. Pechman looked both ways and set off into the crosswalk. From around the corner out of nowhere, a kid no older than eight years old came swooping along on a little motor-ized scooter. The kid flipped his scooter outward and smashed into Pechman's shin. Pechman instantly dropped his basket of grapes and reached for his leg as he yelled at this little Viridis tyke. The little punk yelled something back and put his fists up in the air as if he wanted to fight the lanky six-foot-two Pechman. Pechman just looked at him with disgust.

"Should we help him?" I asked.

Rose answered, "The kid is like eight. Let's see how this plays out."

As the two stared at each other in the middle of the intersec-tion, a second little tyke on a similar scooter came from behind and smashed into Pechman. He looked down as the first kid pulled an object out of his pocket and slashed it across Pechman's arm. The object dropped to the ground and the two little punks rode off, screaming gibberish.

Edwards responded, "Oh, crap! What's going on?!"

I ran out into the street, grabbed the object and helped Pechman over to our side of the road as he was holding his arm.

Beatrice asked in a panic, "Are you okay? What was that?"

Pechman looked at his arm. There was only a little bit of blood. It looked like nothing more than a large paper cut. I showed them all the object in question. It was a small plastic butter knife.

Flip yelled, "What the hell just happened?!"

Pechman looked all sorts of confused, then he checked himself and yelled, "My tablet! Little shitheads took my tablet!"

I immediately messaged Senior Peterson and let him know the details. He initially thought it was funny, then realized the severity of it all. He said he would try to message station and see if they could purge everything on Pechman's tablet remotely.

That evening we found a local pub. We asked if anyone spoke Earth. Apparently here, if you ask if they speak *English*, they don't know that word. We learned if you say *Earth*, they know exactly what you're talking about. Another waitress came by and spoke some Earth—I mean, English. The seven of us ordered drinks. They didn't have beer; however, they had a sort of alcohol cider that wasn't too bad. On their wall there was a huge sign with what we believed to be various names and numbers.

Flip asked our waitress, "What's the deal with that sign?"

The waitress responded, "Game. How much you drink in a honorah."

I asked, "Honorah? What's that?"

She replied, "Honorah. Tick, tick, honorah?"

I turned to Flip. "I think it's a contest to see how much you can drink in a specific time."

Flip looked at the waitress, "I'm in—start the timer and keep them coming!"

That night was crazy. We all drank a lot, but Flip was all in trying to beat some made-up alien record. They had interesting music and Beatrice and Pechman starting dancing to it. The locals gave us weird looks, but we didn't care.

At one point Rose asked me to dance. I had to politely decline. I just don't dance. Besides, Rose wasn't my type. Edwards, however, did dance with her that night. Flip was trying to pick up on the local waitress. This was clearly not working since he was on a mission to drink as many cider mugs as humanly possible.

We were about to get up and leave the pub when we heard a loud bell being rung. We all looked around to see what was going on. The waitress and even the pub manager came out to our table. I was thinking, oh no, what the heck did we do? Maybe we should make a run for it.

The waitress handed Flip some parchment and a pen and said, "Write name down, you won game!"

Flip wrote down his name. The manager brought out a plastic ornamental crown and placed it on Flip's head. Then the waitress went to the huge sign of names, erased the very top name and wrote *Samuel Dolphline*. Our first night there and he was the grand champion of the long-ongoing drinking contest. His name definitely stood out since it was the only one written in English. With a few full cups of cider in our hands, we left the pub in high spirits.

Flip turned to me. "You know what we need? We need to get some food. I could go for some bacon and eggs. We need to find a Denny's. Max! Pull up your map and find us a Denny's. We need Denny's. Which direction, Max?!" Flip then turned in each direction, ready to go whichever way I pointed.

"Flip, we're the furthest from a Denny's that anyone in the history of Earth has ever been. Besides, we can't have eggs."

"I want eggs."

"Dude, the Viridis. They don't eat eggs. Remember, the birds are sacred or something. They won't eat them, won't even cook them. We'll get you something back at our hotel. But first, let's check out this beach."

We headed down to the sandy beach. Beatrice, Pechman, Edwards, and even Rose stripped down to their almost-nothings and jumped in the ocean. Flip, Fisher, and I just stood there laughing at the whole thing, holding our cups of cider. Flip was still wearing his crown of glory.

I looked over at Flip. "Do you know what day it is?"
"I have no idea," he slurred.
"It's 110 day, Flip! Cheers, and happy birthday!"

CHAPTER 30

Ground Control

The whole gang of us returned to station from Viridis unscathed. Well, except for Pechman's brush with death at the hands of eight-year-olds, a number of us getting sunburned, and the one time drunk Matt F. Edwards fell down the stairs and broke his tablet. Other than that, we all survived. Senior Sergeant Peterson did have to explain to Commander Porter why three of his troops had to order new tablets from the IT Department. I'm sure that wasn't fun. All in all, every one of us knew we'd never have a deployment like that again.

Over the next couple years, there were a few more random attacks on the space station. There was an explosion in one of the electrical rooms that started a fire. Two workers ended up getting trapped and died. One wing of the station lost power for a day or so. Another fire was started in the hospital wing. Lastly, several members of top leadership had gotten very sick from what they thought was food poisoning. To this day no one knows who was behind these.

The one constant on Space Station Prime was the never-ending work on the Flightline. I had been running my own shift for some time. T.J. became Senior Sergeant Jackson and took the position of Production Superintendent. Would you believe Flip got called up to be part of Quality Control? He was the last person I'd ever see being part of a team that inspected Flightline maintenance for safety. Even Flip laughed at the thought of it. No one saw that coming. He took the job in stride, and we'd still hang out every chance we got. Flip and I were always at each other's quarters. Other times we'd meet at the Mountain and just enjoy the atmosphere or talk about old times.

Then I finally became an expeditor. This was a challenging yet never dull job. I'd show up early every shift and get the rundown from the previous expeditor. I'd get the flying schedule, the status of breaks for each ship, and a list of priorities for work. I'd also have a roster of everyone on shift. Now it was just a matter of herding cats. Night after night was full of prioritizing who went where. I'd have to know what systems each career field worked and who to assign to what. I would have numerous ships being worked on at any one given time. I'd get calls over the radio left and right from specialists and sergeants asking for a pickup. They needed to go to the Tool Counter, to Parts Supply, to the entry control point, or to and from other ships. It was a never-ending struggle of driving around in circles to get everyone everywhere.

Max: Roger, do you play video games?

Roger: Some, I guess.

Max: I played a few before I joined. Ever heard of an old classic, *Warcraft*?

Roger: Sure, that old game people were obsessed with, playing online for hours with friends and strangers.

Max: No, I'm not talking about *World of Warcraft*. I meant the original stand-alone *Warcraft*. Other similar games that come to mind are *Command and Conquer*, or my favorite, *Star Wars: Galactic Battlegrounds*. All these games had similar gameplay. You start with a limited team of characters that you control to build up your city. You send out the grunts to chop wood or build a house. Eventually you get more grunts to chop more wood, or mine for gold, or build a barracks in order to make new troops. That's the Flightline.

Roger: That's the Flightline?

Max: That's being an expeditor on the Flightline...

I have limited people and limited time. I need to send these ones over here to chop wood and these other ones to build a watchtower. If one troop chops down his last tree, he'll just stand there doing nothing. That's a waste of a good resource. I need to find him something else to do. On the Flightline it's sending this many to preflight a ship, or help with a refuel, or troubleshoot the autopilot. Any idle resource should be utilized—go help your buddies over there and change that spaceship's configuration from a cargo to a bomber. You have to constantly direct them to optimize the limited resources we have. The key is knowing who can do what and what your best options are.

The other thing is knowing when to give them a break. Work hard, play hard. Knowing when they're overworked is also on my mind. If they bust their hump all day, I'll try to give them some extra time off. It's a hard balancing act for sure. The nights flew by fast. I learned so much about what each career field did. We'd sit there waiting for ships to launch and get redballs. Immediately, I would have to know who to send up depending on the problem. I had become a jack-of-all-trades, master of none. At the end of every shift, I'd break it down for the next expeditor.

One night, I was in the flight deck of Ship 1670 when Captain Kirkland showed up.

"Sergeant Morgan, what do you know? I thought I saw you come up here. What are you doing out here by yourself?"

"Just looking over the maintenance logs. We just had our last launch of the night and I had some time."

"Can't you look over those write-ups in the building in the computer system? Also, I noticed your expeditor truck wasn't out here."

"Yep, I could look over all the write-ups, configurations, and fuel loads from the office. However, I find it better to do it out here. I like to look over each ship. I make sure everything matches the logs and ensure there's nothing out of place. It's a lot easier without a truck. All that stop and go. I'd rather just walk from one ship to the next."

"Are you checking all the ships?"

"Yep, all of ours."

"What about the ones not on the flying schedule?"

"Especially those. Things can become in disarray if not looked over frequently. What brings you out here?"

"We have a situation."

"What's that?"

"There's a ship off-station that had lost power."

"Okay, does the pro super know? T.J. usually picks a maintenance team to head out, or coordinates with the other moons. Where is the ship parked at?"

"That's the issue. That's also why I came out here to talk to you about it."

"Go on."

"The ship is 0060. It lost its engines and electrical power right after it left station. It's just floating out there in space. They made a distress call, but it was limited."

"What?! Why didn't you start with that? What's T.J. doing? How are they getting back?!"

I immediately started to wrap things up on the ship and headed to the Production Office.

Captain Kirkland hooked up his harness as well and followed me. "Sergeant Morgan, slow down and walk with me. We have a plan. Senior Jackson is working out all the details. We're working directly with the Special Operations team. The plan is to send a couple maintainers on one of the small personal shuttles to the stranded ship. We were asked not to discuss this over radio traffic due to the nature of things."

"Those little civilian shuttles? I've heard horror stories about those tiny things in space. Okay, so now what?"

We continued to walk fast towards the entry control point.

"Senior Jackson and Diego asked for you specifically to suggest who we send. They say you're pretty good at picking a good team. It should be just an Engine troop and E&E, right?"

"What exactly is wrong with the ship?"

"I don't know exactly, something about losing all power."

"They must have used the backup radio battery to call."

I was thinking of every and any possible scenario that could cause this and what the fix may be. I was going through a list of names and positions in my head. When we arrived at the entry control point, the captain stopped and looked at me.

"Sergeant Morgan, you know this is going to be dangerous transferring from the small shuttle to the ship. Those maintainers will need to wear the spacesuits, work with limited tools, and limited time."

"I was thinking the same thing."

"Which ones have been trained for this, to wear the spacesuits?"

"Trained? No one has. In theory, maybe. In reality, no one."

"I see."

"Let me have a minute. I have a few people in mind. I'll meet you back in the Production Office in a few minutes. I won't take anyone that isn't aware of the risks or unwilling to go."

The captain nodded, and I headed to find my prospective team.

I arrived at the Production Office after a few minutes. I had never seen so many people in there, including Commander Porter and our new chief, Chief Hendrix. T.J. was the only one sitting down as he was on the phone with the flight crew, trying to confirm when this shuttle would head out. Captain Kirkland looked at me. I gave a nod and a look that said I'd found a crew.

Once T.J. got off the phone, he addressed the commander. "We have the flight crew and they're set up. Once that shuttle is prepped and fueled, we can meet them out there on the far end of the Flightline. It might still be about two hours before that happens, though."

Colonel Porter spoke. "I hate the idea of that ship being stranded for so long." He looked at Chief Hendrix. "See if we can do anything to expedite that process." He then looked at Captain Kirkland. "Do we have the maintenance team?"

The captain looked at me. In fact, everyone in the room looked at me.

I answered, "Yes, sir. Sergeant Edwards from Engines. Crew Chief Sergeant York—"

T.J. stopped me. "Good choice on Edwards. I had already suggested him. I'm not sure if we need a Crew Chief. This seems like an engine and electrical issue."

"You may be right, but the way I see it, we only have one shot at this. We still don't know exactly what caused this problem. Marcus...I mean, Sergeant York is more than a Crew Chief. He worked as a Sheet Metal troop for a while and also knows a lot about hydraulics."

T.J. agreed. "He does know more about these ships than anyone. What about E&E?"

"Specialist Fisher is our best bet."

"Fisher is only a specialist."

"I know, but I hate to say it, I'd rather have him than any of the sergeants in his shop. I was deployed with Fisher; he knows his job and can easily think outside the box. I believe that's what we need."

"Okay. Where are they at? We need to get them ready ASAP."

"One more thing," I added. "I would like to go as well."

"You're an expeditor now. Besides, do you think we need Avionics?"

"That's the issue. At this point we don't know what we need. You never know."

Chief Hendrix nodded in approval.

I added, "The other three are just outside the office."

"Bring them in."

Our new team stood there and were told what to bring and when to meet back. We would have to rush to grab the tools and supplies we needed. We were dismissed to meet back soon. Marcus ran to tell Sharyn about the situation. Just as I was leaving, Captain Kirkland asked to see me privately.

Standing in his office, he asked, "So what do you need before you head out?"

"Actually, not much. Fisher is getting the tools we need, and everything else I need I have in my backpack. I'm ready now."

"You know, you didn't need to volunteer for this?"

"I know, I just know how dangerous it is and feel I need to be there for some reason."

"I understand. I do. How did the others take it?"

"They were happy to go. In fact, Marcus was begging to be part of this. Fisher was the only one that was hesitant. I felt bad for asking him, but I really don't see taking anyone else from his shop. I'm hoping I made the right choice."

"I trust your judgment, we all do."

"Captain, if I may ask, why were you so nonchalant about this earlier? We have a ship drifting into space, the crew is on oxygen and we have limited time. Anyone else would have come running to grab me, screaming and yelling."

"Let me tell you something. You see that chair at my desk?"

"The old wooden one? Looks uncomfortable. I hate to say it."

"It was my grandfather's."

"Oh, sorry. I didn't mean—"

"No, don't be. I had it taken apart and shipped it over here in one of my luggage cases. My grandfather was something else. His job in the military was to disarm bombs and sometimes even activate them when needed to clear things. He always told me that after they armed it, they would *walk* away from it, rather than *run* before it blew up."

"Why's that?"

"Running increases your chances of tripping and falling. When given an emergency situation, you need to stop, take your time, and think about your decision. Jumping to conclusions and making rash decisions isn't good for anyone. I didn't want you in a state of panic. Besides, I knew we had time. It's going to take them a while to get that shuttle and crew ready for launch."

"I understand. I understand the chair as well—a reminder of your grandpa?"

"Partly. It also serves as another reminder for me."

"What's that?"

"You're right. That old wooden chair is the most uncomfortable thing known to man."

I laughed.

Kirkland continued, "That's precisely why I brought it out here with me."

"Go on."

"I put it at my office desk for a reason. It's so uncomfortable I can't sit in for too long. It's to remind me not to lead from the desk. I need to get out and be with the team. From what I can see, you do the same thing. Good luck, Max. Bring everyone home safe."

"I will—thanks, Captain."

CHAPTER 31

Major Tom

The four of us maintainers met the flight crew in the briefing room along with a few pilots.

Colonel Sizemore stood up in front of us and went over the situation. "Ship 0060 was only an hour into its flight heading from our station to Viridis when we received the distress call. Their pilot, Major Thomas, was cut off for some reason after only a few seconds. They tried radioing back, but nothing. LT, play the radio call from 0060 to Tower."

The young LT played the transmission. Major Thomas spoke: "Zero-Zero-Sixty to Prime, do you copy! Emergency!"

Station Tower replied, "Go ahead, Sixty, we copy."

"Everything happened at once. Everything just went dead at once. We lost life support, power, gravity. We activated our pressurized suits and secured our helmets for oxygen, but there was no time."

"Slow down—is anyone hurt?"

"Our two passengers are gone, dead—they couldn't...there was no time!"

"We will put together a crew. What are your current coordinates?"

"Let me..."

"Sixty, do you copy?"

"..."

"Can you hear me?"

"..."

"Major Thomas!"

Colonel Sizemore then said, "LT, turn it off." The colonel stopped to collect his thoughts, then spoke solemnly. "As you can see, we don't have much to go on. The two passengers were dignitaries returning to Viridis. It sounds like they just didn't have time to get to the oxygen, or maybe it was the pressure. We don't have all the details."

The tone in the room changed. Everyone in the room felt the heaviness of this situation. The colonel continued, "We will be sending a shuttle craft to the stranded ship. Bill and Del will be flying the shuttle." The two civilian pilots that looked like they were in their sixties raised their hands and nodded. "Our 76er pilots here, Captain Chandler and Captain Hamilton, will ride in the shuttle along with the maintenance team to recover the stranded ship. The crew for Sixty may be in no condition to fly back."

The colonel then asked us, "Is the maintenance team ready?"

I looked at Marcus and nodded.

Marcus answered, "Yes, sir, we have Sergeant Morgan, Edwards, Fisher, and...me. We have our tools and should be good to go."

The colonel wrapped it up. "Great, good luck, team. Oh, by the way, you all should definitely use the toilet before putting on those spacesuits and boarding."

We received a quick crash course on how these bulky white-and-gray fully enclosed spacesuits worked. Enclosed in our space helmets was a short-range radio so we could talk between us. We also had limited oxygen tanks on our backs. We arrived at the shuttle. It was definitely smaller than any of us imagined. It didn't seem much bigger than a minivan on the inside. With limited engine power, these could only be used in space from space station to space station. These shuttle pilots had practiced the transfer between shuttle to ship, or so we'd been told.

We climbed aboard with a couple toolboxes and as much scrounge as we could muster. Scrounge is a term for miscellaneous hardware that has the *potential* to fix anything: screws, gaskets, fuses, circuit breakers, splices, lightbulbs, electrical tape, you name it, we got it. I was determined we would fix this with one go.

The shuttle pilots, Bill and Del, took their seats up front. In the back there were only eight passenger seats total in this cramped tin can. The four seats on each side faced each other. The six of us secured ourselves with the roller coaster–type restraints that came over our shoulders. I then prayed as this flimsy death box shuttle was sling-shotted out to open space. As soon as we left station, we could feel the lack of gravity. I hated this. I hated every moment of it. I had to stay strong. I could see the fear in Fisher's eyes. I had to stay strong.

Trying to remain calm and get my mind off things, I asked Marcus a question. "So how did Sharyn take it? You leaving and all."

"Oh, Max, she was fine. She was fine with me going, but she's been a bit nauseous lately, with her condition and all."

"Her condition?"

"Oh, no, I'm not supposed to say yet."

"Marcus, what's going on?"

"She—she and me—well, we're gonna have a baby."

"What?! I mean...that's great! Marcus, you should have told me. You really should have told me. I would have never brought you here with us."

"Why not?"

"Because you never know. I mean, anything can go wrong."

"Am I more important than the next guy?"

"Yes. I mean, no...I don't know. Don't worry, everything will be fine. Congrats, man, I'm really happy for you."

Fisher and Edwards chimed in, "Alright, Marcus great news! Way to go!"

Captain Chandler spoke over his radio. "Congrats, man, that's great. First one?"

"Yes, sir."

"Wonderful news, but I think I need to remind you all of something. We all have limited battery power for these radios in our spacesuits. I suggest we all keep it quiet so as not to drain them before we get to the ship."

With no windows, we were at the mercy of our pilots throughout this whole journey. We sat in silence during this extremely long shuttle ride. It took a few hours to reach our destination. This was about half as fast as our cargo bombers. Marcus and the 76er pilots spent most of the time sleeping. Fisher and Edwards were enjoying the antigravity, floating a closed pocketknife back and forth between them. I couldn't sleep. I just thought about my deployments, how we were going to fix this ship, and Jo-Leia.

After a long while, we felt an abrupt thud, then heard a whirling sound, followed by a clank.

Del spoke over our headsets. "We made it. You can now disconnect from the shuttle's O2 system and use your reserve tanks. We're sitting on top of yours all ship out there. If we're correct, we should be just about above the top hatch leading to your cargo bay."

Chandler asked, "And if we're not?"

"Then we all made a huge mistake and when you pop open that lower hatch, you'll all be sucked out into the death of space."

We all looked at each other, then looked at the floor to see the round three-foot-diameter hatch. I looked at the 76er pilots. They looked as scared as Fisher.

Bill's voice was heard. "Go ahead and open it. This is what you all came out here for, right?"

Without hesitation, Edwards just grabbed the hatch handle on the floor of the shuttle, unlocked the release points and yanked this thing up. We all gasped and froze.

Edwards then said, "It's just another hatch?"

Del answered, "Good, that means we're in the right spot. That's your BC-76's hatch. Remember, when you open up that one, it's going to fall. Well, with no gravity it may just sit there. Either way, it'll push out."

Edwards opened the BC-76's hatch and maneuvered himself into the ship. As soon as he was through, we saw the crew members of 0060 trying to get into our shuttle.

"Hold on," I said, but then I realized they probably couldn't hear me through my helmet.

Once they realized we were coming aboard, they moved to the side. The maintainers as well as Captains Hamilton and Chandler climbed into the ship. We could see the six flight crew members crowding around the hatch, ready to go in. As predicted, this ship was dark and without gravity. Using the lights embedded in our suits, we could see. The crew of 0060 looked like they were in shock as they each rapidly climbed aboard the shuttle.

Marcus spoke over his helmet radio. "Where're they going? We can't all fit in that shuttle!"

Captain Hamilton then said, "We're not supposed to. They'll be leaving as soon as they're all aboard and we close the hatch."

Marcus exclaimed, "What the hell!"

Hamilton continued, "If you fix this one—I mean, *when* you fix it, I'll fly us home. If you can't in time, another shuttle will come for us."

Edwards asked, "How much time do we have?"

Captain Chandler answered, "How much oxygen do you have?"

I looked over to Fisher. He was just floating and staring towards the back of the cargo bay. I saw it too. Two shapes of people secured to the ground, wrapped from head to toe in a tarp.

"It'll be alright. Fisher, look over your systems, see what you can find."

Just then I saw the last flight crew member try to leave. Edwards was the closest to him. "Edwards, grab him. We need to ask him about the ship!"

I pushed off the wall and flew towards the pilot.

I saw his name tag and asked, "We need to know about the break, Major Thomas! What happened?!"

Through his mask, he tried to talk. Neither one of us could hear each other. Lots of muffled words. I poked the side of my helmet, then put up my hands to indicate confusion.

Edwards asked, "Can't you just talk to him through the radio?"

"We only have the one frequency in our suits, and apparently it's not the same as his."

"What about the ship's radio? You're the radio guy, right?"

"No power, so no."

I then pointed to the flight deck and gave the major a *come here* hand motion. We both floated to the flight deck along with

Hamilton, Chandler, and Edwards. I put up my hands again in confusion. He gave a hand motion of him steering a yoke, then put his fingers out as to indicate a boom while he pointed across the entire instrument panel and even the navigator's station. Major Thomas then put his finger across his neck in a slashing motion.

If this were any other situation, you'd think it was the funniest game of charades ever.

"Okay, so you're flying like normal. You hear a boom and you lose all power."

Chandler interjected, "He can't hear you."

"I know that, but my maintenance team can."

Major Thomas then showed me eight fingers and gave a spinning motion as he pointed towards the wings, along with another finger across his throat.

Edwards then said, "That's when they lost all the engines."

Thomas showed us the circuit breaker panel. They were all closed. He pointed to the top row of breakers and gave a pulling motion.

"Looks like all the main power circuit breakers popped."

The major showed me the motion of pushing them in, then pointed to the battery switch, the auxiliary battery switch, and even the auxiliary power generator, then shook his head no.

"He reset all the breakers but still couldn't get power, not even to the aux power generator."

The major just looked at me and I could see his mouth say *I'm sorry* as he shook his head back and forth. He then gave me the hand signal for pulling chalks. Which meant he was done. I nodded and he was on his way towards the back and out the hatch. Chandler closed it behind him.

I asked over the radio, "What do you guys think?"

Edwards explained and confirmed, "If these circuit breakers popped all at once, we would lose power to all the ion engines, but that makes no sense. Nothing on this ship would cause that. It's a redundant system. This shouldn't happen—this couldn't have happened."

Fisher then said, "Those aren't the only circuit breakers. Some of the main ones are in the back, behind the bulkhead maintenance panel."

I instructed, "Go check. Marcus, help him out."

Fisher had the panel open. We could see several circuit breakers popped; Fisher reset them. Marcus went back to the flight deck and radioed, "Still no power. The aux gen won't come back online."

I asked Fisher and Edwards, "What powers the auxiliary generator?"

Fisher answered, "It just powers. Gets its juice from the main battery."

"Check the batteries!"

Fisher scrambled to the left side of the cargo bay. "I need a three-eighths wrench to open the battery assembly panel."

"Where's your toolbox?"

He pointed towards the top of the ship near the closed hatch.

My heart almost stopped. Had he left his tools on the now-departed shuttle? I looked back at him as he still pointed up. I looked again and was relieved to see his toolbox was just floating up there.

I brought him his toolbox. "Listen, we gotta be careful opening this thing. Just open it a bit and try to find the right wrench. Otherwise, tools are going to float everywhere."

"What do you suggest?"

"I'm hoping most of your tools are still stuck in their foam cutouts. Do you know where the three-eighths wrench is? Think about it—you use this box every day."

"Yeah, yeah, I know."

We slowly opened the box just enough for Fisher to put his huge glove into it. He pulled out the right wrench and I closed it fast. He then opened the panel to access the main battery. I had to hold him in place as he unscrewed the bolts. I even had to make sure I grabbed each bolt as they tried to float away. Difficult with bulky gloves. This wasn't just a regular battery; it was a series of large battery cells. The entire assembly was about two by two by four feet tall.

Fisher asked, "In my left pouch is my multimeter—can you get it?"

"Yeah...here you go."

He checked for power. "Damn, nothing. No volts at all."

"No, that's a good thing."

"Why's that?"

"Now we know the problem."

"Yeah, but this shouldn't happen. These don't go bad without warning. Besides, the auxiliary battery should have taken over. Let me check the aux. It's across the cargo bay on the opposite side."

We flew across to the right side of the ship and checked that one. Fisher exclaimed, "Yes! This one is showing good. Hey, Marcus, try the aux battery switch again."

Marcus called out, "Still nothing."

"This makes no sense. If one battery assembly is out, the other takes over."

Edwards was looking over the aux battery assembly. "Hey, guys, this don't look right."

He shined his light behind the assembly. There was a whole wire bundle that looked like it was cut. Exposed wires were hanging out.

Edwards asked, "Can we fix these?"

I answered, "Maybe, but it's an entire bundle—that'll take forever."

Fisher went back and checked all the wires from the main battery.

After a while, he finally confirmed, "These wires all look good. I even checked them with the meter."

"So, what now?" I asked.

"We can—wait, no, that won't work."

"What won't work?"

"I was going to say we could swap this main battery with the auxiliary, but it's impossible."

"Why? Explain."

"These battery packs are huge. They weigh a ton. We have to get the special forklift set up in the cargo bay just to move them around. The only way to physically swap them is with that special crane. Even with all of us, we can't lift this thing."

"Look at your feet, Fisher."

"Why? Oh, I'm floating."

"Yes, no gravity, ergo easy to lift. If we swap these, what will the system do?"

"Should work—we only need one working assembly."

I then called out to Edwards and Marcus, "Hey, guys, did you hear all that? We need to swap these battery packs around. Fisher, show us which bolts to disconnect. Don't lose anything! Everything floats, remember."

I looked over and saw Edwards and Marcus hovering over a crate near the main battery assembly. "What were you guys doing anyways?" I asked.

Edwards explained, "Marcus was trying to eat the flight crew's food packs from their crate, but he can't figure out how to get them into his suit."

Marcus added, "I'm soooo hungry."

"Dude."

Edwards then said, "Hey, Max, you may want to look at this. Under their food packs in the crate is a weird device that I can't like."

I was perplexed. "What the heck? Fisher, look at this."

Fisher's voice trembled. "That's an EMP emitter."

Marcus responded, "Huh?"

"EMP—electromagnetic pulse. This makes sense now."

"Go on," I said.

"This explains everything. This is a bomb of sorts—must have shut down the systems. All the breakers popped. It's right next to the main battery, the main system. Holy shit! This was intentional... along with those cut wires. This is terrorism!"

Hamilton and Chandler heard us over the radios and immediately came over to look. We all just shook our heads.

The battery packs were swapped without issue. It was fun lifting these huge heavy assemblies with ease and slowly floating them across the cargo bay. We hooked them up and headed to the flight deck. Edwards ran up the auxiliary power generator. We cheered when it came on as well as all the other systems. We had Hamilton and Chandler start the engines and we were off.

On the flight back, we regained our gravity. We had to keep the helmets on since there was no time for the oxygen to return. During the journey back to station, I did a lot of thinking. Then I had a sudden realization as I put all the clues together from all these attacks against Space Station Prime. *I think I knew who did it.* I'd have to inform everyone what I suspected when we returned.

I never thought I'd be so happy to be back on station. The commander, chief, and Captain Kirkland greeted us when we landed, along with a bunch of our maintenance buddies, to include Flip, T.J., and of course Sharyn. It was now safe to finally take our helmets off.

Flip looked at me. "Max, hold on, I gotta get a picture of you, Spaceman Spiff."

"Sure, Hobbes."

The four of us maintainers in spacesuits grouped together as Flip pulled out his tablet and snapped a picture.

Captain Kirkland smiled and said, "Great job, Sergeant Morgan. I knew you'd pull through."

"Thanks, Captain. It was all these guys. I'm just glad to be back."

We all stopped talking and looked towards the back of the ship. A team of medics were slowly carrying out the two from Viridis. We all stopped and bowed our heads as they removed the bodies.

Once they had cleared the area, I said to the group, "I have something to show you. In fact, I need to show everyone."

The entire group followed me back into the cargo bay. I pointed out the severed wire bundle behind the aux battery assembly. Then we showed them the meal crate and what we suspected was an EMP device. I looked over at Marcus. He was already eating from one of the food containers.

Colonel Porter agreed at the suspicion. "We will definitely have this investigated."

I addressed the group in front of me. "I have an idea who could have been behind all the terrorist attacks against our station."

Chief Hendrix looked surprised. "Continue."

"I really don't want to say this, but everything makes sense. I have a sinking feeling that those cooks from Viridis in the chow hall aren't from Viridis."

Flip immediately blurted out, "Dude, what the hell?!"

The commander looked concerned. "Go on."

I continued, "Bennold and Pawly would greet each other with this gesture." I put my fists into the air in a boxing stance. "This was their way of saying hi or whatever. However, when I was at Viridis, some little punk kids used the same gesture the way we use it—to put up a fight, not say hello. Also, on Viridis, they don't eat eggs or even prepare them. The bird is sacred to them, yet these two cooks whip up the omelets with ease and without hesitation. I know it's not much. Earlier a few higher-ups were food poisoned, right? Food prepared by the chow hall?"

Colonel Porter said, "I know, I was one of them."

"Then during this mission, I saw the food container with the EMP device. The cooks are the only ones that have access to those crates before they're loaded onto the ships, right? I'm not saying it's them. In fact, I hope not. I just think it won't hurt to investigate them."

Everyone just stared at me. I was feeling I might have made a huge mistake. Maybe I wasn't thinking clearly. It had been one of the most nerve-racking experiences of my life. The colonel and chief both agreed that they would have them investigated and thanked me for the suggestion. We gathered our gear, returned our spacesuits, and turned in our tools. It was time to relax.

Our small maintenance team, along with Flip, Sharyn and T.J., made our way to the Mountain for celebratory drinks. We all told our friends all about our insane journey aboard the tiny shuttle and working in zero gravity. I even congratulated Sharyn on her baby news. It was so good to be home.

CHAPTER 32

Driving in Circles

A week after my trip into space, Colonel Porter called me into his office. "Our security team did an extensive background on those cooks. Turns out you were right. You were spot-on. They were actually from Calidum. They'd been faking this whole time with phony IDs and all. The chow hall worker and translator Jaycee was the mastermind behind their little operation. Our security teams ransacked all their rooms and found the evidence. Jaycee staged the attack on Space Station Prime, along with the cooks, disabling the gravity generators and seizing up the Flightline space window. They were even behind all the recent random attacks, to include that ship's sabotage."

Colonel Porter continued, "Apparently when the cooks were approached, one started to panic. What was his name? Pawly. Pawly freaked and started to run away. One of the security sergeants shot him in the leg. They even said he pissed himself after hitting the ground. All three of them are in lockup now. There was also evidence recovered of a plan to disable the station's oxygen supply. It was a good thing we caught them now. Outstanding job, Max."

I left the chief's office with mixed emotions. I thought unenthusiastically, *Yeah, we caught the terrorists.* Yet for some reason I felt I had a bond with those guys. How could this be? This would take some time to process.

Two months later I got the word. I was slated to deploy again, back to Calidum. The land of desert and rocket attacks. After Viridis and my bout in space, I was not ready for this. We landed on Calidum at the same airfield as before. Little had changed, only I was an expeditor now. The same hot star beat down on us as the coarse-sand-filled wind pelted me and our crew.

Flip wouldn't be going on this one. It was probably a good thing. He hated Calidum. Besides, with most deployments the Production staff and Quality Control don't easily get along. The Production team, including the expeditors, focus on getting as much maintenance and as many successful launches done as they can, while Quality Control—well, they're just doing their jobs. Which is great, but we all know how much that can be a hinderance.

Being an expeditor here wasn't too different than on station; same things every day. Making sure we launched and recovered each ship and dealt with all the scheduled and unscheduled maintenance. One day during our turnover with the Production Superintendents, we were interupted by Sergeant Dorsey. He was a Quaility Control inspector who wanted to explain some current fails.

The Production Super, T.J., laid into him. "What the hell, Sergeant?! You will wait until after our meeting to talk with me. Stand outside the office and wait until you're called in."

We were all surprised by this.

T.J. explained, "This guy keeps trying to find fails. He's going out of his way to make our maintenance look bad. Doesn't he know we're all on the same team? I know this may look bad, shunning him from our meeting, but back me up, team. He interrupted us."

I responded, "That's the way I saw it."

After our turnover, T.J. let Sergeant Dorsey back in.

Sergeant Dorsey explained, "I evaluated your Tool Counter program and found a lot of discrepancies. Here's the list."

T.J. looked at the list and responded, "I see your concern. Give me two weeks and we should fix these. Can I schedule a time for you to come out again and look at our tool program?"

"Sure." Dorsey pulled up his tablet and set a date two weeks from today.

Day after day was the same thing. Get turnover, monitor launches for redballs, drive the various career fields around. Ensure the Crew Chiefs launch and recover ships. It was a fast-paced, never-ending cycle of the unexpected. Occasionally there would be an avionics fail and I would spend some extra time talking with my troops and making sure they were on the right track.

One day I was in the truck sitting in front of Ship 0060. The flight crew was going through their checks, and we had a couple Avionics guys going up to look at the radio system. I was startled by a deafening BOOM and looked up. To my surprise and horror, a huge explosion shot up directly behind the ship I was parked at. A plume of smoke and debris was almost three stories tall. I was in a panic. We had just been hit! It had to be a rocket attack. Immediately I heard the alarms going off. I shut off the truck, grabbed my hand-held radio, got out of the truck, and lay on the ground. I looked up to see the cloud of debris still lingering in the air.

My two Avionics guys ran out of the ship. The three of us, as well as the flight crew, ran from the ship to the nearest bunker. As I was running, I thought, *There are two E&E troops on the ship next door—I need to see if they're alright.* I did a quick check on the other ship. It looked like they had already run inside or to the bunker. I then met up with the rest of our team in the bunker. We did the quick accountability and waited for the Alarm Green.

I heard many rocket attacks while on Calidum, but nothing that was this close. Twenty more feet and the ship would have been destroyed along with our maintainers, flight crew, and possibly me. Luck was definitely on our side. After the all clear, we evaluated the damage. All in all, three ships sustained damage. The one parked in front of my truck had a shrapnel hole in its wing. I was surprised. After all the debris, we only took one hole. The ship next to it had something shot right through its engine—that engine would have to be replaced. Then, there was a third ship hit by a small piece in its vertical stab. All of those were somewhat easy fixes. We were blessed that day. In fact, we were really lucky. We found part of the rocket that hit our Flightline. It was about fifty yards behind my truck. It actually hit the ground, then flew over the ship and my truck towards the nearby hangar. Any variance of that random rocket attack could have killed a number of us.

The ships were repaired within a couple of days, and we were back on the Groundhog Day schedule.

I asked T.J., "How'd it go with Quality Control? Did our Tool Counter pass?"

He answered, "Hell no, they failed again. Worse this time. Dorsey wrote them up and will be back to evaluate."

"Anything I can do to help?"

"Hey, Max, close the door, will you?"

I closed the door.

T.J. went into detail in a lower voice. "I have Quality Control where I want them."

"How's that?"

"Week after week, their focus is on our Tool Counter, right?"

"Well, yeah, he's right up their—"

"Yes, and every time there's a failure, then they come back to look for more."

"Isn't this bad?"

"No, you don't see the big picture. How often do you see Quality Control on the Flightline, evaluating real maintenance?"

"I guess hardly ever."

"You see, I have them distracted. I don't give a shit what they find in Tool Counter. No one does. As long as it's keeping them busy, we're not getting any Quality Control fails on the Flightline. Those are the fails that really hurt us."

"I see your point. A bit deceiving, but effective."

"I wouldn't call it deceiving, maybe some smoke and mirrors."

On some slower days., T.J. would let Sergeant Dakota drive so I could go to the big meetings with him and Captain Kirkland. These meetings were intense.

Every maintenance unit on base would brief the deployed US Space Military general on everything that had happened the day before. Every break, every fix. Any repeats would be questioned. A repeat was when the ship came back with the same issue it had on a previous flight. These meetings were anywhere between one and two hours. When it got to be our turn, Captain Kirkland would have to stand up and explain everything that was broken on our ships and what we did to fix it.

The problem was that the captain wasn't an expert on these systems. No officer is. They just repeat what the seniors tell them and try to sound intelligent. I must say, Captain Kirkland sounded very smart. We'd have all sorts of officers around the room that had never worked on the ships. They were trying to explain to each other what was happening on *their* ships. Captain Kirkland did his job good. Anytime he had a question, he'd turn to T.J. Then T.J. would stand up and explain how things really were. To this day I still don't understand what these briefings did for anyone. Everyone was just looking at slides and statistics, wondering how they, among all people, could increase the numbers to make them feel better about themselves.

I was in one of these meetings when things got out of hand. This was a monthly meeting that included the general from the Viridis Air Military as well as our US general that was running the meeting. I sat in the back with T.J. as it was getting underway. Captain Kirkland was sitting at the big table. We had already gone through the status of every ship on Calidum and what was being done to fix each one. Then they covered problems such as repeats and fixes that took over twelve hours. I felt like this briefing would never end. I got a text on my tablet from T.J., who was sitting right next to me. I looked down and saw an image of a guy banging his head against a wall. I felt the same thing sitting here. I glanced at him, and he was just staring straight ahead as if nothing had happened.

We got through all the different airframes—I was exhausted. Then the Viridis general stood up and displayed a slide on the big screen. The screen displayed a statue of a large red rooster, about eight feet tall, in front of his HQ here on Calidum.

The Viridis general said in broken English, "This symbol of our group has been stolen. It was there two days ago and now is gone. We must investigate and retrieve my statue. Someone has stolen my cock!"

Our general looked at him with a smirk and concern and said, "You say you lost your cock, General?"

"Yes! It sits among my grass. One morning I woke up and my cock was gone. My cock is large and red. No one has a cock like mine. You can't miss it."

"Well, I'm sure if we find out who did this, we can return it."

"My cock is a symbol of our moon. Without my cock, I am weak—we are weak."

The rest of us were in tears. We tried to hide our emotions, trying not to laugh.

The Viridis general continued, "People will pay for abusing my cock."

The US general addressed all of us. "If anyone has intimate knowledge of the Viridis general's cock, please let me know so we can resolve this matter once and for all. You are all dismissed."

There was a rumor that someone from our maintenance unit had taken the rooster. Once everyone knew the seriousness of the action, the whole thing was resolved. A couple days later, the rooster in question was secretly returned to the Viridis general's lawn. No one really knew who had violated the general's cock.

Back on the Flightline was more of the same. Driving in circles, checking up on each maintainer fixing the various ships. At one point a Security Forces sergeant stopped me in my truck. I stepped out, ready to comply.

She asked me, "What are you doing?"

"I'm doing my job."

"I've been watching you. All I see is you driving around in circles."

"I know, isn't it crazy?"

"Why are you doing that?"

"Well, it's my job to drive in circles."

"What do you mean?"

"I only do it every day. I have to check on these guys, then I check on the others, then I drive someone to get tools, then I check on this ship, then that ship—all day, every day, driving in circles like a madman."

"Can I see your Flightline driver's license and Flightline badge?"

"Sure, here you go. Now can I see yours?"

"What?"

"What, what? I don't know who you are. You just showed up asking me questions. Where are your credentials?"

"Well, I don't have them on me. They're in my vehicle."

"You better go get them."

She returned and showed me her Flightline badge and Security badge. I gave her the okay and she was on her way.

Every day was the same process, different problems. Launch, recover, fix, launch, recover, fix. Driving in circles. Doing the same process every day with different problems impeding our process. Every single day our flight crews had to load the IFF codes. These are the codes assigned to each ship to signify they're part of a single alliance. IFF stands for Identify Friend or Foe. Us, the Nix, and the Viridis loaded the same signature code. When our flight crews interrogated an unknown ship in the air and that specific code came up, they knew they were on the same side. If not, they'd be cautious and possibly engage. Very important to load the right codes while in this type of war scenario.

Before every flight, a crew member has to come out and load the specific codes to each ship. Then our Avionics members come behind them and verify the code is loaded correctly. It's a daily thing. Fairly boring and monotonous. Sitting in the expeditor truck, we see everything. In order to load the IFF, there's a processor located next to the crew entry door. A crew member has to hook up their cryptic unit to the processor and hit "transfer command" to load the specific day's code. The process should take less than a minute. Most crew members squat at the top of the crew entry door, hook up the transfer device and load it. Then our Avionics troop comes up and verifies the correct code if loaded. One and done.

There was a young female lieutenant navigator that would load the IFF codes before each flight. She could never get it right. She would bend over at the crew entry door and try over and over again to load these codes, to no avail. This could all be seen while parked in front of the ship. Most maintainers didn't mind. She was there for four or five minutes bent over with her butt to the world, trying to work this thing. I never knew what the issue was—maybe she didn't have it connected properly, or perhaps she didn't have the code loaded properly in her device to begin with. She'd try over and over, then go back to her building to reload her device and try again. Eventually she'd get it.

Every other day she was bent over with her butt in the air. She wiggled left and right, trying to get it to load. The maintainers on my truck caught on pretty quick and couldn't wait to watch the lieutenant try to load the codes. One day I was sitting there waiting for this same crew member to load the IFF codes. I was alone in my truck this time. Then the pilot walked out of the ship and said something to her. They both approached my maintenance truck.

"Can you take us to the flight crew building?" the pilot asked.

"Sure."

I realized then, this wasn't just the pilot. This was the commander of all the pilots. He got in the passenger seat while she was sitting in the back of my truck. The commander then turned around and laid into her.

He said, "I can't believe you! Every fucking day you can't load the damn codes. What the hell is the problem? No one else has this problem. Next time you need to go to the building to reload this code you will be out here every single launch loading everyone else's codes. Do you understand?"

She nodded. I was driving as stoic as a statue, trying to hide all emotions. I dropped them off at the building and waited. A few minutes later, they both came out. Her codes were reloaded.

As I chauffeured them back to the ship, the commander said, "This better be right this time."

It seemed that she got it right. However, a week later I saw this young lieutenant going from ship to ship, loading everyone's IFF codes. Same process as before, bent over with her butt out to each ship. I guess eventually she learned.

This deployment was interesting, and I'm sure I gained many experience points, but it was mainly work. A lot of work. Between the constant movement of maintainers across the Flightline and the ever-present random rocket attacks, I was done. I was exhausted after it and was looking forward to getting back to station. Our flight back was easy, and I soon found myself back in the luxury of my small single-person dwelling among the grandiose Space Station Prime.

CHAPTER 33

Standing in Line

Max: I don't think I can go to the grocery store anymore.

Roger: Why is that? Did someone's ringtone go off again?

Max: No, it's the people in general that aggravate me. It's not just one person doing one annoying thing. I'd be fine with that. I'm sure I do things that bug others. It's the avalanching effect of a series of people, each one digging away at my nerves.

Roger: Explain.

This starts in the parking lot. Our store has diagonal parking spaces. The slanted ones that line up side by side so it's a little easier to get in and out. It's pretty clear, at least to me, that this is a one-way lane. It'd be difficult to drive the other way and do an almost U-turn to get in a spot. Yet every day, I see cars back into these spots, or pull through to the other side. How are they supposed to get out? Drive the wrong way against head-on traffic, or do some crazy three-point turn to escape?

Then there is me, who doesn't budge. I'll drive my truck down the middle of these one-way aisles. Every once in a while a car will come at me. Then they stop and raise their hands, trying to get me to creep over to the side, to give them just enough room for them to squeeze by. I just stare at them and wait for them to hit reverse out of the aisle. I know I'll probably be shot one of these days. My only goal is just to make them mad enough to think twice about driving down the wrong way. Am I the jerk here?

Roger: In a way, yes. You're certainly not helping the situation. You don't always know their story. Maybe they got turned around and got distracted. Maybe they've never shopped there before. I'm sure you've made your share of mistakes.

Max: I'm sure you're right, you usually are.

It just seems like no one pays attention to the details. After filling my cart with groceries, I head to the checkout. I always use the self checkout nowadays, but even this is frustrating. There's always a long line. I stand and patiently watch the customers in front of me. I stare as they slowly scan each item. They rotate their goods across the scanner a dozen times before they get a beep, failing to find the bar code on multiple attempts. The bar code is on the bottom or on the side near the bottom. It seldom changes. I want to tell them to just look down at the item if they don't know where the code is. However, every customer in front of me just blindly rotates their boxes in all directions over the scanner like they're trying to dry their hands on a washroom blower.

I watched a lady last week scan fourteen boxes of the same cereal. She could have scanned it once and changed the quantity on the screen, or even scanned the same box fourteen times. Instead, I cringed inside when she had to scan each identical box individually, still blindly searching for the bar code, as if it jumped to a different spot for each cloned item. All I want to do is take over and show her how it's done, but I resist because then I would be the *bad guy.*

Roger: So, you don't like the self-service tills?

Max: I love the self-service tills. I just don't like waiting for them.

Once I get up there, I can scan my items and put them back in the cart ten times faster than most of the employees. Plus, I can bag the items the right way. Most times I don't even use a bag, unless I have a bunch of small stuff. The only thing that really slows me down is waiting for the employee to put in the code to allow me to buy alcohol. Even that process bugs me.

I don't mind them verifying that my age is over twenty-one. I think that's a great thing. The problem is that they don't understand the process. Where I shop, they're required to ask for an ID if a customer looks younger than forty years old. I'm fine with that. It's a judgment call on the worker. If there's any doubt, they can check your ID. The problem is when this employee walks up to me and asks if I'm over forty. Then they type in the code and leave. Most of the time they don't even look at me. That totally defeats the purpose. No one selling alcohol should ever ask anyone their age. If there's any doubt, check the ID.

The employee cashiers are worse than waiting. There's a certain standard I have for them, and ever since I returned to Earth, they continually fail my expectations.

I went to the regular checkout for a change. I stood behind a man and his teenage daughter buying a bunch of groceries. This man was buying beer also. He was probably in his late thirties. I could hear the exchange between the cashier and customer.

The cashier looks at him and she says, "Oh, beer?" Then the cashier looks at his teenager. "Is she over twenty-one?"

The man replied, "What's that have to do with anything? I'm buying the beer, it's mine."

"Well, you never know. I need to see her ID as well."

"No, you don't. She isn't buying the groceries, I am."

"Oh, you'd be surprised."

"I am surprised. Why are you asking me this?"

"Do you see the sign there?" The cashier pointed to a small sign next to the till.

I read it as well. It basically said anyone buying groceries that looks under forty must show an ID. The man stopped, then read the sign a second time and said, "So what's your point?"

The cashier just shook her head and said, "You'd be surprised. We do things by the book here," as she continued to ring up his groceries.

What really surprised me was that this man and his daughter bought the groceries and left the store with food and beer in his cart. Neither one of them showed their ID cards. Even if this lady thought she was doing her job right, she failed on all accounts.

I bought my groceries with no issue. Once I had my receipt in hand, I looked at the cashier and said, "You are really a dumb person, aren't you?"

She looked at me with disgust and I felt bad. I can't shop anymore. My expectations are continually lowered. I know most stores have gotten away from uniforms, but when the cashier is in his sweatpants and a dirty T-shirt, it automatically triggers this disdain for him. I know I shouldn't judge people and all that, but how can I not? When I go to a cashier, I expect them to know things and be fast at ringing up the products. Prior to me going to space, the cashiers were professional. They would be fast and ring up the items with ease. They were able to cash checks, ring up coupons, WIC programs, EBT, and so forth. Before the produce-scanning system, cashiers would have to type in a code number for each piece of fruit or vegetable...and they had these codes memorized!

Roger: I understand your frustration. Many people today don't stay in one job very long. They're most likely new and don't know any better. If you don't like lines, why don't you order from home and have it delivered?

Max: Nope.

Roger: Where do you think this frustration comes from?

Max: On the space station, we used to practice standing in lines.

Roger: Practice?

Max: Yes. We had to simulate a deployment process.

Roger: I thought maintainers were constantly deploying to the moons.

Max: They do—we did. We know how to do it better than anyone. Even the new guys have no problem with the process because the veteran maintainers always outnumber them. It's easy to follow in their footsteps.

Roger: Explain to me this process for practicing standing in lines.

Max: Our new commander was Colonel Bucket. We had so many exercises during his era of command.

Roger: Exercise, like running or CrossFit?

Max: No, an exercise is a simulation. To practice the deploying process or practice flying half our fleet all at once, just to see if we still remember how to launch a ship.

Colonel Bucket was there through it all. Every exercise, he stood there with his hands on his hips. It seemed that every chance the colonel got, he'd blurt out, "You need to be ready for a deployment! You never know when our entire unit will be asked to uproot and mobilize to the moons. Everyone needs to have their bags packed and ready to go at a moment's notice. You never know. You may just show up to work and find out you're deploying that same day. You never know!"

The deployment exercise is designed to help all the parties involved. It's designed to help every other agency know how to ship out a massive group of people at the same time. However, in order to practice herding a massive group, they need a whole lot of guinea pigs. That's where the spaceship maintainers come in.

The first step in this process was for everyone to have their luggage inspected. We packed our bags with all the required items based on a checklist we were given before the exercise. Of course, we all unpacked our bags at the end of this practice deployment. We stood in lines waiting for our bags to be checked by inspectors as they recorded the results. They were only checking off the minimum items that were on their made-up list. Which was completely unrealistic.

We were fake-deploying for a six-month trip to the moon Calidum, yet their checklist required three T-shirts, four coveralls, three pairs of socks, winter gear, and so forth. We were basically going through the motions to get our lists signed off. Even though these checklists were most likely written by people that had never deployed to a moon. First of all, you would never survive anywhere with three shirts or three pairs of socks. You need at least double that, usually more. Four sets of coveralls? Two is all you need, but it's best to bring three just in case one rips. Winter gear? This is Calidum. What are we teaching our specialists—just pack what's on the list? They need to think about where they're going and what they really need.

If anyone is missing a required item, it's logged in by an inspector. Every aspect of these exercises is recorded through a point scale. Then at the end of the exercise, they display our total scores to see where the problem areas are. Then Commander Bucket would have to explain the importance of being ready to deploy at a moment's notice again.

On one of these exercises, I saw a specialist getting frustrated because he forgot to pack a towel. The list said he needed to have one towel. I pulled out my pocketknife, cut my towel in half, and gave the specialist one. The inspector was watching all of this in disbelief.

I told him, "One towel each, it doesn't specify the size."

He just shook his head and let us go. After our bags were checked, we went and stood in another line. This one had the Personnel troops checking over our deployment records. You'd go to the front of the line and give them your name. Then they bring up all your records on their screen and ensure everything is checked off.

If not, we're dinged a few points by the inspectors. Why the line? They're just looking at records in this manner. Could they do this on their own time? We don't even need to be here for that. They already have the list of deployers. Do we really need to be present for all this? Anyways, once we get through this ordeal, we need to get issued our weapons.

However, since we weren't deploying, they wouldn't give us guns. We had to stand in a line anyways. There were twelve people in front of me going through the motions. No one was getting issued a weapon. This took forever. After an hour and a half, I got to the window. The armory troop over the counter just looked at me with a dark, blank stare.

After a full minute, I asked her kindly, "What are we doing?"

Specialist Rooks responded, "We're simulating me not getting you your weapon or ammunition."

"Why are you not issuing anything?"

"We can't because this is just an exercise."

"So now what do we do?"

"I have to wait eight and a half minutes before you can sign the form."

"Is eight and a half minutes how long it would take to issue out a weapon and ammo?"

"That's what they say."

"How long would it take *you* to issue one out?"

"I've only issued out weapons a couple times. It would probably take longer for me since I haven't had much practice."

"Wouldn't it make more sense if we spent this time handling real guns and ammo to get you some practice?"

"I was told we can't do that since this is an exercise and we can't give out real weapons."

"How much time do we have left?"

She looked down at her tablet. "About six minutes."

After an extremely long and painfully awkward six minutes, she handed me her tablet, which displayed a serial number, along with a small piece of paper.

Specialist Rooks instructed, "Now you'll need to look at the serial number on the paper and make sure it matches the one on the tablet. Once you verify the numbers match, you'll need to sign the tablet here to indicate we issued you that number for your simulated weapon."

"The serial number is two. You need me to verify that two matches two?"

"It's just for practice."

I signed my name. "Okay, now what?"

"You need to walk to two paces to your left to the weapon-clearing station and say the word *clear* to clear out your weapon that I didn't give you."

I walked to the clearing station. I did a hand motion of clearing my imaginary gun and kept walking.

Specialist Rooks then yelled, "Sir, you didn't say *clear*. You need to clear your weapon! You can't pretend to deploy if you don't pretend to clear!"

Now was the fun part. Our deployment exercise fake briefings. We all sat in a cramped room. Already frustrated by the process. Tired, hungry and angry, we just wanted to be done with this so we could call tonight a total wash and then actually get some real work done on the Flightline.

First on the agenda for our deployment briefing was someone from the Medical division. He gave us a briefing on how having sex in a deployed location with others can have an adverse effect on our health and welfare. I thought to myself, *We're deploying with the same people we work and live with. How is this any different in another location?* Next up was a briefing by an intelligence officer. He said this would not be a real briefing on the location since that might compromise classified information. Instead, he projected on the screen a globe of a made-up moon with made-up terrain and made-up people. He told us which inhabitants of this moon were dangerous and what type of hazardous weapons they might use against us. This information wasn't helping anyone. Could we at least get a brief history lesson on some real events on these real moons?

The briefings continued. We heard from Finance, the Support Group, the Legal office—even the chaplain gave a briefing. After that we waited. Then waited some more. Finally, they walked us up to the Flightline Entry Control Point Five. We were loaded onto a bus that used the same track system as our expeditor trucks. We sat on that bus for two hours until they said the exercise was over. We didn't even drive anywhere. We then departed the bus, walked back to the so-called terminal and had the joy of trying to find our individual deployment bags among a hundred identical bags.

Standing in lines. Practicing standing in lines for hours, and for what? I could never figure this out.

Roger: You were taught to pay attention to detail, correct?

Max: Only every day.

Roger: You also learned specific processes, and how to streamline the system.

Max: Okay.

Roger: You've been taught for twenty-plus years how to be organized, act professionally, and make smart decisions.

Max: Where are you going with this?

Roger: Did you know all this before you joined?

Max: Of course not, I was an idiot.

Roger: When you go to these grocery stores or anywhere else in public today, you have certain expectations. You want to see the process, you want to see people following the rules and acting professionally. You get frustrated when people don't see all the details around them as you do.

Max: I suppose I do.

Roger: You had the unique experience of learning all these skills. You need to realize most of the people you encounter have never been through what you have. They don't see the world the same as you.

Max: I hate to say this, but that makes sense.

Roger: You shouldn't let this bother you. Be thankful for all you have, for all you've been through and all you've learned.

Max: You're right.

Roger: That's what I'm here for.

Max: I can still hate standing in lines, right?

Roger: Sure. Just change your mindset a little.

Max: Oh, one more thing I almost forgot. That Colonel Bucket that was always saying that we might deploy without notice.

Roger: Yeah?

Max: They needed a new commander to replace the one on Nix. Colonel Bucket was picked and was gone within two days without much notice, deploying by himself.

CHAPTER 34

The Slow Death

Max: Well, Roger, this was an end to an era.

Roger: Why is that?

Little by little, my brothers and sisters came to the end of their military careers. Senior Diego served his time and was out. Chaplain McKinley had left and was replaced. Even Marcus and Sharyn called it quits as they went back towards Earth with their little boy, Aaron, who we'd grown to love. Left and right, more and of my family was leaving. Of course, we always had new specialists and sergeants come in, but it was never the same.

With everyone leaving, my focus was to just get through each day and count down until my time was up. Now it was Flip's time. He had served his twenty and was ready. I was happy for him, yet sad at the same time. There was a bunch of us there for his big going-away. We had a picnic of sorts in the courtyard of Barracks Texas. It was great but bittersweet. I couldn't believe how many people from station showed up. I was overwhelmed as everyone wanted to talk to Flip. Part of me wanted to stay by his side, but he was bombarded with people. I just kept my distance for the most part.

The next morning, I walked with Flip to the Medical Bay. There he would be put under, put into cryo-sleep and sent off onto the Space Bridge. I didn't even know what to say. Neither of us did. We were both at a loss for words as we walked the cold corridors towards Medical.

We arrived, and I said, "Well, Flip. It's been real."

He hugged me and said, "I know, I know. You'll come back soon now, right?"

"Yep, I'll be right behind you. Good luck, man."

"You too."

And that was that. Flip was gone.

Roger: So now what?

Max: The craziest thing happened several months after Flip left. I thought I was almost done with my enlistment, then I found out something.

Roger: What's that?

Max: I made senior sergeant.

Roger: Wow. Good for you.

Max: I don't know then I'd be stuck.

Stuck in an office, off the Flightline, in meetings, counseling, and APRs. A slow death. I had a few months before I was actually the new rank. As those months went by and I continued to be an expeditor on the Flightline, I knew my time was approaching and for some reason I was fearful of it. It had come. I sewed on the rank of senior sergeant.

My new job would be in the Resource Office. Toiling over endless APRs and going to countless meetings. Meeting upon meetings. We would even have meetings before meetings to talk about what we should talk about during the next meeting. I would sit through an early meeting with our Production team along with our new LT and Chief Clavin. The previous Production shift would cover everything they did the night before. Then the LT would take that info and go to the next meeting to explain it all to the Maintenance commander, Major Kirkland. Then there would be an additional meeting where Major Kirkland explained everything to the space station general. It was a long game of telephone, and I sat through all these meetings, hearing the repeated information as each group was questioning why things were done the way they were and what could have been done better.

T.J. and I would sit through these meetings and secretly text each other funny messages or pictures. They would discuss the mission-capable rates to determine how these unscheduled random breaks were impacting our fleet and how we could prevent them from ever happening. They looked at the number of times a break came back after being fixed, called repeats. They would record every time a part was canned, or discuss how long it took our maintainers to make their repairs.

Other meetings went into detail concerning the manning of our Flightline. We would talk about how each section had limited people. They would try to determine how we could move people from one low-manned position to another low-manned position in hopes it would fix the problem. I would look around the room and count the number of higher-ups. The combined years of Flightline experience in this room was astronomical as we spent all our time going from meeting to meeting. I thought I could see why they were low-manned on the Flightline.

We would have other meetings with our commander to discuss the problems with our people. Countless slides of those that missed appointments as we struggled to explain why they missed, what we were doing to stop it, and how we would prevent this from ever happening again. Other times we would have countless discussions on our *problem* specialists.

The ones that are constantly getting into trouble. No matter what we do, they're always messing up. Show up late for work, miss roll calls, failing barracks inspections. People getting into fights with each other. Then there were the never-ending Quality Control fails. It wasn't just the fails, but the lack of trying on the Flightline.

The crazy thing was that the majority of these issues only came from a very small sample of the specialists. We would spend ninety-five percent of our time on the five percent. We'd take them into the chief's office and counsel them, trying to figure out what the deal was. Most of the time there were other factors involved causing them to make poor decisions. We'd try to get to the root of these issues. People would be written up. Some sergeants would be demoted to specialists. Others would just have to be sent back to Earth.

All my years of Flightline maintenance and here I was spending the last couple years in this slow death. I couldn't wait to get out, get back to the Earth I knew. Night after night, meetings, counselings, and the dreaded APRs.

Roger: Did you ever have a chance to sit still after spending all your time running or driving around in circles?

Max: While working in the Resource Office I would sit at my desk all day long toiling over the dreaded APRs. Annual Performance Reports or APRs evolved over the years to become a grueling exercise of utmost futility. The purpose of the APR is twofold: rating the member via a point scale while showing their accomplishments.

The US Space Military are rated high to low, five to one, over categories displaying their overall performance. Most of my career, almost every maintainer was given an overall rating of five, anything less was questioned. These ratings greatly impacted their promotions, which is why so many were hesitant to give out low ratings. Years went by with almost everyone getting fives and only a few fours, it was unheard of to see any score less. Points were intended to separate the maintainers into a point range, all this did was hurt the few that got a four.

Roger: It seems nonsense to have a point scale if no one will use them to differentiate between the specialists.

Max: Once decided to utilize the scale the correct way it was like pulling teeth to get a good range of numbers. The other major aspect of APRs was capturing all the accomplishments they made over an entire year's span. Every year higher-ups would add more and more requirements for how to write these performance statements. Countless statistics had to be incorporated into each bullet statement, regardless of what the person really did.

Numbers had to be everywhere; this many space flights launched, or this many pounds of munitions delivered. We'd add mission-capable rates and repeat rates, which made it more about the unit and less on the individual. You could look at a whole stack of APRs and could only differentiate them based on whose name was on top. These would be written and edited by supervisors, the Resource Officer, and then end up on the chief's desk. There were times we would embellish a menial task to see how far up the chain it would go; take this example. *Fostered American/Nix holiday festival; secured 8 specialist's transportation —fortified intergalactic relations.*

Roger: I don't see a problem with this; contains an action, an impact, and a result for a clear concise statement.

Max: What it doesn't state concerns a group that got drunk on St. Patrick's Day on Nix, then one called a taxi.

Roger: I'm beginning to see what you have here, by taking some truth and disguising it; may I have another?

Max: They wanted all the APRs to have volunteer lines, even if they only worked the Flightline; take this one. *Selflessly contributed to the cause; donated over 14 hours/2,000 Space Bucks—boosted local community funds.* In other words, a Specialist Frank went to a local casino establishment and gambled away his whole paycheck.

Some specialists were injured and could only work jobs like Debrief; this would make a difficult line like this. *Protector of information; secured potential transfer of 3,000 sensitive documents; thwarted insider unit threat.* This is an exaggerated way to say the member spent hours and hours shredding the chief's obsolete paperwork.

Roger: This all seems very insane for all of you, how many man-hours were wasted on these detailed reports?

Max: Too many to count, an endless endeavor to ensure all APRs were written and edited to pristine perfection.

CHAPTER 35

Hello Darkness

Roger stopped by our usual spot at the hospital. "Max, Max, Max! What's going on? You're not yourself today. Tell me. Max, look at me. Are you alright?!"

It took me a second to reply. I finally looked at him. "I've been better."

"You don't look good. Tell me, what's going on?"

"Do you know how old I am?! Take a guess—take a wild fucking guess!"

"Whoa, Max, I don't want to. Why are you yelling? You're scaring me."

"How old? I need you to answer!"

"I don't know, I guess midforties. This doesn't matter, Max!"

"Nothing matters!"

"Why are you crying? Come on. We all matter. Tell me what's going on. I'm scared."

"The world changed. Everything I know is different. I hate this place. I hate it."

"I've never seen you like this. Tell me."

"This world, everything I know, the lies. The damn lies."

"Look at me, look at me. Focus. Tell me."

"I don't know how."

"Tell me. Tell me."

"...Flip is dead."

"Flip dead? How? What happened?"

"I got the message. Nothing matters."

We both sat in silence for about a minute. I could tell Roger wanted me to continue.

I started, "After everything he's done, everything he's sacrificed, all the lives he's impacted. He talked about going out in a blaze of fire, but no, he just got sick. They still don't know. He went to the hospital. They said he had problems. He just got worse. They don't know why. He was dead in two weeks. They didn't know. They couldn't even help him. I couldn't help him. I never knew. Never knew he got sick. No one told me."

"I can't imagine what you're going through. I'm only here to help."

"Why?"

"I'm here."

"Why, dammit!"

"I'm here."

"I need."

"What do you need?"

"I need…"

"Take me back to the last time you saw him. Max, take me back to last time you saw him."

"It was the party back on station."

"Good. Good, Max. Who else was there?"

"Everyone. It was at the courtyard at our old barracks. Our entire Avionics crew, most of the specialists, most of the Crew Chiefs. Resource Office, expeditors, people from all over station, everyone. It was his big send-off. It was a party. We had a huge feast, and plenty of drinks. T.J. brought out an electric keyboard and jammed on it for half the night. Funny thinking about it. We were making so much noise that the Security Police were called."

"Go on."

"They showed up. We thought we were busted; thought we'd have to shut it all down. They were about to shut it down until they realized it was for Flip. They knew him. Hell, everyone on station knew Flip. They joined us and even had a few drinks with us. This was a huge thank you and congratulations. It was a send-off before he went back to Earth. It was…it was…sad to see him go. I can't believe he's gone."

"Sounds like he was loved by everyone."

"Everyone. I never saw him after he left. Why didn't I see him?! I returned to Earth later and never saw him. I never saw him."

"You've kept in touch. You told me that."

"But not gone to see him! Messaging him at random times is not seeing him."

"You kept asking me how old you were. What was that all about?"

"Do you remember what Flip told me the first time I met him, about the Space Bridge?"

"I'm sorry, but I don't."

"He said, 'Space Bridge does some freaky shit.' When I finally left the Stella system forever, I felt so many emotions. I was happy to have experienced so much. I was proud of all my accomplishments. I was tired, I was so ready. I was so ready to return to the Earth I knew."

"You deserved it. You did well."

"I went through the Space Transport. They put me in cryo-sleep. Oh, did I sleep. We all did. The whole set of us coming back to so-called regular life, but that wasn't the case."

"What happened?"

"I'll tell you. What was it? Two months? Two months the Space Bridge was supposed to take?"

"I think so."

"Back in the day as a specialist it took me seven months. Remember, to go from Earth to Stella, Seven months. Not this time. Oh no. We got stuck, or rerouted, or slowed down—who the hell knows? It was eighteen! It was eighteen life-sucking years traveling in cryo-sleep."

"No! You never said."

"Eighteen years. I came back to a world that wasn't even close to being the same. How old am I? I have no clue. Based on my birth year, I'm sixty-four. The years I've been awake, actually aged, actually lived. Somewhere around forty-six."

"I heard some transports had complications coming back. I had no idea it was that long. No idea. Why didn't you tell me? All this time, you should have told me. You should have told me."

"I didn't think it mattered. I didn't want to trouble you. I don't know. This was my internal problem. My problem, not yours."

"We're in this together, Max. I'm here for you."

"I know, Roger. I didn't want to show weakness. It was the lies. All the lies that came in. Numerous transports came back late. The cover-ups, the cover-ups, lying to the public, lying about the delays. It's like swimming upriver through that wormhole coming back. So unpredictable, so disruptive of our lives. What kills me is that they knew this. They knew the whole time. Sending transport after transport to and from. They knew about the delays but didn't care. It wasn't important. All that was important was to send as many of us as they could to help with this situation. And why? Why? So they could be friends with the aliens, get more technology from them. At our expense. They knew, dammit."

"What now?"

"Earth has changed so much I don't know how to live in it."

"How old would Flip have been?"

"His Space Transport took almost ten years to get back. I don't know, somewhere in his mid-fifties."

"What now?"

"I need a break. I need to think."

"Promise me you won't do anything stupid."

"What's left to do? They've already taken away half my life and my best friend. I'm done. I'm so done."

"I'm with you, Max. We're going to pull through this together. I'm not leaving you. I won't."

Roger took me to my home and spent the night in my spare bedroom. I would like to think I wouldn't have done anything harmful that night. But then again, I wasn't in the right state of mind. His presence saved my life. He saved me more than once. I needed this. I needed him to express my thoughts and he was always there. I needed to just have someone listen, and it was Roger. It was always Roger.

CHAPTER 36

My Old Friends

A couple days later, I approached Roger where he worked at the hospital. "Hey, I have an important question for you."

He responded, "What's that? You seem better today."

"I am. I'm feeling pretty good considering everything. Roger, I don't know if you understand the significance of our talks. You have helped me more than I ever thought possible. I just want to thank you for everything. I also want to ask you for one more favor."

"What's that?"

"Next week there will be a funeral service for Flip. It'll be in Omaha."

"That sounds great. You're going, right?"

"I am. I was also hoping you'd come with me. It'll be a cool road trip across the country. I'll pay for everything."

"You know, let me see if I can get time off. That sounds like it could be fun."

The next week, Roger and I departed Phoenix and headed east. I drove my truck and we did a lot of talking along the way. I made him a promise.

I said, "I've done most of the talking on this incredible mind warp journey. I want to hear everything about you, Roger. No more stories from me."

Roger told me all about his exciting life. He was raised on the East Coast, primarily in New York. Although he'd never served in the military, his résumé was impressive. Roger worked at some elite colleges, to include Yale for some time. He even spent a brief stint working directly for the governor of New York.

I asked him, "How about your family? You said you're still married to your high school love, right?"

Roger responded, "Yep, still married to Zuri, forty years come this April."

"That's awesome. Really, what's your secret?"

"No secret, just tell her she's beautiful and tell her she's always right."

"I can see how that would work. You told me she works at the hospital as well, correct?"

"She still does. She's a nurse in the maternity ward."

"Good to hear. What about your kids?"

"Two daughters and four grandsons."

"Great. Why did you move to Arizona again?"

"For Zuri. Her parents moved here to escape the New York winters. Zuri got a job at the Arizona Medical One, so naturally I followed and ended up getting a job there as well."

We had a great road trip, and I even had Roger drive for part of the way. I could tell he really loved driving my new truck. I learned more about Roger. In my mind he was a saint. He didn't have to put in this amount of effort for me. Who was I? Why did I matter to him? All these talks with him over the last year or so really put my life in perspective. He had become a true friend that I felt I could never truly repay. We stopped in a small town in Texas overnight, then continued our journey. We talked endlessly as we trekked across this great country. Our final stop was a small hotel in Omaha.

The next day, we put on our nice suits and made our way to the funeral service in the evening. I didn't know who would be there, or if it even mattered if I was there. I had no expectations, I just thought I should be there. Standing outside the chapel, Roger and I waited. I didn't want to go in just yet. We saw groups of strangers arrive.

Then a heard a voice. "Max?"

I looked up, and it took me a while to place their faces. "Sharyn? And Marcus?"

Sharyn said, "Yes. Wow, look at you."

I replied, "You look different. I mean, you look—I almost didn't..."

Sharyn answered, "It's been a long time, Max. A real long time."

Marcus gave me a big hug. "You look good, Max, almost like you didn't age much at all."

I responded, "You're right there. Space Bridge, minus eighteen years."

Sharyn looked shocked. "Wow! I'm so sorry. It was only minus six months for us."

"Where are you two at now?"

"We're good. Living in Colorado, enjoying retired life. Our kids are grown now. Eighteen years, Max? Are you okay?"

"I am, I really am. I want you to meet my good friend Roger. He's been my saving grace."

Just then another familiar face showed up.

T.J. approached. He was walking with a cane and from the looks of it had a prosthetic leg.

He greeted us. "Well, would you look at this sorry group."

"T.J.!" I said. "Wow, great to see you."

Marcus looked perplexed as he pointed to the leg.

T.J. explained, "I know, I know."

Marcus asked, "What happened?"

"A blessing and a curse. I got real bad after my enlistment. Space Bridge minus thirteen years for me. I took to drinking hard. One night I thought I could drive home, tried to beat the train signal. I have no idea what I was thinking. My car got sideswiped by the train and I hit a barrier. Lost the leg."

Marcus asked, "How is that a blessing?"

"Haven't touched the juice since. I cleaned up and started counting my blessings."

Sharyn responded, "That's so sad, yet great for you. We are just happy to see you. I guess it could have been much worse."

T.J. added, "You're right, I was so lucky. Besides, I still have my arms. I can still tickle the ivories."

Roger informed me, "Looks like everyone is heading in."

We all made our way into the chapel, and we all sat in the same pew. The chapel was full of people that we didn't know. The ceremony was what we could expect. The minister gave a nice sermon. As I sat there, I felt bad. Flip had no real family. His grandparents that raised him had already passed. Although Flip had many close friends, he had never married nor had children. Towards the end of the ceremony, I was feeling remorse and hurt. Would I end up the same? Dying without a family member at my side?

As the ceremony came to a close, the minister said Samuel Dolphline had an additional request. He then played a video on a big screen.

The video started with an older Flip speaking from what looked like a hospital room. "Hey, guys, it's Sam here. Some of you know me as Flip! The doctors tell me this is it for me. The end is near, my friends. I have a few things I need to say. First of all, no regrets. We have all experienced the good and the bad. No matter what, we learn from those events, and we all need to move on. Look up and forward. Take your experiences and use anything positive from them. Life is short, and my doctor says my life is even shorter than yours, ha! We all have a choice. We can complain and whine about the insane world around us, or we can appreciate this crazy adventure we're on. The question is, would you rather be happy or miserable? I choose happy! Enjoy this video..."

The next video was a series of clips and pictures Flip had obtained over the years. The first set included some antics he had talked about while he worked on the radio show. Him swimming in the mall fountain, the lot of them rerouting cars through the middle of town. A selfie of Flip in his underwear departing for space the very first time. Him and Turtle drinking at the Mountain. Really cool photos of the space station Flightline with the dome and open space in the distance. Some random pictures of Flip on Calidum.

This was better than I could imagine. I looked around the church, seeing everyone in awe of the pictures. It was all smiles and tears. The video continued, showing me standing in front of a ship waving my arms wrapped in aluminum foil, then all of us in the courtyard, watching the great mattress exchange. The York wedding, followed by pictures of us at the Christmas dinner party. There were pictures of us all on the beach on Viridis as well as the maintenance response team in our spacesuits. Other pictures included an array of friends he had acquired from the last ten years or so back on Earth.

Flip came back on the video. "Well, that's it, my friends. I love you all. If the funeral service followed my instructions, there should be an open bar following this. Cheers." Flip raised a glass and took a final drink.

Immediately after the ceremony, we all met in the small reception area. True to his word, there were drinks available to us.

Roger turned to me. "Max, this is wonderful. I can finally put some faces to the names you've been giving me."

Just then I heard a familiar voice.

"Hey, bub, whatcha doing?"

I turned around fast. "Jo-Leia?!"

"I snuck in after the ceremony started."

"Wow, so great to see you. You look...amazing!"

"Space Bridge, minus twenty."

"Oh. What are you up to? Can we talk after this?"

Flip's reception was wonderful. Our group stood around for a long time, reminiscing about the video and the great times we had in the Space Military. I said my goodbyes to T.J. as well as Sharyn and Marcus. Afterwards Roger went back to our hotel and Jo-Leia and I went to a local coffee shop.

I found out a great deal about her. She had come back after being suspended for almost twenty years in the Space Bridge. She was in a state of despair and immediately ended her military service. She had gotten married and had two kids. Unfortunately for her, Jo-Leia got divorced after some time and continued to raise her children. However, she did pursue her dream of flying and got her license. She even bought herself a small airplane and now had a business of flying tourists around the Grand Canyon, near where she lives. To my surprise, she had flown out here to Omaha on her small plane.

I headed back to my hotel room alone after the great talk with Jo-Leia. The next morning, I knocked on Roger's door and he answered.

I greeted him. "You want to get some breakfast?"

"Sure, Max."

Over breakfast, I told Roger, "I'm so glad you came out here for this. It means so much. You know, Flip is right about focusing on the positive. I know I complain a lot. However, the US Space Military is truly the best thing that has happened to me. So many of us are going through the same experiences."

Roger asked, "What about all the stuff about the coverup and lies?"

"That's all politics. Those were the people well above us making all the bad decisions. The men and women I worked with every day had nothing to do with that. We did our jobs. We toiled day and night and helped each other get through it. Everyone worked and everyone struggled through it. Even though the nights were rough, I can't take that back. I won't take it back. Just the memories alone are worth more than anything I can imagine. I loved what we did, and I'm proud of all those that served."

"What about coping with the fact you came back and everything had changed so much?"

"That's just the thing. Did I lose eighteen years, or did I gain eighteen? I can't change the past, at least as far as we know. However, I can always choose to change my attitude moving forward. In fact, in most situations, that's all I can change."

"That's wonderful. How did it go last night with Jo-Leia?"

"Amazing. I was going to ask you something."

"What's that?"

"I've been thinking, and this is a big one."

"Go on."

"Would you mind terribly if I gave you my truck and you drove yourself back to Arizona alone?"

"What exactly do you mean?"

"Jo-Leia flew out here in her airplane. She's returning to Arizona and asked if I'd fly back with her. I have a good feeling about this."

"Well, good for you. I guess I can drive your truck back. It may take me longer; I don't like driving more than five or six hours a day."

"Two things. One, I'll pay for all your hotel stays. Second, the deal was if I *give* you my truck. It's yours—you can have it. I'll give you the title once I get back."

"What? Your truck is almost brand-new. I couldn't!"

"No, really, take it. For everything you've done for me, the truck is yours."

"Why would you do that?"

"Roger, you have done so much for me and deserve it. Besides, as the saying goes, 'new guy oversleeps, new guy pays for drinks.' Those eighteen years frozen on the Space Bridge weren't for nothing. I was still paid a nice sum for my military service. Take the truck."

"Max, thank you! We'll keep in touch."

"Always."

Jo-Leia and I walked out to a little Flightline, seeing a row of small planes. Her aircraft was a sweet-looking twin turboprop. It was fueled and I helped with the preflights. Tower gave the okay and we taxied to the runway. We got the go-ahead then we barreled down the runway until the wheels lifted off the ground. Jo-Leia had control of this marvel of flight as we took to the open blue skies.

Epilogue

The hospital's top staff of a dozen doctors at Arizona Medical One was nearly at the end of their meeting.

Dr. Dumas sat at the head of a large boardroom table. "That almost wraps things up. Before we conclude, Dr. Steven, will you give us a brief recap, please?"

"Yes, Dr. Dumas, we discussed the current nursing shortage. We plan on revising their schedule again. There are two new doctors coming from California on Thursday, with whom Dr. Megan agreed to meet and get them set up. The north staff parking lot will be paved next week, so we need to find an alternate staff lot. Lastly, we will finally receive the new EEG machines by the end of the month."

"Thank you, Dr. Steven. I see we have one last piece of business. Dr. Megan, you said you wanted to discuss a matter concerning the cafeteria?"

Megan responded, "Yes, there's a matter of that gentleman that we see sitting at the same table every morning."

Many doctors around the table grumbled at the same time: "Not this again." "Who cares?" "Do we really need to discuss this?"

Dumas stopped them. "Continue, Dr. Megan."

"It has come to my attention that many patients and staff are wondering why this gentleman is always there. He spends most of the nights here. They say he talks to himself sometimes."

Dumas asked, "Is this man a patient of our hospital? Does anyone know his name?"

Silence as they all stare at each other.

Megan said with concern, "I think that's the problem. No one even asked him what his name is."

Dr. Dumas continued, "We have almost a hundred doctors in this building alone. Which brings in thousands of patients and even more visitors. As long as this man isn't bothering anyone or posing any danger to himself or others, it's not our concern."

"Should we be concerned?" asked Megan.

"We have enough patients with real problems. If he needs anything, I'm sure he'll make an appointment. He's probably just visiting. He must know someone."

Steven raised his hand. "I do see him talking to that night janitor every time when I come in for breakfast. I can't think of his name. Do you know which one I'm thinking of?"

"Like I know any of the janitors' names—come on," scoffed Dumas.

"Does anyone know? He's the one that's always cleaning and fixing the toilets, among the other crap around here."

Megan said, "Hold on, I'm pulling up a picture on my tablet. Is this him?"

"That's the one," Steven replied. "The janitor's name is Roger."

Outtakes

Prologue. Take 1:

Max: When the Flightline engulfs you, like it does every maintainer over time, you see every fine detail. I don't just see a row of planes.

Director: Cut! It's a *spaceship*, not a plane.

Director:

Flying scene. Take 1.

Max: Fear has engulfed me. I start to feel the enormous airplane shift its weight as we roll down towards...

Director: Cut! Stop using the term air*planes*. These are *ships*—space*ships*. Just not planes or airplanes. How many times do we have to correct you?

Getting Hammered scene. Take 4:

Turtle: Everyone calls me Turtle. Do you get it?

Max: Yeah, named after the—

Turtle: It's because nothing bothers me. I have a strong shell that deflects everything.

Flip: No, you're Turtle because you're short and you're ugly!

Director: Cut! The line is "You're short and you're slow," not "ugly"!'

Getting Hammered scene. Take 5:

Turtle: It's because nothing bothers me. I have a strong shell that deflects everything.

Flip: No, you're Turtle because you're short and you're fat!

Director: Cut! Short and slow, short and slow, he's a turtle, for crying out loud.

Night One scene. Take 5.

T.J.: Alarm Yellow! Max, close the toolbox, lock it up! Make sure your harness is still connected to the stand!

Sharyn: Put your mask on! Flip the switch!

T.J.: You still have that O-ring?! ...Good, don't swallow it!

Sharyn: This is awesome! Alarm Red on a maintenance stand!

Director: Cut! Cut! Turn off the blowers! Bobby, we can see you shaking the stand in the frame. Keep your head down next time.

I Don't Have Three Arms scene. Take 1.

Max: What are you doing?

Flip: Nothing, just checking on you (Laughing) 'Thrrrp!'

Max: Dude! You're not supposed to fart for real!

Flip: Just go with it. Make it believable.

Max: (Laughing) I'm sorry, I can't. Dude, what did you eat?

Director: Cut!

The Walk scene. Take 1.

Another night, another roll call. Senior Sergeant Tillhammer went through the long list of names.

Tillhammer: Jackson?

T.J.: Here.

Tillhammer: Dolphline?

Flip: Present.

Tillhammer: Morgan?

Max: Here.

Tillhammer: Bueller? Bueller?...

Director: Cut!

Flying Beds scene. Take 7.

Mattress falls from the second-floor stairs and gets wedged.

Director: Cut! The mattress needs to do a cartwheel down the stairs, a cartwheel.

Flying Beds scene. Take 8.

Mattress falls from the second-floor stairs, turns over once and falls off the railing.

Director: Cut! Try again. Make it do flips. Cartwheels!

Flying Beds scene. Take 9.

The mattress falls down the stairs, turns over once and lies down.

Director: Cut! Skip it. Let the special effects figure it out. I don't care if they CGI it.

Field Trip scene. Take 4

Max: Did I mention we're on Nix? All that time standing and waiting in the extreme cold, freezing your ass off.

Director: Cut!

Max: What? Wasn't that right? *What'd* I miss?

Director: You said *ass.*

Max: Okay?

Director: Max never curses until *Hello Darkness.*

Max: Oh, I forgot. Is *ass* really a curse word?

Director: Yes, it is. Say *freezing your butt off.*

Field Trip scene. Take 12.

Max: It's—it's bloody Stonehenge!

Diego: Stonehenge!

Big Marcus: Stonehenge!

Marge: Stonehenge!

Ian: It's only a model.

Everyone: (Laughing)

Director: (Laughing) Cut!

Medical scene. Take 5.

Dr. Kim: Did you sexually harass anyone or did anyone sexually harass you?

Max: No.

Dr. Kim: Are you currently sexually harassing anyone or is anyone sexually harassing you?

Max: No.

Dr. Kim: Do you plan on sexually harassing anyone in the future?

Max: That all depends—what are you doing later tonight?

Dr. Kim: (Laughing).

Max: I'm kidding!

Director: Cut!

Take Me to Church scene. Take 2.

Diego: The chapel on station is a one-stop shop for all religions. Did Jo-Leia tell you about the big cross behind the altar?

Max: What about it?

Diego: There's a huge cross for the Christian services. However, the cross can be swung to reveal a crucifix for a Catholic Mass. They call it the Swinging Jesus.

Director: Cut! Can we say that? Swinging Jesus?

Mr. Writer: I don't think we should.

Director: What about in the outtakes?

Mr. Writer: Let me think about it...I'll allow it.

———————————

Preparations scene. Take 6

On the eve of my deployment, I needed to clear my head. Flip, Turtle, and I sat at our usual table at the Mountain. Flip stood up and raised his mug.

Flip: To Sergeant Max—oh crap!

Just then Flip's hand slipped and he dropped his mug. It hit the table and drenched Turtle.

Turtle: Dude, beer all over me.

Flip: (Laughing) Sorry, man. At least it's not real beer.

Director: Cut!

Max: (Laughing) Why isn't it real beer?

Director: Really? We can't have you all drinking on set. Flip can't even hold it right sober.

———————————

Dinner Guests scene. Take 3

Big Marcus looked at Flip, "you're on."

Flip stood up and raised his glass for a toast, "I pledge allegiance to the flag..."

Director: Cut!

———————————

Tough Life beach scene. Take 2.

Max: Well, let me look around. We're the only ones on this beach drinking beer. The only ones wearing long shorts that go down to our knees. You're the only one out here taking pictures. The only ones speaking English, if that wasn't a dead giveaway. Also, I'm pretty sure none of the locals have seen American football.

Flip: This is a tough life.

Max: Sure is. Roger?! What are doing out here in shorts with your feet in the sand?

Director: Cut!

Roger: You guys get all the fun. I wanted to come out and enjoy what you're going through. It gets boring sitting on the same set day after day, only talking to Max.

———

Tough Life, hotel scene. Take 1.

Opening the doors was a glorious shock. We each had a small porch with a spectacular ocean view. I stepped out onto the porch, then reached over and knocked on my neighbor's back door. Flip opened it and was dumbfounded by the view.

Flip: Well, this place certainly sucks.

Max: What do you mean? You don't like the ocean?

Flip: The ocean? Oh crap, sorry, everyone! I thought we were looking at the desert or something.

Director: Cut!

Flip: No, really, all we're looking at here is the giant green screen. It's hard to keep track of where we are. We keep moving between sets!

———

Birds of a Feather scene, Take 4.

Pechman: Multiple issues: radar won't display an image, interphone in the left rear cargo bay is out, the air conditioning wasn't heating, number seven engine showed low power, the Flex Capacitor isn't flexing...

Max: Flex Capacitor?

Pechman: It's...what...makes...time...travel...possible.
Director: Cut!

———————

The Slow Death scene, Take 2.
Roger: Did you ever have a chance to sit still after spending all your time running or driving around in circles?
Max: I did in the Resource Office; I'd be at my desk all day messing with those dreaded APRs.
Director: Cut!
Max...?
Director: In this APR section you must say every line *word for word* from the script.
Max: Will do. Why's that?
Director: Apparently the writer wrote each sentence to fit across one line of page if used under *Times New Roman.*
Max: That's crazy! Is he completely insane?
Director: It's late, we're all tired, just read the damn lines.

———————

My Old Friend scene, Take 1
Sharyn: It's been a long time, Max. A real long time.
Marcus: You look good, Max, almost like you didn't age much at all.
Max: You look old as dirt. What the hell happened to you?
Sharyn: Marcus, don't let him talk to you like that.
Max: I was talking to you, Sharyn.
Director: Cut!
Max: I'm kidding. No really, they did a great job in the makeup department. Great job!

———

My Old Friends scene, Take 2.

T.J. approached. He was walking with a cane and from the looks of it had a prosthetic leg.

T.J.: Well, would you look at this sorry group.

Max: Wow, great to see you.

Marcus: You got a new leg, Lieutenant Dan!

All: (Laughing)

Director: Cut!

———

Megan: Hold on, I'm pulling up a picture on my tablet. Is this him?

Steven: That's the one. The janitor's name is Roger.

Director: Cut! That's a wrap! Thank you, everyone!

About the Author

Timothy M. Lander was born in 1976 and raised in Southern California. In 1998 Tim joined the Air Force and served for over twenty-one years as an Avionics troop primarily working on B-52s and C-130s. He served alongside truly exceptional aircraft maintainers in North Dakota, Texas, and Arkansas; while deploying to such places as England, Greece, Iraq, and Afghanistan. Tim currently resides in Chandler Arizona along with his amazing wife Erica as they raise their four awesome kids currently guiding them through High School and College.